Neglected Souls

Neglected Souls

A novel

By

Richard Jeanty

RJ Publications, LLC

Newark, New Jersey

The characters and events in this book are fictitious. Any resemblance to actual persons, living or dead, is purely coincidental.

RJ Publications
rjeantay@yahoo.com
www.rjpublications.com
Copyright © 2005 by Richard Jeanty
All Rights Reserved
ISBN 978-0-9769277-1-6

Printed in Canada

September 2004

11 12 13 14 15 16 17 18 19 20

Introduction

After reading a novel by another young author on my roundtrip flight from New York to Atlanta last summer, I found myself inspired and compelled to tell a story of a different kind. It was a story that I had witnessed from many different stories that developed into one. I'm fed up with the excuses that people use for their failures and I want to offer something different.

I know of many successful stories in the hood, but I haven't seen too many of them in print. We're so encouraged by negativity and the frenzy perpetrated by the media continues to add fuel to the negativity that our common folks have to deal with on a daily basis. I want to offer a situation, which might seem extreme to most, but is not that extreme at all to many of us. I want to put certain things in perspective to encourage others and inspire many more.

The fact that we have many success stories in the African American community that's never made their way to the bookshelves or even the publisher's desk, never sat well with me. I'd like to offer the common folks an alternative to what's out there. Sometimes being alive as a Black man in America can be more of a burden than anything. We always have to prove ourselves to people.

The cops assume the car we're driving is stolen before even asking to see proof of ownership, our classmates think we're all attending colleges and universities across the nation on athletic scholarships, people assume we're all deadbeat dads who don't want to provide for our offspring, we're not supposed to be in the upscale neighborhood unless we're cleaning it, carrying our cell phones on our hips in New York City can be a death sentence imposed on us by trigger happy, cowardice New York City cops, and some people even assume we only wear suits when we have to go to court.

Whoever said it was wrong for us to capitalize on our athletic abilities anyway? The NCAA makes enough money to offer scholarships to half the struggling kids in the ghetto, but why would they give them a penny if they can't get ten dollars in return? The characters in my story made the best of their situations and some of them came out victorious. Life is a struggle; none of us have the final answer to our destiny. The mystery is about creating one.

Acknowledgements

First, I'd like to take this opportunity to thank my father for inspiring me to write this book in a manner that I could have never conceived on my own. Dad, you may not have thought highly of the little discussion you and I had that night about my book, but it was your words that inspired me to add a different moral to my story. Thanks for taking the time to talk to me and showing interest in my work.

I'd like to specifically thank Stacey Murphy for all the support. You're one in a million.

I'd like to also thank the following people in no particular order. All my readers from the focus group: Carline Gele, Mindy Perilus, and Melissa Robinson for taking the time to read the book and offer their opinions.

Very special thanks to my friend Elaine Sylvester for taking time out of her busy schedule to dedicate to my book.

Special Thanks go out to all the bookstores around the country that carry my books and all the book vendors around the country. I would like to acknowledge my man Henry, in New York, Hakeem in Philly and everybody else in Brooklyn, the Bronx, Queens and all the burroughs. I can't forget my man Lloyd in Boston from the Black Library. Your memory lives on.

Last, but not least I'd like to thank all the people who encouraged me to pursue my dream of becoming a writer and all the readers who walk away with a new outlook on life in the inner city after reading this book.

Stolen Innocence

Katrina and her children were very close in age. She was just fourteen years old when her daughter, Nina, was born and sixteen years old when her son, Jimmy, was born. Neither father was involved in the kids' lives. As a matter of fact, the fathers were unknown to both children. Katrina could've never told Jimmy who his father was anyway. She would have had too much explaining to do. Nina's father on the other hand, was a man of Hispanic descent who had sexually violated Katrina. He was an older boy from the neighborhood where Katrina grew up.

When Katrina found out she was pregnant with Nina a month after she had been raped, she told her very religious parents what had happened but they did not believe her. There was a rumor going around the neighborhood that Katrina had slept with another boy in the neighborhood. That rumor ultimately tarnished her reputation with her own parents. Once she revealed to them that she was pregnant, it basically confirmed the rumor that she was promiscuous.

Katrina's parents never gave her a chance to explain how she was impregnated against her will through a rape. Her account of the event did not matter to her parents. Her parents turned their backs on her and called her all kinds of trifling names and immediately kicked her out of the house. She left with her supposed bundle of joy in her stomach and never went back home. Katrina gave birth to Nina all alone in the hospital. At the age of fourteen years old, she had to find a way to provide financially and emotionally for her daughter.

Katrina was a loner in high school who spent most of her time studying, but she would always get giddy and nervous around boys. She didn't know how to react to advances from the boys and shied away from most kids her age because they were always making fun of her. Jose saw Katrina's alienation from her peers as an opportunity to try to befriend her. Jose was about five years older than Katrina; he had just graduated from high school that past June and was waiting to be shipped out to the military.

It was early October when Jose had his first conversation with Katrina. Jose Ramirez was a short and chubby man who was about a sandwich away from being obese. He was no taller than five ft five inches and weighed about one hundred and seventy five pounds. He had spiked hair and enough pimples on his face to earn him the nickname "Pizza Face" back in high school. He was also an abrasive man who could turn a sweet old lady into a modern day bitch. He was rude and had the confidence of a super hero around younger women. Nobody could tell Jose he wasn't God's gift to young and impressionable women. Around people his age, he clammed up in a shell that nobody could open.

Jose had so many different complexes it would take a lifetime to list them all. However, the one apparent one was his Napoleon complex to compensate for his lack of height. He felt the need to dominate young impressionable people around where he lived. He didn't have any friends his age. He would always try to gather the younger kids on his block to tell them glorified, fictitious stories about himself in high school. Most of the kids figured he was lying because he would always stop talking when the older guys from the neighborhood who went to school with him showed up. He was a super hero in his own mind.

Katrina lived with her parents in Hyde Park, which was a small suburb of Boston, near the Dedham line. Back in the seventies and early eighties, the city of Boston provided those ugly yellow cheese buses for transportation to all students who lived more than five miles away from their school. Every student who rode a school bus had an assigned stop to board the bus every morning. It was usually a block or two and no more from a student's home.

Because Katrina lived so far away in Hyde Park and her school was located near Fenway Park, she was assigned a school bus. Katrina boarded her bus two blocks away from her house every morning at 6:35 AM in order to get to school by 7:20 AM and the bus would drop her off at 2:30 in the afternoon everyday. It was a routine schedule and Jose had figured out exactly how to talk to Katrina without her parents finding out. He would go to her bus stop every afternoon to wait for her so he could walk her home. At first, she was irritated by him and didn't really pay him any attention. But his persistence finally paid off two weeks later when she finally opened her mouth to ask him why he continued to bother her everyday even though she ignored him.

He became cocky and told her that he knew that she would eventually come around to her senses. Jose was the type of guy who took a turn down as an invitation to come-on to a woman. In his own mind, she had always wanted to talk to him. However, as time went by, Katrina started to see a different side of Jose. She saw a desperately confused young man who was seeking the approval of his friends, and their personalities were pretty similar. They became friends and she made it clear to him that it was all that they could be. The thought of anything more never even crossed her mind.

Kissing boys was the furthest thing from Katrina's mind when she entered high school early that fall. She still saw boys as pests whose jobs were to make fun of people all day. She was grossed out by the idea of someone shoving his tongue down her throat to kiss her. One can only imagine how appalled she was on the day Jose tried to steal a kiss from her. He came out of nowhere, without any warning, and planted a big wet kiss on her. It was literally wet because Katrina's mouth remained closed while he was trying to stick his tongue in her mouth. The first word out her mouth was "yuck!" as she ran away from Jose. She couldn't believe he had physically violated her like that after just two weeks of befriending her. She realized that she should not have let down her guard around him so soon. She ran the whole way home hysterically angry.

Katrina was never attracted to Jose and found his body odor to be rather offensive, but she never felt comfortable enough with him to tell him. Katrina had set the parameters on their friendship from the beginning and Jose had crossed the line. She couldn't forgive him and did not want to forgive him for what he had done. From that day on, she believed their friendship was over and there was no way she was going to change her mind about it.

A week had passed and by this time Jose had become repulsive to her. He was still relentless in his pursuit to rekindle the friendship he and Katrina once shared. She wanted none of it and Jose's ego was crushed. Jose wasn't ready to deal with another rejection, especially by a young, impressionable chick. The day Jose planted the kiss on Katrina's lips, he had hoped for it to be this fairytale situation he had dreamed up in his mind for weeks. He never factored in the fact that it took two people to tangle. He felt like an idiot standing there when she ran away from him after his romantic attempt at kissing her the week before. Jose wanted to know the reason why Katrina had not grown to like him. She enjoyed his jokes and they formed somewhat of a friendship.

Katrina was not a rude or open person, so she kept all her feelings inside. She was rather timid while Jose was clueless. He was always projecting his feelings onto other people without communicating with them. He found out the hard way that his advances were not welcomed. Katrina ignored him for two weeks and for two weeks he kept trying to get her attention. One particular week, he went and dropped a rose on her front porch every morning with a note saying he missed their friendship. She never responded to his effort and Jose was once again embarrassed.

Katrina had never told anyone about the incident with Jose. She didn't have any friends to confide in and her parents who were very old fashioned weren't the kind of parents she could go to with boy issues. They tried as much as they could to shield their kids from the sins of the world or what the bible made them believe to be sins. Katrina was the eldest of three children; she had a younger brother and a younger sister that followed. Katrina was five years older than her brother and seven years older than her sister. Her parents had set high expectations for all their kids and if they didn't do as they were told they were shunned.

Katrina always had a hard time getting up for church on Sundays and she had made her parents late for service on numerous occasions. She had earned the reputation of a rebel early from her parents. She once told her parents that she didn't want to go to church because God could care less if she prayed in church or at home. Her parents were furious that she had talked back to them in such a manner. She was grounded for a week. Katrina's parents didn't want her to have a negative influence on her younger siblings. They tried as much as they could to keep her siblings away from her. Katrina's parents had started to develop preconceived feelings of mistrust towards their daughter because she didn't agree with them all the time. They never took the time to get to know their daughter; instead, they became preoccupied with shielding their younger children from her. Katrina's parents never allowed her to be an adolescent.

Katrina's innocent, rebellious behavior was not at all innocent to her parents. Katrina's parents took their daughter's occasional defiance seriously. They had on numerous occasions made it clear to Katrina that they didn't want her walking through an abandoned field, located a block away from their house. And not a moment too soon, her younger brother had seen her cutting through the field from his bedroom window. He alerted his mother who saw Katrina doing exactly what they had told her not to do. When she got home, she was confronted and she lied about it. She had started to build a barrier of mistrust between her and her parents.

A neighbor once told her parents that they had seen her wearing jeans coming out of school. Her parents forbade Katrina from wearing pants. They were strict Christians and they didn't want their daughter to bend any of the Christian rules. Katrina was slowly becoming the black sheep of the family. She would buy clothes prohibited by her parents with her allowance and would carry them in her bag to school and change in the bathroom. The more they tried to control Katrina, the more she pushed their buttons and the more defiant she became.

Jose had it all planned in his head. He wanted to get Katrina back for rejecting him and he thought he came up with the perfect plan. It was a wonderful sunny Friday afternoon in the fall of 1984 and Jose was set to leave the following day for the army. He hadn't seen or bothered Katrina in weeks. She was glad he was no longer pestering her about being his friend. However, on that fateful day, "Pizza Face" showed his ugly head once again. This time, Jose didn't go through the same routine at the bus stop; instead, he waited for Katrina about a block from her house.

As usual, Katrina defied her parents' orders and walked through the abandoned field as a short cut and Jose knew this. As she cut through the field, Jose approached her with a gun in his hand and told her to shut up or he would kill her as he put the gun to her head. He threw down her book bag then smacked her and knocked her down to the ground. On this day, when Jose confronted Katrina, she was wearing a long skirt that her mother had laid out on the bed for her the night before. While Katrina was on the ground, Jose covered her mouth with his left hand while lifting her skirt up with the gun in his right hand. He brought her skirt up to her waist then proceeded to rub the gun up and down her vagina through her underwear. In his sick mind, he kept telling her that she liked it and wanted more of it. Jose then pushed Katrina's underwear to the side with the gun then stuck it inside her vagina as she winced in pain.

Katrina was not sexually active and had never had any object in her vagina prior to this heinous incident. It hurt to have the barrel of a gun thrust inside of her. He went on about how he could blow her up and have her guts spill out by pulling the trigger while the gun was still inside of her. Katrina wanted to fight back but she couldn't; he got on top of her and overpowered her with his weight and the gun pressed against her head. The sorrow in her face could only be described as innocence lost. Tears ran down her face as she lay on the ground with her eyes closed.

A few minutes had passed and Katrina was no longer responding to Jose's sick remarks, he grew angrier and he decided that raping her would be the ultimate revenge. He pulled her panties to the side, rammed his short penis inside her vagina while holding the gun in her mouth. He must've humped her for about a minute before he came. When he got up he told her that he would kill her if she told anybody and would kill her brother and sister as well. He left her lying on the grass powerless and ashamed.

She blamed herself for the whole incident because her parents had told her many times not to walk through the field. Other women had been assaulted there at all hours of the day in the past. Poor Katrina didn't even have the strength to get up from the ground to walk the rest of the way home. She felt no longer pristine and had lost her virginity to a despicable rapist.

She finally mustered the courage to get up after about forty-five minutes and headed home. When she got home, she went straight to the shower to wash off Jose's dirty paws and sexual aggression he'd forced upon her. After she got out of the shower, she went to her room where she sobbed for the rest of the night. She did not eat dinner nor did she speak to anybody about the incident. Her parents didn't even bother checking up on her. Her parents were old school and they didn't know how to talk to their daughter. No attempt was made to reach out to Katrina and she felt isolated and alone in a house full of people. Katrina felt she had contributed to the rape because she had defied her parents' orders to avoid the abandoned field. She dealt with her dilemma the best way she could that Friday night and that day she just wanted to sleep away the whole experience.

After trying to sleep her problems away for twelve hours, Katrina woke up on Saturday afternoon feeling worn out. With no one to talk to about the situation, Katrina contemplated suicide. She wanted to pour a glass of Clorox mixed with milk down her throat to end her life. She went downstairs to the washroom in the basement and started pouring Clorox in a cup. When her little brother came down looking for her to play hide and seek, she decided that it was not worth it. She took one look at him and smiled and went back upstairs to play with him for a little while. But her brother only provided temporary relief from her problems.

Soon after, Katrina started thinking about the whole ordeal again. She became withdrawn and went back upstairs and locked herself in her room. Katrina didn't eat anything that day and she was a nervous wreck. Every little noise only increased her paranoia. Finally, her younger sister came knocking on her bedroom door that evening to see how she was doing and why she hadn't talked to her all day. Her sister loved to play with Katrina's long and thick curly hair. She came in the room with a comb in hand and wanted to play hairdresser with Katrina, but Katrina had a pounding headache. She told her sister it wasn't a good time to come back later. Her sister sadly left the room.

It was Sunday morning when Katrina was awakened by the pounding knock of her father's fist on her bedroom door. She had once again overslept and only had a few minutes to get ready for church. Her father told her she had five minutes to get ready or she would have to catch a bus to the church and meet them there. Katrina didn't have the strength to ride the bus that day, so she quickly got up, took a quick shower and threw on the first dress she could lay her hands on.

On the way to church, all Katrina kept thinking about was how God must've punished her for disobeying her parents' directives. She started feeling guilty and thought she deserved what happened to her. She could not wait to get into church to get on her knees and ask God for forgiveness and the strength to deal with her problems. Katrina was quiet the whole way to church and everyone in the car on that particular day seemed somber.

They arrived at the church just in time to catch the pastor announce his sermon topic of abortion and premarital sex. It was as if the gods were watching Katrina. The pastor talked about how the female body is a temple and it is up to women to protect it and at no time should they allow temptation to get the best of them. He also went on to preach that even in extreme cases of rape it is still considered immoral to abort a baby.

Katrina sat through church service for three hours; listening to this man babble on about how women have to take the initiative to protect themselves from men. The whole service felt weird to Katrina because she was raped two days ago and now this pastor was preaching about fornication and abortion. When it was time for prayer, Katrina knelt down and asked God to forgive her for the times she had disobeyed her parents and she promised she would never do that again. But she also asked God why he didn't protect her from Jose.

She left church feeling puzzled that day, thinking that although her parents were overly religious, their prayers did not even protect her from an attacking perpetrator. Katrina started questioning everything, thinking that maybe they didn't include her in their prayers when they prayed. During the ride back home, her father reiterated everything that the pastor had talked about to his children. Her father went on and on about how women who wore tight jeans and miniskirts were doing themselves a disservice. All was quiet in the car when her father was talking and that only increased her loneliness and Katrina felt even more ashamed about what happened to her.

Katrina's parents acted like slavery never ended. Mrs. Johnson was very submissive to her husband and she adopted a few of his bad habits in the process. Mr. Johnson's word in the house was bond and no one was allowed to question his decisions. There was loyalty in their home, but it was rare for the parents to express love to each other and their children. It was understood that the whole family was loved, but daddy didn't know how to express it.

The Johnsons only had a sixth grade education and were forced to join the workforce when they were very young to help support their very large families. Mr. Johnson grew up in a household with fifteen children and a single mother while Mrs. Johnson had ten siblings in a single-family household growing up. The Johnson's had continued to follow a negative cycle that existed in their families for many generations. Their grandparents were ex-slaves who were forbidden to express love to their children and they passed those traits on to their offspring. The Johnson's believe that children were to listen to their parents and that was the only opinion that mattered.

A Life Changing Meeting

Katrina was only fifteen years old when she met Tony and she already had one child that she was raising on her own. She had no job, a ninth grade education and no employment experience. In addition to being a young African-American female, the odds didn't work at all in Katrina's favor. She had been living off the welfare assistance she was receiving from the state of Massachusetts. They barely gave her enough money a month to take care of her daughter, Nina, so she couldn't afford an apartment of her own and being a minor made it all the more difficult for her to establish herself.

For a year since Nina was born, she moved from shelter to shelter with her daughter. Katrina had dropped out of school a few months before her daughter was born. Boston Public Schools at the time didn't allow pregnant students to remain in school once their stomach started to show. She attended a prestigious exam school in Boston. When Katrina became pregnant she was just in the ninth grade, impressionable and book smart. Everyone had high hopes for her, everyone except those who were supposed to be the closest to her in her family. They never supported Katrina the way parents should have. She was a straight A student at one of the best schools in the city and she was never shown any appreciation by her parents. Katrina's motive in life was under suspicion by her parents most of the time for no apparent reason.

Katrina struggled for a long time with her daughter, so when she met this guy named Tony she thought her prayers had been answered. Tony was smooth, caring, giving and charismatic. When Tony met Katrina she was living in a homeless shelter for women called The Cozy Place with her young daughter located in the South End section of Boston.

Katrina was referred to the shelter by the hospital staff where she gave birth to her daughter.

She met Tony on a breezy summer morning while he was driving on Massachusetts Avenue in the South End. She was pushing her baby carriage on the way to Boston City Hospital for an annual check up for her one-year-old daughter Nina. Even though Katrina was living in a homeless shelter, she was able to look neat and clean and she wore the hell out of those donated clothes given to her. On this particular day, she was wearing a nice pair of skintight, blue Jordache jeans, a baby blue t-shirt with a nice pair of baby blue Puma sneakers.

She was nonchalantly walking and pushing the baby carriage Nina was sitting in like nothing else in the world mattered to her. Katrina was easily noticeable because of her natural beauty. Her dark skin was flawless, and she had a complexion that any super model would kill for. Katrina's long and thick curly hair was one of the assets she had inherited from her mother. She didn't need to use a perm like many other women who shared her African ancestry. She was average height for her age and well proportioned physically. She was looking good that morning and her face was glowing. Tony had slowly driven passed her and almost crashed his car into on-coming traffic trying to get a better glimpse of Katrina's body.

He finally pulled over to the side of the road and waited for her to walk by him. As she got closer to his car, he rolled down the passenger side window of his freshly painted Cadillac Seville. He asked if he could talk to her for a minute and she ignored him. Realizing that his attempts would be futile if he continued to talk to her from inside the car, he quickly parked the car and jumped out to walk alongside her.

Given the situation, most women in Katrina's predicament would have been impressed to meet a guy like Tony who owned a nice car and who was good looking and suave. Tony was tall, dark and very handsome. He stood about 6 feet tall, weighed about 190 pounds of solid muscle. Tony was wearing a wave cap on his head to hold down his waves. He had on a nice black Adidas sweat suit with white pinstripes and a pair of crisp white on white shell toe Adidas sneakers, which were very popular at the time. To top it all off, he wore a pair of Gazelle glasses like the ones the famous rap group Run DMC used to wear during that era. Tony tried talking to Katrina as she continued to push her daughter in the stroller along Massachusetts Avenue headed towards Boston City Hospital. Katrina didn't utter a word to Tony the whole time he was trying to talk to her, until he told her that she was the kind of woman most men dreamed of meeting. She asked him what he meant by that.

He started to tell her all the words she yearned to hear from her father as a little girl. He told her how beautiful she was and from the way she spoke she seemed very intelligent and articulate and she should have a man in her life that could take care of her. Tony came at her from a different angle and hit all the right notes at the right time. Suddenly, Katrina keyed in on Tony. He offered to give her a ride the rest of the way, but she declined as she was already close to the hospital. Tony wanted to keep in touch with Katrina and asked for her phone number. Katrina, however, at the time didn't have a phone number to give to Tony and she was ashamed to tell him that she was living in a homeless shelter. Instead, she took his number and promised to call him later that day.

From Bad to Worse

Sometimes a simple phone call can take a person to a place they never imagined they would go. While it was true that Katrina was struggling with her daughter Nina, Tony would only prove to be a source of temporary relief or worse, he would add more to her problems if anything. Katrina made a simple phone call to Tony, which resulted in a date with him at one of the most expensive restaurants in Boston, a place that Katrina had never been to or even imagined going to. Elated, she made plans to leave her daughter with a friend at the shelter in order to go out with Tony that night.

Tony wanted to impress Katrina the best way possible, so he made a reservation for 8:00 PM at Maison Robert by the pier in Boston. Katrina wore one of her best outfits on that day. She was always able to find some of the best clothing items in the pile of clothes donated to the shelter. She wore this little red mini dress she'd found that barely came down to her knees and since she had a gorgeous body, the dress accentuated her every curve. She also wore these red high heel pumps she also found in the donated stock at the shelter, but she could hardly walk in them. Her steps were awkward, but any admiring fan would be drawn more to her body than the way she walked. Her beautiful full lips were glistening with the cherry red lipstick she had smoothed all over them. She was definitely lady in red that night and she wore it well.

Katrina had planned for Tony to pick her up a block from the shelter; she wasn't ready to tell him that she was living in a homeless shelter. As Tony approached the corner, a block from where the shelter was located, he first noticed the curvaceous body in the red dress and then the legs wearing the high heel pumps. At first he thought it was another woman and was getting ready to hit on her with his best game, but as he got closer driving his squeaky clean

Cadillac Seville with wheels so shiny and covered with enough Armor All to cause a major sliding accident on the road, he realized it was Katrina.

Tony couldn't believe his eyes when he saw Katrina; she was exactly everything he was looking for in a woman at that moment. Her transformation was amazing. She was a beautiful, sexy woman with a body to die for and most importantly she still looked young and definitely had the energy that he sought in a woman. It was on that particular night that Tony realized that Katrina was built like a Thoroughbred ready to take over a racetrack. After a few minutes of admiration, Tony realized that he hadn't yet gotten out of the car to open the door for Katrina. He quickly jumped out from the driver's side and went over to the passenger side to open the door for Katrina. She felt like a princess as he ushered her in the car with a bow. After she got in the car, he stood there for a few seconds more to admire her beauty. She timidly asked him to stop and he hopped in the car and they took off for the restaurant.

After a few minutes of driving, Tony reached around to the back seat and pulled out fresh, nicely arranged dozen of roses and handed it to Katrina. Her face was flushed and she didn't know what to say, she thanked him and told him he didn't have to go through all this trouble. That was the first time anyone had ever given her nicely arranged flowers in her whole life.

While Katrina and Tony were in the car driving, she started taking inventory of his clothes. Tony was wearing a cream-colored polyester and gabardine-blended suit with a buttoned down, shiny polyester brown shirt, a brown belt, shiny paten leather shoes and a brown Kangol hat. Tony's jewelry complemented his outfit; he was wearing about four gold chains around his neck, three gold rings on each hand, and enough cologne to make a grown woman dizzy. Nevertheless, she was very impressed with Tony's attire and jewelry and thought that maybe Tony was just a hip, well-to-do guy trying to set himself apart from the rest.

She was so used to seeing her father wear those three-piece suits to church on Sundays; anything new was a breath of fresh air. Everybody at her church dressed conservatively, Tony's outfit was a break from the norm for her. Katrina also noticed that Tony had a mature face with a few earned laugh lines and newly formed wrinkles around the forehead. She wasn't sure how to go about asking Tony his age and she also didn't want him to know how old she was. She left the subject on the back burner for now, but she'd hoped to bring it up later.

Tony was so pleased with the way Katrina looked; money wasn't going to be an object that night. He told her to order anything she wanted on the menu and not to worry about a thing. At this time, Tony became the hunter and she was the hunted. While they sat and waited for the waiter to bring their food out, Tony pulled out a little black jewelry box and handed it to Katrina. Surprised, she asked, "What's that for?" He told her, "It's my way of showing appreciation to a special, beautiful lady for coming out with me". She opened the box and inside she found a nice gold necklace with a gold cubic zirconium adorned heart piece.

Katrina was in awe because she had never received any gifts of this magnitude not even from her father. Tony asked if she'd like to put it on and she said, "Yes". He walked over to her side of the table and clasped the necklace around her neck. She asked if the sparkling glass around the heart was diamond, he confirmed with a nod. Tony knew that there was no diamond on that piece, but Katrina didn't know any better. She would have been happy to have gotten just a necklace.

By the time the food arrived, Tony and Katrina had been deeply engaged in a conversation about their upbringing and experiences, she kept a lot from Tony and he pretty much did the same. She ordered the seafood plate consisting of lobster; calamari and shrimp with white rice and Tony ordered a steak with mashed potatoes. It didn't make a difference to Tony whether or not she was of legal age to drink; he ordered a bottle of Dom Perignon along with dinner just to impress her. They looked so mature as a couple, the Maitre D didn't even bother asking Katrina for identification before serving the champagne.

That night would mark the first night that Katrina ever had champagne. Tony focused all his attention on her through dinner and she felt like she and Tony were the only people present in the room. He complimented her from head to toe every chance he got. He occasionally rubbed her knees under the table just to make his presence felt and he knew she liked it. Katrina had never been given so much affection in her life. By the time they were done eating dinner, Katrina had a buzz from gulping down most of the champagne. It was around 9:30 PM when they were done eating, they called the Maitre D over and Tony paid the two hundred and sixty five dollar tab along with a thirty-five dollar tip before they left.

Katrina sat back observing the transaction and she was thoroughly impressed by what she saw. Tony asked her if she wanted to come by his place for a little while, she said she couldn't because she had to get back to her daughter. He then asked if he could come over to her place. She screamed a loud "No!" not wanting Tony to discover she was just a homeless teenage mother after the wonderful dinner they shared. He was shocked that she had turned him down and told her "I wish this night could last forever". She tried to explain to him that she didn't mean that she didn't want him to come over. She made up a quick excuse by telling Tony she was in a situation where she was staying temporarily with a friend and she couldn't have any company over.

Knowing she had a buzz and incoherent, Tony drove directly to his place and when he got there he begged her to come in for a few minutes. Against her better judgment,

Katrina agreed to go upstairs to Tony's apartment for a few minutes. It was about 9:45 when they went upstairs and she failed to keep track of time. They went upstairs and Tony opened a bottle of Moet and got her even drunker than she already was. She loosened up and all her inhibitions just went out the window and a naughty side of Katrina was unveiled. Tony loved every minute of it. She hadn't been with a man since she was raped, but that night she talked like a pro and acted like an amateur through her actions. They didn't do anything sexually exciting that night, as they were both too tipsy to recognize or control their actions. She and Tony fell asleep together on his bed after they had sex.

   Tony and Katrina awoke the next morning around 10:00 AM. Katrina couldn't believe that she had spent the night out leaving her one-year old daughter with a friend. But even worse, she had jeopardized her space at the shelter. The shelter had a strict 10:00 pm curfew for all their residents and Katrina knew she had violated that rule and might be back on the street by the time she got back to the shelter. To make matters worse, it was clearly explained to her many times when she first went to the shelter that she could not sleep out and if she did, she would automatically be kicked out of the shelter. They told her there was a line of people waiting to get in the shelter and the facility wasn't going to put up with anyone who broke their rules.

   She hurried off the bed and ran to the bathroom where she found all kinds of female clothing and make-up products. She didn't really have the right to say anything, so she kept quiet about it. She tried to get Tony to hurry to take her back to the shelter. Tony acted like he didn't understand why she was in such a rush. She told him she couldn't explain it to him, but she had to get home as soon as possible. At this time, she didn't even know where her daughter might be because the shelter also had another rule that all the residents had to be out by 10:00AM daily.

All shelter residents had a schedule that they had to follow in order to secure their space at the shelter. They were expected to be out looking for work everyday so they could transition themselves out of the shelter life. All kinds of crazy thoughts ran through Katrina's mind. She thought her girlfriend might turn her daughter over to the staff and they might call the Department of Social Services on her for neglect. She was losing her mind and Tony felt her sense of urgency and quickly threw on a sweat suit and some sneakers to take her home.

Tony was trying to drive as fast as he could down the Roxbury streets in Boston. He acted like he was really concerned about Katrina's well being, so he asked her why she was so anxious to get home. She didn't answer and he knew she was keeping something from him. He tried to comfort her by telling her whatever it was, he could probably help her with it. She wasn't comfortable enough to allow him into her world just yet, so she sat in the car silently, thinking of the worst-case scenario for her daughter.

Having had enough of her silence, Tony pulled over and demanded that she tell him what was going on. She finally broke down and told Tony that she was living in a shelter and they had a curfew of 10:00PM that she had violated and furthermore, she would be expelled from the shelter for staying out with him. Tony pulled her near him and told her not to worry and that he would help her out and she won't have to live in the shelter anymore. She let out a sigh of relief then went on to tell him that that wasn't all of it, she also had to find her daughter. She explained the rule of in by 10:00 PM and out by 10:00AM and that she wouldn't know where to find her friend who was watching her daughter. The only thing Tony could tell her was everything was going to be all right.

When Katrina and Tony finally made it to The Cozy Place in the South End, she was relieved to find her friend standing in front of the shelter with her two kids in tow and

Nina in a stroller and all of Katrina's belonging in a duffle bag. Katrina knew she had been kicked out of the shelter when she saw the duffle bag. She recognized that duffle bag from a mile away because it was the only memory she still carried with her from home. The reality of the whole situation hit Katrina that morning around a quarter to eleven o'clock. She quickly asked Tony to give her a few minutes to talk to her friend to find out what was going on. Her friend Christine wasn't even mad that Katrina had stayed out; Katrina had been so depressed lately, her friend was happy to see her go out and have some fun.

She didn't have to tell Katrina that the shelter had kicked her out and before she could even utter the words Katrina cut her off and said, "I know" with tears flowing down her face. Christine asked if Tony would be able to help her and she said, "he said he could". Christine felt better knowing that Katrina wasn't going to be on the street with her daughter.

That morning Katrina looked like a street hooker whose luck had just run out as she walked back to Tony's car with the duffle bag on her back while pushing Nina in front of her in the stroller wearing a bright red dress and high heels. When she got to the car, Tony simply rolled down the passenger window and she stuck her head in to ask if she could get in. Tony looked at her and raised his head to the sky and said "sure'. He didn't bother helping her with the bag or her daughter and he sat there and watched her as she struggled to get her daughter and her belongings in the car. Katrina and her daughter finally got in the car knowing very little of what the future held for them. Katrina's nightmare had become a reality and she was now dependent on a stranger's kindness to make it for however long it would take. It was at that moment that she realized she was at Tony's mercy.

Introduction to the Game

Something about Tony didn't tell the whole story. At first, he seemed like the knight in shining armor that Katrina was looking for. He showered her with a nice expensive dinner, flowers, a nice gift and a wonderful night completely. But they say "everything comes with a price and if it looks too good to be true, it probably is" and boy that saying couldn't be more in tune with this situation.

It had been a week since Katrina had been living in Tony's house. During that week, she saw two women wearing the skimpiest of outfits come and go at all hours of the night. Tony lived in a four-bedroom apartment in one of the roughest streets of Boston. Katrina never asked any questions about the other women and nor did she care. She was trying to hold out until she could find space in another shelter. Meanwhile, Tony was kind to Katrina and gave her everything she needed; he even had the other two girls in the house move into one room so Katrina and her daughter could have their own room and privacy.

Katrina was trying to ride the gravy train for as long as she could without questioning the source of the gravy. Tony tried his best to make Katrina feel at home, but she always felt a sense of urgency to get out of Tony's house. Something just didn't feel right to her. He hadn't tried anything sexually with her or forced her to do anything she didn't want to do. However, Katrina showed she was grateful by cleaning and cooking everyday for Tony. While it may have been a nice gesture, Tony was interested in more than just cleaning and cooking from Katrina and Tony had known all along that Katrina was staying at a shelter, because he had been down that road before with other girls. Presenting himself as a savior was the first step in his plan.

It was the beginning of the second week when Tony knocked on Katrina's bedroom door to ask if he could speak to her. She opened the door and invited him inside. Asking, "What would you like to talk about, Tony?" Tony sat down on the bed, took a deep breath then started to ask her if she enjoyed the lifestyle he had been providing for her. She told him "Of course we like and appreciate all that you have done for us. It has been the best that we have lived in the past year". As if Tony was expecting anything less, he then told her "That's good, I was hoping you'd like it". Tony then went on to tell her that he wanted to take care of her but she was going to have to help a little too. He asked Katrina "How come you never ask about the other women in the house?" She told him it wasn't her place to ask because it's his house. He said to her "Good! A woman who minds her own business is always a good thing".

Tony started explaining to Katrina that when he met the other women they were all in the same situation as Katrina and he took them in and provided them with a roof over their heads, food and everything else that they needed. Before Tony could get to the point where he wanted to tell her that the money to help those women had to come from somewhere, he received a beep on his pager and told her he had to go, but promised he'd continue the conversation later. Tony walked out the room leaving Katrina to wonder what it was that she was up against and what he could possibly want from her.

After Tony left, one of the other women knocked on Katrina's door. She reluctantly opened the door to find a big, tall attractive girl named Candy standing in the doorway with a joint in her mouth. Candy was about five ft eleven inches tall, one hundred and sixty pounds but appeared to be more like a giant Statue of Liberty with the five-inch heels she was wearing. She towered over Katrina and her voice was authoritative and territorial. She was wearing acrylic, colorful fingernails that were about two inches long and her badly sewn weave came down to her back. Katrina asked, "What can I do for you?" Candy answered, "You can do like the rest of us, get off your ass and go out there and work to contribute to this house".

As Katrina stood there stunned by her comments, Candy continued to chastise her saying, "You ain't no fucking princess, we all have to work and you do too, bitch. We ain't gonna have you lying up in the house all day and all night while we out there busting our ass". Katrina was scared and she didn't know how to respond to Candy's comments. She told Candy " I don't have to talk or explain myself to you, I'll wait till Tony get home and talk to him", she then slammed the door in Candy's face as she stood outside the door yelling " You're gonna get what's coming to you, bitch!"

Five hours had passed when Tony finally returned to the house. He came back to the house with a box from this cheap store that was more like a run down version of Fredericks of Hollywood called "Booties R Us". In the box, there was a red g-string teddy that he bought for Katrina. He went to her room and knocked on the door. Katrina thought it was Candy coming back to bother her again so she rushed to the door with a pocketknife in hand and screamed, "You better leave me alone, bitch or I'll cut you". She was shocked to find Tony standing there with his right hand behind his back. She quickly apologized and he asked her what happened. She explained to Tony her little run-in with Candy earlier. Tony told her not to worry about Candy, stating that he'd take care of her. He told her he had something nice for her and reached around from behind his back and handed the box from Booties R Us to Katrina. He told her he wanted her to put on what was in the box and to wear the same red high heel pumps she wore the first time they went out and left the room. She was in no mood to put on any lingerie, but the tone in Tony's voice was convincing enough for her not to refuse.

Tony came back a few minutes later wearing a robe and nothing else. He stood behind her with his arm wrapped around her, rubbing her stomach and kissing her gently around her neck area. He then slowly made his way down to her lips where he passionately French kissed her like she had never been kissed before. His tongue and hers moved in unison.

Tony had a way of making a young girl feel good physically, sexually and emotionally. She was enjoying the way Tony was gently touching and kissing her. Suddenly, she stopped acting like she wasn't interested and started getting into it. She threw her arms around him bringing him closer to her in a tight hug. He proceeded to smoothly caress her breasts with one of his hands while leisurely sucking hard enough on her nipples to force a little bit of milk to start coming out of them. She was quietly moaning in pleasure, trying to contain herself so her daughter wouldn't wake up.

As it started to heat up in the room between them, Tony slowly picked up Katrina and carried her to his room. He lay her down on her back with her legs spread wide open on his bed and proceeded to give her the best oral experience she's ever had. His tongue was like an Anaconda tastefully devouring a surprised dessert, savoring every drop of her juice in his mouth. No one had ever performed oral sex on Katrina before and she had never had anyone make her feel so good. As Katrina's passion rose, her moaning and screaming became louder and she grabbed Tony's rising manhood gently stroking it back and forth trying to get it as hard as she could to pleasure him the same way he was pleasuring her. He had his index and middle fingers inside her while gently licking her clitoris. She was enjoying it and screaming for him to take her.

Tony was not done with Katrina yet and ignoring her pleas, he effortlessly grabbed her and flipped her upside down so her legs rested on his shoulders, putting her kitty cat in his mouth so he could lick her clit some more. It was like a choreographed move from the movie "Enter the Dragon". Slowing the motion of his tongue, Tony delicately licked her clit until she reached orgasms multiple times. Sexually satisfied, Katrina wanted to return the pleasure given to her and attempted to blow him. While Katrina's desire to please Tony could not be contained, her teeth got in the way making it too painful for Tony to enjoy. She didn't have enough experience to return the favor just yet; Tony wanted it to be all about her, anyway.

By the time Tony placed Katrina back on the bed, she was engulfed in a passionate flame that she didn't want to flicker. He could see that she was yearning for more, so he laid her on her back then spread her legs open so he could gently finger her back to submission once again. She wanted to climb on top of him and start winding and grinding on him like a top running its course around a cement floor. She was ready to take the real thing whichever way he was going to give it to her. He dropped his robe, grabbed his nine-incher and proceeded to slowly enter Katrina. He stroked her slowly back and forth while she lay on her back until she started screaming "Harder! Harder!" The harder she screamed, the more forceful he became and the more she begged. He flipped her over and gave it to her from the back doggy style while rubbing her clitoris with his fingers. The motion of her round booty circulated even more blood from Tony's brain down to his manhood.

He was banging her like he had never banged a girl in his life. She was in a state of ecstasy that she had never experienced. She blurted out "I love it! It feels good and I want more of it!" Tony knew he was skillful in the bedroom, so nothing she said at the time was going to make an ounce of difference to what he already knew. He had been there many times before with so many women. He banged her until she had no more energy left in her. By the time Tony reached orgasm, Katrina was ready to fall asleep. Tony knew sexing Katrina was business as usual for him. However, Katrina viewed it differently. She felt loved by him and that ultimately transformed into full grown and developed emotions for him. Katrina felt she had found a father figure and a lover in Tony.

Katrina woke up the next day with a new outlook on her situation. She was starting to feel wanted and more comfortable in the house. She was starting to have strong feelings for Tony and wanted more of his time, and Tony was more than willing to oblige. Tony was sexing Katrina on a regular basis and satisfying her more each time they had sex. The more he slept with her, the more attached she became and the more her feeling for Tony grew. By the third week, Katrina was completely turned out and Tony felt it was time to lay out his plan for her. Tony had made her vacate the other room and moved into his room with him. Nina was now sleeping in the other room by herself. Katrina believed that the move not only solidified her relationship with Tony, but also raised her status within the house. Besides Candy, there was another woman named Chocolate who lived in the house. A drug user, Chocolate slept most of the day and was only able to stay alert at night to work the streets. Prior to the time Katrina moved into the house, Chocolate and Candy each had their own separate rooms.

Tony had set the rules for his plans for Katrina. She was in love with Tony and couldn't get enough of him. He did everything for her and she appreciated everything he did. Tony had boosted Katrina's self esteem to the point where she started feeling like a princess around him and other people. She wanted to please him and wanted to see him happy all the time the same way he made her happy. Katrina had no idea that there was a method to Tony's madness and she would soon find out.

The Plan Unfolds

His plan firmly in place, Tony waited two weeks before continuing his conversation with Katrina. When Tony came home that evening, it was business as usual, he sexed Katrina the way she liked it and the best way he enjoyed. After having sex with Katrina that evening and confident that he had her in the palm of his hands, Tony started to divulge his plan to Katrina. He and Katrina were still laying in bed together when he started to tell her how it was time for her to carry her own weight like everybody else around the house.

Katrina still hadn't questioned Tony about the other women in the house. He thought she must've figured out what was going on and was ready to partake in the activities or she was just really gullible. Just to make sure there was no misunderstanding, Tony decided to go into details about what the other women meant to him and why they were in the house. Tony knew that Katrina's feelings for him had blossomed to a point where she was under his spell.

He wanted to test Katrina's devotion to him, so he asked her the easiest and stupidest questions that he could come up with. His first question to her was the typical "Do you love me?" and she resolutely responded with a "Yes". He then asked her "What would you do to prove your love to me?" She told him she'd do anything for him. He wanted to make sure, so he asked her " Anything?" she responded with a resounding "Yes". Tony had pretty much set the mood for any type of conversation at this time.

Tony looked deeply into Katrina's eyes and he asked her to do what she'd never imagined that the man she loved would ever ask of her. Tony asked Katrina if she would sleep with other men if that made him happy. Katrina jumped to her feet and said, "Why would I wanna sleep with other men if you're my man?" Tony then told her that it didn't have anything to do with her love for him or his love for her, it was more about survival. He told her he knew she loved him and wouldn't take it personal if she did it because it's part of the business. And that's when she asked, "what business?" He told her "The pimping business, I'm a pimp". She still couldn't understand what his being a pimp had to do with her. Even though Katrina had been on the streets for a year with her daughter, she still didn't understand everything about the streets.

He was tired of going around the subject so he finally said to her, "As a matter of fact, I want you to do it". Still puzzled, Katrina asked again, "You want me to do what?" Tony reiterated "I want you to go out there and earn some money by sleeping with other men. What don't you understand?" She was shocked and didn't know what to say. Tony started explaining to her that there were bills around the house to be paid and gifts to be bought for her and her daughter and the only way those things could happen was if she slept with other men for money.

Katrina had no idea that Tony was about to unleash his pimp game on her. A forceful edge in his voice, Tony told her that she had no choice, she either did it or he'd stop loving her and she would have to go back to the streets. Katrina thought long and hard about the decision she was faced with and decided to sleep on it for a night. She asked Tony if she could give him an answer the following day and he agreed like a nice pimp would. Katrina didn't know that there was no such thing as a nice pimp.

Katrina had grown accustomed to the life that Tony provided for her in the last month or so and she didn't want to go back to the streets. She was lying in bed thinking about alternative ways to get out of the situation, unaware that she was already indebted to Tony. She had no friends and she didn't want to crawl back to her family who had turned their backs on her. She was lying in the bed with tears running down her face hugging her daughter Nina when Tony walked in the room. True to the game, he placed his arm around Katrina and her daughter comforting her like a father would.

That night Tony explained to Katrina that she was his family now and he would do whatever it took to provide for and protect her and her daughter. He told her that he was the only person in the world who loved her. He took Nina away from Katrina and placed the child on his shoulder. He stepped a few feet away from Katrina and started talking to her like her daughter's life was now depending on the decision she'd make. Tony authoritatively told her "I know you don't want to wake up tomorrow to find yourself alone with your daughter on the streets again, right?" He had this deadly look in his eyes that she didn't know how to react to! The fact that he also brandished a 9mm glock revolver around his waist as he was talking to Katrina instilled all the fear and reinforcement he intended it to.

Tony told Katrina that she was an ingrate and he didn't like ingrates. He brought her into his house, took care of her, made sure she didn't want for anything and she owed him. Tony stepped up the guilt trip routine by running off the numbers for the money he spent on Katrina. He pulled out a list of things and the money he spent on Katrina and her baby for the last month. Katrina felt like she was stuck in a zone and her back was against the wall. He handed her back her baby then walked out the door leaving her no other choice.

Katrina thought long and hard about running away but she didn't have any money and Tony had enough connections on the streets to find her within days, if not hours. Katrina had eavesdropped on an earlier conversation Tony was having with another man over the phone when she first came to the house and it brought out a streak in Tony that she didn't want to see again. She overheard Tony threatened to chop off the head of another pimp who was trying to do business on his turf and he was serious. She had dismissed it as an isolated incident, but she was now faced with the same consequences.

Later that night, Tony came home with blood all over his hand from a fight he had with another man. He was cursing and screaming at Candy telling her that he had cut off the man's tongue and left nut for messing with Candy and next time he'd put a bullet in the man's head for messing with one of his bitches. After witnessing that episode, Katrina knew there was no way out for her. She was young impressionable and scared. Katrina felt cornered and had no other choice but to accept Tony's proposal to sell her body to men for money.

Following the incident from the previous night, Katrina had slept in the other room with her daughter. She awoke early the next day anticipating a confrontation with Tony, but she had already made up her mind that she was going to become one of Tony's bitches. She was ready to assume the role without actually knowing the meaning of the term as it related to the streets. She figured as long as she didn't have to worry about food and shelter for her daughter, it was worth not having to go back home to face more humiliation from her parents. Her parents' attitude forced her to make a tough decision very easy.

When Katrina walked into Tony's room she did not anticipate finding him in bed with Candy who was riding sucking him off the same way that Katrina had done the previous night. She ran out of the room horrified, no longer feeling special. Tony called for her to come back and join them but she ignored his request and went to Nina's room and locked the door. The clicking of the door lock only intensified Tony's anger as he walked out to the hallway and demanded that she came out of the room and into his bedroom. Candy was anxiously waiting to have Katrina watch some of her best work; she volunteered to go drag her out of the room into Tony's room.

Tony didn't really like to display physical violence in front of his women; he commanded respect through his tone and instilled fear with his body language. When he told Katrina he wanted to talk to her and commanded her to open the door, she didn't think twice about it. After Katrina opened the door, Tony walked in and ushered her back into his room so she could watch him and Candy go at it.

Tony wanted Candy to teach Katrina the tricks of the trade. He told her one of the most important things in this business is getting these guys to climax very quickly, because once they climax the date is over. He made her sit on the chair in the corner of his room to watch Candy go to work on him. And that she did. Candy was a veteran in the game and could get an impotent man to cum. She got on her knees and aggressively sucked Tony so hard, she almost separated the skin from the rest of his penis. She dipped his balls in her mouth like a teabag being dipped in a hot cup of water. After about three minutes of sucking, Tony came all over her face. He then turned to Katrina and asked, "Did you see that?" Candy wanted to show off more of her skills to Katrina like she was competing for Tony's love.

He sensed Katrina was uncomfortable so he asked Candy to leave and give him a few minutes alone with Katrina. Candy walked out and closed the door. He pulled her near him in a bear hug then slowly went down on her and proceeded to eat her like she was cotton candy at a state fair. Katrina gave in to the sensation throbbing between her legs. She was holding Tony's head between her legs screaming she loved it. He turned her over for a quickie and she obliged. He rammed her from behind and with a few strokes he ejaculated all over her back. He kissed her and told her he loved her then walked out of the room.

Getting Sucked In

Tony told Katrina he wasn't gonna put her out on the streets by herself just yet because she was still inexperienced. He wanted her to be under his watch, so he told her he'd be bringing a couple of gentlemen to the house later and she was to take care of them. He told her to make sure Nina was asleep by 10:00 PM because he didn't want to expose any babies to his business. Tony left specific directions for Katrina to follow. He'd bought her a few more skimpy outfits from the same trashy lingerie store in the combat zone and ordered her to put on a crotch-less black teddy that he had bought her. Katrina took a shower and got dressed as planned. She rubbed this inexpensive oil that Tony had bought all over her body and sprayed the cheap perfume around her crotch and neck area.

It was exactly 10:00 PM when Tony showed up with two disgusting looking white men in their fifties. One of them was wearing an expensive gray business suit, blue shirt and a yellow tie. He wore a gold antique watch on his left wrist and sported a conservative haircut. She took him to the back room and as this guy started to undress she couldn't believe her eyes. He was wearing a garter belt, bra and female underwear like a woman would. He was a cross dresser looking to get poked from behind by a dominatrix and Katrina was no dominatrix just yet.

This guy pulled out a big dildo from his jacket pocket and asked Katrina to strap it on and bang him from behind with it. She couldn't believe it. She thought she was going to be the one getting sexed by this disgusting man, but she ended up giving it to him from the back and to her surprise, she enjoyed humiliating him. After they were done, he left five hundred dollars on the dresser then walked out. She couldn't believe how easy it was, but not all her clients would be that easy to deal with.

Katrina walked out of the room feeling confident and asked for the next guy, but he was already pleasured without her even knowing it. The whole time she was banging the man with the dildo; the second man was watching and jerking off through the peephole in the back room. Tony was the kind of pimp who had special clients, some he had to accommodate at home and others he didn't know from a hole in the wall. Tony had especially set up the back room in his house to accommodate his white-collar clients who feared getting caught in the back of a car on the street. Those were his regular nonthreathening clients that he'd bring to the house to break in his newer, inexperienced women.

Katrina couldn't believe how quick and simple it was to earn those five hundred dollars. She got a taste of the game and was sucked right in by the fast and easy money. Katrina had never even seen five hundred dollars in cash in her life; much less earn it that quickly. The two gentlemen were escorted out by Tony and she was left alone in the apartment gazing at the money in her hand. She once again thought she could walk away unscathed by taking the five hundred dollars and move to another state. But money is the root of all evil; she wanted another score to satisfy her financial needs. The money was tempting; the thought of being able to get away from Tony and still be financially secure was even more envious.

When Tony came back a couple of hours later, he found Katrina lying on the bed with the five hundred dollars spread on the bed like she just won the lottery. She was happily smiling and knew that making more of this money could only bring more happiness. Tony sat down next to her on the bed and told her if she thought that was something, there was a lot more where that came from. Tony allowed her to keep the whole first score and Katrina thought that would be the deal all the time. Tony told her he'd take her shopping the next day and she could spend the money on anything she wanted. She told him she wanted to make love on the money spread around the bed. Tony threw another thousand dollars consisting mostly of five and ten dollar bills on top of the five hundred dollars that she had earned and told her she'd have fifteen hundred to spend the next day when they would go the mall. She was so happy; she reached for Tony's belt and pull down his pants before he could say "whoa!" She took him in her mouth and went to work like Candy had taught her. She gave Tony the blowjob of his life. She had Tony ejaculating all over her mouth within minutes.

Tony took notice of Katrina's improved sexual skills. This time around, Tony didn't really care to be gentle with Katrina. He banged her as hard as he could until her coochie started bleeding. She was screaming in pain, but enjoyed most of it because it was Tony. After he was done with her, he explained to her that she may come into contact with rough clients who would want to get rough with her the exact same way and she would have to be ready to take it. Tony was all about getting his investment ready for the market.

Nina woke up around 9:00AM the next morning, crying, she wanted to see her mommy. She walked out of her room and right into Tony's room to find her mother sucking Tony off early in the morning. Although she was only a year old, the look in her face was sad and disappointed. It was almost as if she interpreted a shameful act in her own little mind. Katrina quickly jumped up when she realized her daughter was standing there watching her. She took her back to the other room and comforted her. She went to the kitchen, grabbed a bottle of Gerber apple sauce to feed Nina.

It was noon when Katrina walked in the room with a tray full of fruits, eggs, bacon and toasts to serve Tony breakfast in bed. She had put her heart and soul into making him breakfast that morning because she was looking forward to spending the day shopping with him. Katrina had also started to reconsider her position with Tony. She was no longer seriously thinking about running away. Instead, she was looking forward to the perks that came with being a prostitute. Tony glorified prostitution to young Katrina by showing her old movies depicting the high lifestyle of the call girls in Hollywood. He told her he would simply play the role of her manager while she did the work and as manager, he would provide everything for her including protection, jewelry, fur coats and even a car when she got her license. Tony's plan was to solicit clients for Katrina until she was comfortable enough to solicit them on her own.

Tony and Katrina showered together while Candy watched Nina in the other room. Tony was very imposing in the house and when he gave an order it was to be followed. He told Candy to watch Nina while he and Katrina took a shower. Even though Candy was pissed that Tony was spending all his time with Katrina, there was nothing she could do about it. She knew that Katrina was the new girl and Tony had to break her in. Candy received the same treatment when she first moved in the house. The day was going to be all about Katrina and Tony didn't want to have any other disgruntled woman complaining.

After a few minutes, Tony and Katrina quickly got out of the shower and got dressed. Tony made sure the dress Katrina wore was an eye catcher and was as revealing as it possibly could be to any man who was shopping for pussy at the mall. He wanted her to leave very little to the imagination. If the dress were any tighter or shorter, she would have been arrested for indecent exposure. Tony was a street hustler whose mind was always on hustling. Katrina may have felt that it was all about her, but Tony had a way of shopping his girls around. He may have set out to spend fifteen hundred dollars on her at the mall, but his master plan was to also pick up about twenty five hundred in business while Katrina was shopping.

Tony and Katrina arrived at the Galleria Mall around 5:00PM on a Saturday afternoon, when the mall is usually crowded with all kinds of people and especially men who were looking for sexual favors from women. Most men can't seem to control their urge to look at a woman's curvaceous body, no matter how whorish she looks. That was the trap that Tony wanted to set at the mall. While Katrina was having a great time picking out some of her favorite outfits at different stores, Tony was trying to solicit clients for her. All they had to do was glimpse at her and Tony knew he had the men hooked.

In a span of two hours, he had set up about nine appointments with ten different men for Katrina at two hundred and fifty dollars a pop. Two of the men wanted to have a three-some with Katrina and they were willing to pay a grand. Tony had secured enough business for Katrina for the night, so he went back to the store to assist her with her items. She was happy paying for her own clothes and Nina's without any worries. By the time they left the mall, Katrina had spent about fourteen hundred dollars on clothes and shoes. She still had one hundred dollars left and she wanted to treat Tony to dinner. They went around the corner to TGI Friday's for a quick meal before leaving the mall. She spent all her money because she was betting on making more by continuing to sell her body.

Getting Down and Dirty

Katrina had no idea what Tony had in store for her. There's no such thing as working hours for prostitutes as she would soon find out. They start working at nightfall till dawn and Katrina was about to get a taste of what it took to live the ghetto fabulous life of a prostitute. Tony had made arrangements for Candy to take Nina to the sitter for the night so Katrina could work all night. Her first client showed up at 7:00PM and she couldn't believe what kind of guy he was. He was a young corporate, Christian brother who wanted to simply have oral sex with her because his Christian wife had denied him that pleasure since they got married.

He explained to her it was his first time and to go easy on him. Katrina hadn't fully mastered the art of oral stimulation completely yet, but this guy had nothing to compare her skills to. She unzipped his pants as he sat on the edge of the bed and pulled out his already erect penis to put in her mouth, he stopped her, and asked if he could eat her first. She gladly obliged. He ate her for about fifteen minutes until he satisfied his hunger then she sucked him off for about five minutes until he climaxed. His wife didn't believe in having oral sex period. He was a quick and easy customer who gave her no problems. He handed over the agreed payment of two hundred and fifty dollars to Katrina.

Tony had subsequently scheduled the appointments a half hour apart. The corporate young man was done by 7:20PM and Katrina had ten minutes to freshen up for her next appointment scheduled for 7:30 PM. Her next appointment was a middle aged white man who had driven all the way from Dover, Massachusetts to Roxbury for some black ass. He was rich and married to a twenty something young white woman with two young children. This guy was of a strange and different breed. He wanted her to drink a glass of water and wanted to be in the bathtub with her. She took him in the shower where he took all his clothes off. He laid flat on his back in the tub, he then asked her to scoop down and urinate on his face and chest while he jerked off. After guzzling down a couple of glasses of water, it was easy flowing for her. She urinated all over the freak until he came. After coming he quickly showered, put his clothes back on then head back to his suburban wife in Dover. He left two hundred and fifty dollars on the sink in the bathroom.

Katrina couldn't believe how easy the money was flowing. She hadn't had sexual intercourse with any of her clients and she was in the black for five hundred dollars. She couldn't wait to see what was next. She knew eventually someone was going to want sex and she was ready to do it, but not the way her sixth client wanted it. Tony had left her a box of condom for protection and he was adamant about her using them.

This particular client didn't want to put on a condom and wouldn't let up about it. She was finally fed up with fighting with him, she reached out under the pillow and grabbed a knife that Tony had left her just in case something like that went down. She put the knife to the guy's throat and threatened to cut him if he didn't get up and leave. The guy sensed that she was serious; he quickly got up and left. As he ran outside, Tony was around the corner making sure she wasn't harmed. She signaled to him that she had a problem with this client. Tony grabbed the guy by his neck then pulled him to the side, beat the crap out him and took the $250.00 he was supposed to pay Katrina.

Tony had everything covered. He had told Katrina that he'd be around the corner where she could always see him through the window and if anyone gave her a hard time to just go to the window and wave. He knew she wasn't a pro yet and wanted to make sure she was safe. Tony also knew the clients wouldn't feel comfortable in the apartment knowing he was there, and that was one of the reasons why he waited outside around the corner. None of the men who went in to see Katrina even noticed Tony standing outside around the corner. He camouflaged himself like a lion waiting for a prey.

After the sixth guy left, Katrina had an hour break before her next date would show up. Tony went upstairs and asked Katrina for the money she had earned. It was about fifteen hundred dollars and he wanted it all. She couldn't understand why she had to give up all the money to Tony. He explained to her that the money she earned was placed into a special bank account so when she needed something he could buy it for her. He told her he didn't have time to go into the details about the monthly expenses and that he would tell her later. He brought her some Chinese food from the restaurant around the corner. He was happy she was having a good night, but she still had four more customers she had to see before calling it a night. She was a bit tired but he didn't want to hear it. He was slowly breaking her in and he didn't have room for any lazy horses in his stable. Katrina was young, good looking, energetic and the best prospect that Tony had.

Any tricks for the right price

Tony had a way of keeping his women in line. Candy was his favorite sex partner and he'd give her his all every time they had sex. Candy was freaky and there was no limit to what she'd do to Tony. She was an expert in "rim jobs" and Tony loved the feel of her tongue around his anus. Candy was the first person who introduced Tony to a rim job. She'd learned about it from a white customer who wanted special favors for a large sum of money. When the customer asked Candy for a rim job for the first time, she had no idea what he was talking about.

After the guy explained that a rim job is the art of slowly licking the anus, she was disgusted and said "no way!" However, once the guy demonstrated to her how it was done by slowly using his tongue to lick around her anus and occasionally sticking it in. The sensation almost left her orgasmically crippled. She knew she would do it for the right price. And every hooker has her price. The offered price of a thousand dollars didn't even completely roll off the guy's tongue before Candy told him she'd do it". Candy pulled out some kind of oral condom that covered the tongue, stuck it in her mouth, and then went to work on the guy's anus. She's been a rim job expert ever since.

Tony stopped kissing Candy the day after she started performing rim jobs on customers. Condom or not, Tony had his own standards too. She did, however, always clean the customers' asses herself before she'd lick them in addition to wearing the oral condom. She just couldn't resist the temptation of a thousand dollars. Her many attempts to try to get Tony to perform a rim job on her were futile. Every pimp has his limits. Candy was trying to be as patient as she could with Tony; he hadn't slept with her in over a week and she wanted some loving from him. Tony was the only guy Candy ever made love to. Even though she slept with other men for a living, she was able to distinguish between love and sex. She always professed her love for Tony because he was there for her when she was down and out.

Candy had performed other tricks for men that she kept hidden from Tony. She had developed an obsession for money that created no boundaries between sex and money. Candy was enthralled by the ghetto fabulous lifestyle way before ghetto fabulous was in vogue. She would go to any length to perform a trick as long as the price was right.

Getting Caught in a Trap

Deep down in his conscience, Tony knew that Katrina was young, but he didn't bother to ask her age. It had been a few weeks since Katrina had been turning tricks for Tony in the apartment and it was time to move her to the street to get her own clients. Katrina made her debut on the streets on a hot Friday night. She was dropped off on Washington Street around 10:00PM in the Combat Zone, downtown Boston. Katrina flagged down her first customers who were two young, suburban white kids looking to get quick blowjobs because they could afford it. The driver must've been driving his parents' Volvo station wagon.

When they pulled over to let Katrina in the car, their hearts were beating louder than a police siren. They were both nervous and Katrina even more nervous than they were because she had never worked the streets before. She knew they weren't old enough to be cops, but they could've been pulling some adolescent prank in the Combat Zone. Katrina commanded one hundred and seventy-five dollars each for a blowjob and the guys didn't refuse; they pulled out the money and handed it to Katrina. She directed them to a side street where they took a left down a dark alley so Tony could keep watch over her. The two white kids took less then a minute each to climax and they were happy just to get their shit off that night.

By midnight, Katrina already had ten customers and most of them were just looking for blowjobs. She had given more blowjobs in the span of two hours that could last her a lifetime. Her eleventh customer pulled up in a darkly tinted Chevy Blazer. He was a thirty something white guy who sounded a little too hip for the streets. She hesitated at first, but after the guy pled with her for about 10 seconds she hopped in the car and drove back down to the alley. When Tony saw the truck pulling in the alley, he took off running and Katrina knew there was trouble. Before she could say anything, the guy pulled out his badge, read her rights then placed her under arrest for prostitution.

Katrina had only been working the streets for one night and she was already arrested for prostitution. She was taken to the fourth precinct downtown where most of the nightwalkers were kept. She was in a cell with a bunch of career hookers who acted like it was normal procedure for them to be locked up every night. Katrina was crying hysterically and screaming that she was only fifteen years old. One of the hookers overheard her and called a cop over to let him know that she was just a child.

Katrina was given one phone call and she called Tony to pick her up. She explained to Tony that he had to tell them that he was her father. Tony looked old enough to be Katrina's father. He was in his late thirties, but he dressed like a twenty something so he could talk to young girls. Tony, however, didn't know that Katrina was only fifteen years old. He thought she was at least sixteen because she had a child. Tony was apprehensive about picking Katrina up form the precinct because he wasn't sure if she had told the cops that he was her pimp or if he'd slept with her. He didn't want to chance it. He called on good old reliable, Candy, to go pick up Katrina from jail. Candy first had to leave the streets, go home and change into some decent clothes so she could look convincing enough as an older sister to Katrina.

The thought of going to jail for fifteen years for statutory rape was running through Tony's mind as he pulled up in front of the police station to drop off Candy. He told her he would be down the block waiting in case the police were looking for him. He handed her a thousand dollars and told her that it should cover the bail. After Candy left the car, Tony drove down the street mumbling "the bitch has only been on the streets one night and already she's costing me money, but that's my bad, though. I should've warned her about fucking Petey and his fucking Blazer".

While Tony was in the car pondering his next move, Candy was inside the precinct trying to get Katrina out. She was asked to show ID and her ID revealed that her real name was Patricia Cabot. When they asked who she was bailing out, she told them Katrina. When the cop asked if Katrina had a last name, she quickly told him Cabot. The cop called to the back to have Katrina Cabot brought out. When the cop in the back called for Katrina Cabot, no one responded. He called a second and a third time, and then finally Katrina put two and two together and figured that Tony had probably added the Cabot to her name. She was released into her older sister's custody and no bail was necessary because she was a minor.

Katrina was surprised to find a woman standing at the front desk in the police precinct wearing her Sunday's best. At first, she couldn't make out who the person was, but when Candy slowly whispered under her breath "it's me, Candy!" Katrina quickly ran to her, gave her a hug and thanked her for getting her out. The cops asked if that was her sister and she confirmed.

They returned her belongings and told her because she was a minor she won't be prosecuted this time, but next time she would be sent to a juvenile hall. She took her belongings, including about a thousand dollars she had made that night and placed it in her purse. Before they walked out of the precinct, Candy pulled her to the side and told her that Tony didn't have to know about the money she made because sometimes when dirty cops arrest them, they would keep the money, especially "Dirty Petey". She told her to keep the money for herself and to tell Tony her bail was a thousand dollars if he asked.

As much as Candy resented Katrina when she first came to the house, she hated seeing another young woman go through what she went through with Tony. She was already in the game and had grown accustomed to the highs and lows of that life, but she wanted to protect Katrina in her own way.

Katrina for the first time felt a bond between her and Candy. And for the first time since they met, Candy made Katrina feel welcomed.

Establishing Who's Boss

When Katrina and Candy got to the car outside, Tony extended his hand out to get the money Katrina had earned. Candy noticed that Katrina couldn't lie to Tony so she quickly intervened and told him that "Dirty Petey" had taken all the money. She also told Tony that she thought Katrina should go home and rest for the remainder of the night. Tony was pissed at Candy for suggesting that Katrina should go home. Tony started going off on Candy saying, "Fuck that! On a Friday night, I ain't gonna make no money. This bitch went to jail, I had to take you off the streets to bail her out and she came out with no money, fuck that!" Tony then asked, "How much was her fucking bail, anyway?" Candy replied "A thousand dollars". Tony angrily screamed at Candy "A thousand dollars! This bitch gonna have to work!" Candy interjected and told Tony she'd cover Katrina's half for the night. Katrina was in the back seat of the car in tears. She had just realized the kind of situation she was involved in and what kind of person Tony really was. Tony may have been kind to her in the beginning, but he was a monster who was out to get what he could from the women he recruited.

Tony had psychological control over all his women. He molded them, and made sure that they all felt like he was the only person in the world who loved them. Chocolate and Candy had been living the prostitution lifestyle for about ten years already and were used to Tony's aggressive ways. In the meantime, Katrina was introduced to yet another side of Tony on the night she got arrested. She saw a side of Tony she never thought existed. First he brandished a gun near her daughter's head and now he was getting pissed about losing money because she went to jail.

She realized that night that crossing Tony might possibly place her life in jeopardy. She also realized why Candy was trying to hide money from Tony. Although Candy seemed like she was happy with the life she was leading, she also made it clear to Katrina that it was never too late to leave. Candy didn't want Katrina to get caught up in that lifestyle. And she was also concerned with Nina's welfare. Candy herself had a baby, but her baby was taken away by the Department of Social Services when she neglected her for the streets. She just couldn't stand to watch another young girl go through the same thing she went through.

Tony may have been in control of the women, but they always had a choice to make. Candy tried her best to show Katrina how to establish herself in the game and how to walk away with something. Candy taught Katrina how to pull extra tricks on the side where Tony couldn't watch her. She wanted to make sure Katrina worked more for herself and less for Tony. Candy was as slick as they came in the game and for every thousand dollars that she earned for Tony, she earned about five hundred dollars for herself and had it stashed away in a safe deposit box.

Candy took Katrina down to the bank where she had her deposit box and opened an account for her. Candy kept her deposit box key on a chain around her neck. She had the key plated with silver, and when Tony asked about the key she told him it was a key given to her by her mom as a child as a symbol of her being the key to her heart. She suggested that Katrina had her key plated with silver and put it around her daughter's neck.

Candy was trying her very best to cover every corner while she was schooling Katrina about the streets. One of the major things she wanted to cover was identity. She explained to Katrina that she should never, ever, under any circumstances, use her real name on the streets or with the police. The first thing she needed to do was to create a new name for herself that she could always use on the street and with the police, should she ever get arrested again. Katrina shook her head in agreement then asked Candy what kind of name she thought would be appropriate or best suited for her? Candy took a long look at her and decided that Star would be a good name for her. Candy turned to her and told her "from now on you should call yourself Star". Katrina liked the name, but she asked Candy "why Star?" Candy didn't really have an answer but she made one up anyway. She told Katrina that she would have to be her own star looking over her shoulders on the streets. She made plans to take Katrina to the Chinese store in Chinatown the next day to get a fake ID with the name Star Bright.

Katrina was fascinated by Candy's intelligence and she wanted to absorb everything that Candy was dishing out. Katrina started to see in Candy the big sister that she always wanted. Candy may not have been the best of role models, but she was all Katrina had available to her. Candy had made it clear to Katrina that she had plans to leave the streets and didn't see prostitution as a career. After all, Candy was only twenty-five years old and didn't want to reach the old ripe age of thirty still turning tricks. One of her concerns was not allowing Katrina to get absorbed by the streets. Candy had already been on the streets for about ten years and it had become so hard for her to leave, she wanted to make sure another young person didn't waste her life on the streets.

Katrina became Candy's protégé for all but six months because Candy's plan to leave wasn't going to be extended beyond that time. She tried her best to school Katrina about pulling tricks, saving money, staying away from harm and danger, and putting her daughter first. Katrina managed well while Candy was around. She was saving money and doing all the things she needed to prepare to leave Tony. But somewhere along the way, greed had taken over Katrina's mind, body and soul.

Addicted to the Oldest Profession

Katrina had been on the streets for a couple of months and the money was flowing like water coming out of a fire hydrant in the middle of a hot summer day. Katrina was averaging about three thousand a week for Tony and another two thousand for herself. She tried her best to save some of her money but every now and then she would splurge on a few expensive items then lied to Tony about where they came from. For the most part, Tony covered all of Katrina's expenses from the money she handed in to him. It was always the usual skimpy outfits, anything to keep his merchandise moving.

Tony and Katrina were living the lifestyle of the ghetto rich. They might have as well lived at the mall because they spent most of their time there. They were spending thousands of dollars everyday on bullshit items that had no resale value. She was buying big gold "bamboo" earrings; name rings, big rope chains and some of the most expensive but hideous hooker boots she could find. Tony was trying his best to emulate the rappers and ran around with this up and coming rap group he was managing. They actually never made it.

Tony wasted a lot of money trying to make stars out of three knuckleheads whose rhyming skills were lackadaisical at best and they actually thought they were the best thing since sliced bread because of their association with Tony. He was paying for VIP admission everywhere they went and they drank the most expensive champagne on the menu while Katrina was on the streets breaking her back. Tony had also bought a couple of nice cars to park on the street where he lived. Although no one messed with Tony's cars on the street, it was funny to hear Tony brag about owning three cars, but never once mentioned buying a home.

Katrina made sure that Tony was aware of her new street name, Star. When he asked her how she came up with it, she told him it was a secret. Life was good for Katrina and Tony and they were getting along great. Katrina started to fall in love more and more with Tony along the way. She used to daydream about a normal life with Tony and her daughter. She thought that Tony would make good on his promise to stop hustling and settle down and become a family man. Tony continued to feed her lines to keep those dreams alive. He had set a deadline for them to reach their goals and Katrina was looking forward to that day.

She was not an observant person and didn't pay much attention to Tony's spending habits. If she were paying attention, she would've known that Tony wasn't the kind of guy who knew how to save or wanted to save his money. Whatever amount of money Tony was carrying in his pockets was pretty much all the money he had and it wasn't unusual for Tony to walk around with ten thousand dollars in cash in his pockets. Tony didn't trust leaving his money anywhere or with anyone.

Katrina was bringing in so much money she never really kept track of how much money she had earned. She had started to choose work over her daughter. She had developed a list of clients that she could book during the day. She would often drop her daughter off at this old lady's house that used to watch her for a hundred dollars a week. Her daughter spent most nights over the old lady's house. The woman didn't mind because she was retired and living alone at her house and enjoyed the company. Nina kept the old lady sane for the most part and she didn't mind the extra income. Money had become Katrina's priority and being estranged from her daughter was the last thing on her mind. She had developed spending habits similar to that of socialites. She was buying everything and anything that her money could buy without letting Tony know she was holding out on him.

Somewhere along the way, Katrina had developed an insatiable appetite for sex, as well as the desire to control men during sex. She'd often get wet and horny while thinking about some of her clients. She always considered Tony to be the best sex partner she ever had, but she was also into variety and she especially loved the men who performed oral sex on her. Once Katrina became a full-time prostitute, Tony rarely performed oral sex on her. Tony was very oral in the beginning of their relationship, and he knew that was the highlight of their sexual encounters. In a way, he sort of made her feel dirty because he'd started to deprive her of the very sexual favors he used to entice her. She looked forward to having this specific client, named Leon eat her out every time they met and this guy expertly ate her to the point where she would occasionally do him for free. Katrina became addicted to money and sex in a matter of months. All her priorities and plans to secure a better life for her and her daughter were out the window. She became selfish and uncontrollable in just a few months.

From Bad to Worse

Six months had passed and Candy left the house and the streets as planned. Katrina no longer had a friend to confide in and she was all alone in this hell she had created for herself. Tony had also kicked Chocolate out of the house because she wasn't bringing in enough money. Chocolate was in her thirties but the streets had worn her out so much, she looked like she was in her upper forties. She had also fallen victim to the new epidemic known as crack. Chocolate was strung out most of the time and was taking up space that Tony didn't want to spare. He figured if he no longer had any use for her why should he allow her to stay in the house?

It was a sad day when Chocolate left because Tony was especially harsh to her right in front of Katrina. He called her "a washed up ho who couldn't control her urges on the street". He also told her " dumb bitches like you is the reason why the world is full of retarded kids" Katrina saw firsthand what she had to look forward to, but she was convinced that Tony loved her enough and would never treat her like that. Katrina and Chocolate never took the time to get to know each other. Chocolate was actually the first girl that Tony was able to influence to the point where she was selling her body on the streets to support him. Chocolate was the guinea pig for Tony's mastery of the art of turning out and breaking down women.

Candy left Tony without leaving any clue behind. He spent days looking for her all over Boston, but she was nowhere to be found. Candy had moved to Phoenix, knowing that Tony wouldn't have the brain to think about that part of the country. Tony did not know that Candy had been saving money, so he thought she'd still be on the streets somewhere in Boston trying to make a living. Candy didn't even tell Katrina where she was moving to; she figured that Katrina would eventually wake up just like she did to find her own way out. There was no goodbye, no teary eyes and no hugs. She simply vanished. She couldn't risk having Katrina leak information to Tony about her whereabouts. She left wearing a business suit with a shoulder bag containing fifty thousand dollars in cash.

Tony had really made it seem like it was all about him and Star, as he started calling Katrina after Chocolate and Candy were out of the house. He was paying more attention to her and doing more recreational activities together. Tony did his best to gain Katrina's confidence and trust. One could say that he had her wrapped around his finger. Most men think it is okay to go out and play when they have their girlfriends in check and Tony was no different. While Katrina was sleeping during the day, Tony would get up early in the morning to go look for new recruits to fill the empty spaces he had in his house and his pockets. Tony was a lavish spender and had no money management skills whatsoever. The more money that was brought in, the more money he spent and Katrina had stopped holding out on him after a few weeks of Candy and Chocolate's departure. She had increased her net income by almost fifteen hundred dollars a week and Tony spent an additional fifteen hundred dollars a week trying to keep up with the Joneses.

Katrina believed Tony when he told her he was trying to save money so they could leave the street life. She never once questioned his motives or asked to see any kind of proof that money was being saved. She was enjoying the fact that someone was taking care of her and providing for her every want and needs, even though she was really the one earning the money. Psychologically, Tony had screwed her up so badly, she really believed that Tony was her caretaker and they had a future together.

When Tony brought a new run-away teen named Trisha to the house, he told Katrina she was his cousin and that she was only going to be in the house for a few weeks and that was it. Katrina felt it was very thoughtful of Tony to bring his young female cousin into the house to help her, so she didn't question it. However, Tony was up to his old tricks again. Trisha was not related to Tony at all, nor did she know him; he had met her the same way he met Katrina. Trisha was going to be Tony's new belle on the streets and he was setting the stage for acceptance by Katrina.

Tony was now spending the money Katrina was bringing in on Trisha and she grew suspicious. The first sign that something was wrong was when Tony came back from the mall with Trisha; all she bought were skimpy outfits and hooker gear. Katrina was mad but she didn't say anything to Tony or Trisha. Tony dropped her off on the corner of Washington and Tremont Street in the combat zone around 10:00 PM that night. She was apprehensive the whole night because she was bothered by the fact that Trisha might be taking Tony's attention away from her. She decided to take a cab back to the house around 11:00PM.

Katrina may have been young in age but she had started to develop the maturity and rationale of an adult since she had been on her own. Katrina had decided to go with her instincts that night and went home early. It was a good thing that she went home early because there was a big raid in the Combat Zone and fifty prostitutes and johns were picked up. Her instincts kicked in just at the right time because when she got home she could hear moaning and groaning coming from Tony's room. She didn't even bother knocking on the door, she went right in to find Trisha riding Tony like a horse pulling a carriage. She couldn't believe what she was seeing; she started pulling Trisha off Tony. Tony quickly got up and got between them before they could get at each other. There was a lot fussing and cursing between Trisha and Katrina, but Tony wasn't worried because he knew that Katrina wasn't going anywhere. Trisha was a beautiful young girl, but she wasn't stacked like Katrina and didn't have the sex appeal that Katrina had. Tony knew he had a lot of work to do before Trisha could become a moneymaker for him.

Katrina was mad at Tony for a whole week. She didn't yet fully understand how the pimp game worked. She refused to do anything with Tony and his futile efforts to win back her affection fell short. He tried buying her back with her own money, but it didn't work because she was already used to him buying her stuff. He needed to use a new approach to get her back. She'd left his bedroom and moved into the old bedroom where Chocolate and Candy used to be. Katrina's heart was torn and she didn't know what to do. One of the solutions she came up with was to retaliate by doing what Tony did to her with another man.

Katrina had never slept with a man on the street without using a condom, but on this very day she would allow her favorite pussy-eating client, Leon to have sex her without a condom. She actually paid for the hotel room so she and Leon could be together for a few hours. Leon was a smooth, seventeen year-old street- hustler, who didn't have time for a girlfriend, so he used prostitutes, especially Katrina to get his kicks. He liked Katrina because her body was firm, she was pleasing to the eyes and they had a few things in common. Leon was only a year and a half older than Katrina and most of the things he talked to her about were things she could identify with and age related.

That one particular night, when Katrina and Leon had sex for about two hours, they did it like two young rabbits whose days on earth were numbered. Tony was going crazy trying to locate her for the two hours she was with Leon. She always had a good excuse to get Tony off her back. In the past, she only had Tony to make her feel like a woman, but that night Leon did things to her that Tony had never done. By the time they were through, she had vowed she would never charge Leon for sex again, and that sex with Leon from then on would take place in a hotel room every time. They couldn't really get their kicks in the back of the car anymore. She enjoyed the touch of Leon's hand and the fact that he was much gentler with her made it all the more appealing. She was starting to develop special feelings for one of her customers, which was totally against industry rules.

Leon and Katrina continued to see each other and had sex regularly for about a month. She had started to consider leaving the streets to be with Leon. She thought about the reality of having someone normal in her life even though Leon's life was also complicated with all the hustle he was involved in. Leon may not have been a pimp, but he was involved in more hustle than any pimp on the street. He did car insurance jobs, he was involved with money counterfeit, and he also did the occasional gun dealing with his close clients. Leon was also a small time weed dealer who was out on the streets all day everyday getting his hustle on. It almost seemed like Katrina was only attracted to the street hustlers who were available to her. After all, they were the only kind of people she was exposed to.

It had only been six weeks since Katrina and Leon were sleeping with each other when she met with him at the Eastside Motel to tell him that her menstrual cycle was off after they had just finished having their usual sex session. She told Leon there was a possibility that she might be pregnant and he was definitely the father. Katrina knew for sure that Leon was the father because she hadn't slept with Tony in weeks without a condom since Trisha moved into the house. Tony would occasionally have her perform oral sex on him and that was the extent of their sexual relations for a while. Leon couldn't believe that a prostitute was standing there telling him that she was pregnant by him. He didn't want to hear it from her. He told her "I can't have no baby by no ho". Katrina couldn't believe her ears. The man she'd been secretly seeing saw her as nothing but a ho. Leon said nothing more to her; he got dressed and left the room never to be heard from again. It was at that point that the reality of the situation hit and Katrina had to figure out how she was going to tell Tony she was pregnant by another man.

Starting Over

Katrina was able to keep the pregnancy from Tony for three months and by that time Tony already had Trisha on the streets working and bringing in even more cash than Katrina did. It was an early morning day in June when Tony got horny and went to Katrina's room to try to have sex with her and he accidentally took notice of the change in her stomach. Katrina refused Tony's advances and tried her best to shield her belly from Tony. That morning Tony was just too horny to be turned down by Katrina and no pimp would allow one of his bitches to say no to him anyway. Tony pulled the covers off Katrina and he got on top of her while she was lying on her stomach. It was like being raped all over again for her, but this time her daughter was laying next to her on the bed.

As Tony tried to force himself on Katrina, she realized she couldn't allow herself to be raped again, she mustered all the strength she had and pushed Tony off her with her hands. He fell to the floor off the bed and took a couple of openhanded swing at Katrina, which landed on the side of her face. He told her " No bitch is gonna disrespect me in my own house" as he continued to try to smack her. She finally got up and tried to fight back and Tony for the first time noticed that Katrina was pregnant.

All hell broke loose when Katrina's pregnancy was finally revealed. Tony knew that he couldn't be the father, but he asked her in his own way to establish that he wasn't. He told her "I know there's no way in the world that you're pregnant by me, but I want to hear it from you". She angrily told him that he wasn't the father and she wouldn't want to get pregnant by him anyway. Those words out of Katrina's mouth went directly to Tony's ego. He hit her as hard as he could with a closed fist after she told him that and Katrina fell to the floor. Tony went into her drawers, lifted the window and started throwing all her belongings out the window. He told her to get the fuck out of his house and that he was keeping all the shit he bought for her.

By the time Tony was done ransacking the drawers and the rest of the room, all of Katrina's clothes and her daughter's belongings had been thrown out the window in the muddy waters that was left from the rain the night before. Everything was ruined and she was back on the streets on her own once again.

Tony threw Katrina out because he no longer needed her and knew that because she was pregnant she would be of no use to him in a few months. Katrina was once again faced with the reality of being on her own. This time would be different because she had work experience, though it was as a prostitute, at least she'd be able to provide for herself and her daughter. Katrina had also saved a significant amount of money when Candy was around. Now was the time that the money that Candy had encouraged her to put away would come into use. Katrina had never gone back to retrieve the money at the bank.

When Katrina was faced with the reality of not having any money, no clothes for herself and her daughter, she took a long hard look at her daughter and realized that her daughter was wearing around her neck; the key to the safe deposit box that Candy had made her obtain. Katrina felt relieved and for the moment, all her worries went away. Katrina had never kept track of the money she was putting in the safe deposit box and when she went back to count the money, she realized for the first time that she had close to twenty five thousand dollars saved. For close to six months she had put away a thousand dollars a week and she never once realized how much the money had accumulated. Katrina was now 16 years old, a year wiser, pregnant again but with twenty five thousand dollars in cash in her possession.

After Katrina left Tony's place, she decided to rent a room in this local motel for four hundred dollars a month. It wasn't luxury living, but she had a roof over her head, two double beds and enough space for her and her daughter. Since she had cash, the hotel clerk didn't even bother asking her for identification. Katrina wanted to secure an apartment for her family before her next child arrived. She had stopped working the streets and was trying to focus on Nina and her unborn child. Katrina had also gone back on welfare so that the state could pick up the tab for the delivery of her new child. She diligently searched and searched and finally she was able to find an affordable apartment in Dorchester a month before her new son, Jimmy was born.

Katrina moved into a small two-bedroom apartment with her two children, Jimmy and Nina, on the second floor of a three-story house located on Kentworth Street off Norfolk Street in Dorchester. The apartment was initially a one bedroom but she converted the dining room into another bedroom making it a 2-bedroom apartment. The kitchen was small with a couple of cabinets on the wall opposite the sink and there was one window above the sink that provided sunlight into the dimly lit kitchen. The kitchen floor was covered with an old style linoleum tile that was representative of all the foot traffic it had endured for the last twenty-five years or so.

The flooring was coming apart on each end of the room and a person could easily trip over the lifted pieces of tiles around the corners of the kitchen. The kitchen walls were covered with layers and layers of wallpaper from the ceiling to about the sink level going across the room. From the floor up, the old stained board paneling connected with the wallpaper to form the ugliest union since Frankenstein and his bride. While wallpaper and board paneling were prevalent in the 60's, it's beyond anyone's comprehension how and why people still found it aesthetically pleasing to the eye. Almost half of America's homes built more than twenty-five years ago fell victim to the wallpaper trend. Katrina firmly believed that whoever invented wallpaper should have been put in jail for the idea.

The board paneling was darkly stained to prevent the kids' handprint and all other kinds of mess from appearing. It's not that the homeowners didn't want any mess on their walls; it's more about keeping the mess from being noticeable to the eyes. The ugly board paneling can hide anything, including roaches. Board paneling had become a safe haven for roaches and they were smart enough to discover that. The wallpaper in the kitchen was an orange and yellow floral mix that did not belong in anybody's kitchen.

At first glance, it looked like the kind of paper that a hardware store could've easily placed in their "10 cents bin" in an attempt to get it out of the store without giving it away for free. Most business owners' figure there's always going to be a sucker out there to buy whatever crap that they were selling. And they were right in this particular situation. The owner of the building where Katrina lived surely thought he was getting a bargain too. Years after, Katrina would still remember the pain that the wallpaper brought to her eyes upon first seeing it. It also brought laughter because she had never seen anything so ridiculously funny in her entire life. The whole kitchen was repulsive, but it didn't make much of a difference to Katrina because she spent very little time in there, anyway.

Kentworth Street was a short street located in an awkward corner off Norfolk Street. At night, the sounds of gunshots dominated the air and drug dealers ran the streets. Drug transactions were taking place conspicuously along the street everyday and during all hours of the day. It was a shabby neighborhood full of depressing tenements and derelict old homes. Crack had slowly taken over the whole neighborhood over time and prostitution was at an all time high in Dorchester.

Young women ran through the streets at night looking for johns like rats rummaging through garbage cans and raw sewage looking for food. The big wall built by the old high school to keep the kids and the school grounds separated from the hard life of crime, was riddled with bullet holes. It almost seemed like the Boston Police department purposely avoided Kentworth Street. It had become the black hole of Boston and specifically of Dorchester. Even Stevie Wonder could've seen the drug deals and other crimes happening on Kentworth Street. It was one of the hottest streets in Boston at the time and anyone walking through that street had better be ready for some type of drama.

The path which Katrina and her kids' life would take was almost unavoidable. The seed was planted and it was just a matter of time before it blossomed and became part of the forest. Poor Jimmy and Nina didn't really stand much of a chance to make it in the cruel world where they lived. Katrina couldn't afford to give her kids a better chance. In a way, what didn't break them was going to make them stronger and more resilient. Outside those apartment doors on Kentworth Street, lived the nightmare of every parent and child in America.

Unfortunately, Katrina and her kids didn't have much of a choice as to where they wanted to live. Katrina had made the best choice she could afford for her kids at the time and that choice would ultimately be the turning point in their lives. There was a greater probability that Nina might follow in her mother's footstep. Jimmy had no male role model in his life and he would find it even harder to establish his own identity. Jimmy's path to follow was to be set by him. So, it seemed.

A few months after Katrina left Tony, she found out in the news that a rival pimp on the streets had killed him. The guy whose testicle Tony had cut off came back for revenge and caught Tony off guard. Tony was savagely beaten and stabbed to death in the Combat Zone section of

Boston. There was no police investigation to apprehend the assailant. The police department in Boston didn't like to waste too much of their time trying to solve murder cases involving criminals. Tony had become a well-known violent pimp on the streets by hookers, pimps and cops alike.

A Desperate Situation

It wasn't long before Katrina's money ran out. She lacked the money management skills that she needed in order to survive. She still had guilty pleasures and they were expensive. She had spent most of her money buying a few pieces of furniture and unnecessary brand name clothing for herself and her kids. She blew twenty five thousand dollars in a matter of months. There were a few men along the way who also took advantage of her kindness. She had loaned money to a friend to buy a car and she never heard from him again. Katrina never had anyone in her life for too long. Everyone who came into her life needed something from her and they never stuck around after they got what they wanted. She was just being used and abused, but she could never put a halt to it.

Jimmy was only five months old when Katrina was forced back on the streets. She had prepaid her rent for six months when she moved into her apartment and the six months had come and gone. She was faced with an eviction and nowhere to turn. Katrina decided to go back to her old ways to provide for her kids, however, this time it would be different. She no longer had to give most of her money to a pimp, but she also didn't have the protection he would provide. This time around, Katrina was in the Mecca of prostitution activities, she didn't have to walk too far to get clients, the clients knew where to go and the prices in the neighborhood was only a fraction of what she used to get downtown. Most of the women on Kentworth Street were crack heads turning tricks for their next hit. That ultimately meant that the johns who frequented that area were a bunch of broke men looking to humiliate themselves and the prostitutes for the ten dollar service they sought.

Katrina had another dilemma in her life, not only did she not have a babysitter, but now she had two kids. She really needed to stay close to home if she were to continue working as a prostitute. All the luxuries of being a downtown prostitute had gone out the window; there were no men driving up in nice cars or special alleyways with lookouts. These crack heads were turning tricks in the bushes, in the backs of dirty run down pick-up trucks, behind crack houses, inside the crack houses and anywhere that could shield them from being totally conspicuous.

Katrina thought long and hard about her decision, but she felt she had no other options. She had to go back to prostitution because a job at the local grocery store wouldn't pay her enough to pay her rent, a babysitter and put food on the table. Katrina was no fool and she knew what was happening on her street and the kind of women that were out there. At night, anyone on that street could hear the prostitutes fighting over customers. Some of them had missing teeth, black circles around their eyes, hair looking like they've been electrocuted and they smelled like they hadn't showered in years. Sixteen-year-old Katrina was about to enter a new territory and she would stick out like a sore thumb among these women.

Katrina was attractive, young, clean, and sexy but most importantly she wasn't on crack. There was no substance controlling her mind. The owner of the house where she lived had threatened to go to court and vowed to have her out by the end of the week if she didn't have the money for the rent. Since the owner of the house didn't live there, she knew that whenever there was a knock on her door during the day it was him. She would hush her kids and not answer the door, but she also knew it was a matter of time before the landlord could have an eviction executed at the local courthouse. The owner of the house was too afraid of the neighborhood to come around at night, so Katrina decided if she was gonna be a prostitute she might as well do it at home.

Inauguration Night

The first night Katrina went on the street was five days after her rent was due. At the time she was only paying three hundred and fifty dollars a month for her apartment. When Katrina was working for Tony she had no problem earning four to nine hundred dollars a night, but this time things were going to be different. The customers in the area where Katrina had to work consisted of horny men with menial jobs who didn't have much money to spare. These men were so used to paying ten dollars to get a blowjob from the crack heads, they would laugh at the one hundred and fifty dollar asking price that Katrina used to charge downtown, anyway. This place wasn't downtown but Katrina was no crack head, not yet anyway. A compromise had to be made on the part of Katrina for survival's sake.

She first stepped out on the street looking like a cover girl compared to the rest of the prostitutes on that street. All the men walked by the other prostitutes as if they didn't exist when Katrina was out there. They were looking to get a taste of the new, clean, beautiful, stunning and curvaceous girl who just moved in the neighborhood. It was almost childlike the way these men got excited about Katrina. It was reminiscent of a child moving to a new neighborhood and all the boys were fighting for her heart, but only this heart came with a price tag that these boys weren't used to.

The first guy who tried to solicit a blowjob from Katrina only had twenty five dollars to his name and when he asked her how much for a blowjob, he was confident that his pocket was heavy enough for the demand. Astonishingly enough, Katrina told him it was a hundred dollars for a blowjob. The man took off laughing and went back to his friends and told them "this bitch had some nerve to ask for a hundred dollars for a blowjob when everybody else charges ten". He went on and on to his friends about how "this is Dorchester, not downtown and if this bitch wants to charge that kind of money she needs to go downtown". After rambling for about ten minutes, his friends looked at him and told him that he was only pissed because he didn't have the money, knowing damn well she would have been worth every penny. He shook his head in agreement then said, "The bitch is bad for real, though".

Katrina had been on the corner for close to an hour and she had no customers. She only had this one white customer from downtown she kept in touch with who was bold enough to come to the black neighborhood looking for action. This guy was a regular client of Katrina's. He would carry a big knife in his jacket pocket every time he came to see her. The one regular customer that Katrina had wasn't enough for her to make her rent money and feed her kids every month. Most of the men who came by couldn't afford her asking prices for services.

Being the business woman that she had grown to be, she decided to drop her price down to seventy-five dollars for a blowjob for the next man who approached her. The man who was next in line was a construction worker who had heard about Katrina being on the block from one of his friends who couldn't afford to get services from her. Armed with the knowledge that Katrina was good looking, clean and might be worth every dime, this man came prepared. He left his house with a hundred dollars in his pocket that he didn't plan to bring back home with him. He wasn't the type of guy that Katrina was used to, but on that desperate night she needed to break the dry spell. The man was still wearing his construction clothes and was probably funky from working hard all day. He asked her how much she charged for a blowjob and she told him seventy-five dollars but he didn't just want a blowjob, he wanted to have sex with her as well. She negotiated down her price to a hundred dollars because mama needed to pay the rent. She took the customer up to her house and performed more tricks on him than any of the crack heads on the street could ever perform sober. It took all but fifteen minutes for her to make him cum then she sent him on his way. He was the first customer to go back and brag about her services and how skillful she was in the bedroom. This first customer pretty much set the standard for Katrina's clientele.

Katrina would go on prostituting herself for the next eleven years. By the time Nina was ten years old, she had stopped the flow of traffic inside her apartment. She didn't want to start answering weird questions especially from bright-eyed Jimmy. Too many men in the house would have definitely raised the suspicions of her kids. She would occasionally allow this guy named Tyrone who she called her boyfriend into the house to sleep over. Tyrone had developed a special relationship with Katrina's kids.

On different occasions he would stop by the house at night to check up on the kids while Katrina was working the streets. Tyrone never had a problem with Katrina being a prostitute even after claiming her as his girlfriend for close to five years. However, there was something terribly bad about Tyrone's relationship with Nina and Jimmy. The kids dreaded his presence after a while and they didn't want him around. There were times when he offered to take them out for ice cream and they would both flat out turn down his offer.

Katrina never took the time to talk to her children about their feelings towards Tyrone. She figured they were growing up and sometimes kids tend to stray away from certain people in their lives as they get older. Tyrone also saw the lack of attention from Katrina to her kids as an opportunity to violate their trust. The less attention Katrina paid to her children, the bolder Tyrone became with the children and the more frequent he visited the children. Only God knew why Tyrone was so infatuated with Katrina's children.

Coping as a Single Mother

On this early autumn morning in September 1992, Katrina Johnson woke up early to make breakfast for her family. It was one of those rare occasions where she was able to get up by sunrise. The sun was beaming that day and temperatures were expected to climb to the low 80's, ideal for early September. Katrina usually slept very late and the kids seldom saw their mother before they left the house for school. On this day, however, there was no school because it was the first day of the month and Labor Day weekend extended the summer vacation for a few more days.

Katrina must've had a good night the night before because she was in a great mood and wanted to show her children some form of appreciation. Katrina threw on her robe and walked to the small bathroom to brush her teeth and wash her face. Her bathroom was located on the right side of the apartment on the way to the kitchen pass the kids' bedroom. The bathroom was old and neglected; however, the eye can easily see that at one point in time beauty existed in that bathroom. The walls were painted a shabby white, there was a window located on the right side where the cast iron clawed tub was located. There still existed a few ceramic tiles on the back wall in the shower to keep the water from damaging the plaster behind it.

The ceramic was covered with mildew and other foreign stains that could hurt somebody's eyes. Katrina's and the children's hair were caught all over the drain keeping the water from flowing easily down the pipes. The ceilings were painted a bright white and that was the only part of the bathroom that kept its integrity. The once stainless steel faucets were starting to rust and were hard to turn in either direction. The mirror above the bathroom sink had also deteriorated to something that resembled smog. One could hardly make out an image from this mirror; nevertheless, it was the Johnson's only bathroom.

Katrina was always pretty as a young girl, but she had developed into one of the most attractive women any man could easily wake up to in the morning when she was taking care of herself. However, on this particular morning her hair looked like she had been through World War III with a lady tiger and her make up ran down her face like she was fighting her way upstream through Niagara Falls.

For the most part, Katrina was an even better looking mature woman who can pretty much stand out in any crowd. Katrina inherited some of her mother's best assets. Her African features stood out like those of a queen from the old throne who had been pampered for years by her servants. She had the most beautifully bright dark brown bedroom eyes that God could've bestowed upon her. One of the most outstanding features she had was her luscious lips. Her lips could actually run a man's imagination wild, especially when she wore her favorite red colored lipstick. Her lips were full, thick and defined like God himself had taken a pencil to draw the perfect lips on her face.

She was also slightly bowlegged which gave her a leg up on the competition when she walked. She had the strut of a sex goddess with a body to die for. She was a perfect size 6 and stood about 5ft 5inches tall. She weighed about 125 pounds with the weight evenly spread to all the right places. Her curves were more dangerous than the hairpin turn in western Massachusetts. She was physically every man's fantasy and every woman's envy. For the most part, women like Katrina end up being more of a nightmare than a fantasy for most men. Katrina looked too good to be domesticated and her kids were too skinny for her to make that kind of claim.

From the look on Katrina's face as she walked into the kitchen, it was apparent that the kitchen was not her favorite place in the house. As repulsive as the kitchen looked, it had nothing to do with the expression on Katrina's face that morning. It just seemed like a strange place she occasionally visited out of guilt for her children. Katrina had the grandiose aura of a socialite trapped in a struggling woman's world. To say the least, she did not enjoy cooking but she tried going through with it on this particular morning. Katrina walked to the empty fridge to take out the last three eggs sitting in the dairy compartment. While in the fridge, she decided to check if the milk carton was just there for show, she shook it and as expected, it had one tiny sip left in it. She also checked the orange juice carton and had the same result. The empty plastic bag that once contained sliced bread was sitting on the kitchen counter, giving a clear indication that they had run out of bread as well.

About this time, an attempt at a good gesture had worn out Katrina's patience. She decided she didn't want to cook breakfast anymore because there was nothing in the house to cook or eat. Katrina wasn't the kind of mother who would go above and beyond for her children. Most mothers would run to the nearest store to find something for their kids to eat, but not Katrina; she only provided the bare necessities for her children. She was overly consumed with the streets and the cheap low fashion clothes she could get her hands on.

Katrina headed to the living room to do what she normally did all-day everyday, which was watching television. Katrina's converted two-bedroom apartment was very small according to the standards at the time. Her living is the former dining room converted. In her living room, Katrina had an old red leather couch that looked like it was bought by one of her suitors when she was still a knock out in her teens. The couch just didn't belong in that room. The lines running through the leather were apparent signs of the couch's age. The chair that accompanied the couch looked like trash that some old lady hoarded because her subconscious wouldn't let her get rid of it. It was brown tweed with darkly stained wooden arms, the material covering the chair was torn all around, but it served its purpose.

She had an old Zenith color television that hadn't been made since the early seventies. It looked like the introductory model when they first came out. The colors were fading and the people never quite looked human because of the distortion of the colors and the lines running up and down and across the television screen. It was sitting on a small wooden table that looked like it was on its last legs. The living room had a funky disco style light that was transformed from an old chandelier hanging down from the ceiling. It was covered with enough dust that could span three generations of inhabitants in that apartment. The walls were covered with some type of bright faux red velvet wallpaper to accentuate the couch. The living room was a scene out of one of those Blaxploitation films from the seventies. The most beautiful part of the living room was the pristine hardwood floor. Somehow, the floor managed to maintain its integrity and looked like something from an early 19th century Victorian home.

Katrina was one a few people with the ability to find something amusing in anything on television. It was as if she were an analyst, analyzing everything she watched. She made Sesame Street sound like a show on Broadway when she described it. She paid great attention to details. Katrina could have easily been a critic for television shows. She spent so much time in front of the television during the day; she became a human TV Guide. She knew the schedule for every show on almost every station. However, she had her favorites. Good Times and The Jeffersons were two of her favorite shows. She wouldn't miss the reruns for the world.

Katrina seemed like a happy go lucky person when she was in front of the television. However, when examined closely, it was quite evident that she was suffering from the pains of life. The world hadn't been so kind to Katrina and her family. She led an almost brutal life and never received any breaks from anyone since she was a child. She wasn't sure what kind of hand life had dealt her but she was trying her hardest to turn a lousy pair into a full house. She wasn't content with her life and the life of her children. Katrina always wished she could do more.

It was 10 o'clock in the morning when 10-year-old Jimmy finally woke up from his bed. He ran to the living room to watch his favorite cartoons. Without asking his mom, he turned the channel on the television to his favorite morning cartoon show and hopped on his favorite chair. Jimmy loved that old raggedy chair like he loved his mama. It was where he practiced his acrobatic wrestling moves, his superman flying attempts, his jumping jacks and anything else you can imagine a child could do on a lonely chair.

After Jimmy quickly changed the television station without asking his mom's permission, an argument ensued between him and his mother about his rudeness. His mother called him rude and inconsiderate. Jimmy didn't have any idea what inconsiderate meant so he started screaming at his mother. He told her he was tired of her calling him names every time he did something and asked what inconsiderate meant. His mother explained that it was someone who gives no consideration to the way other people feel when they do something. Jimmy and his mother used to engage in a lot of futile verbal matches.

Katrina's parenting skills were almost nonexistent, as she didn't have much practice. She was absent in those kid's lives even though she lived with them. She finally walked away from the television and Jimmy allowing him to watch what he wanted. As she headed back to her bedroom, Jimmy yelled that he was hungry and asked if she was gonna make breakfast. She told him to get up and find something to eat on his own, knowing damn well there was nothing to eat in the house.

All the commotion going on in the living room between Katrina and Jimmy forced Nina to finally get out of bed. Nina's bedroom was her sanctuary; it was the one place where she could lie down on her bed to read her favorite books without being disturbed by her brother. It was as if she blocked out the rest of the world when she was in her room. That was the only place she found peace. Nina and her brother shared a small room right across from the bathroom. The room was slightly bigger than a college dorm room. There were two single beds, one on each side of the wall across the room, a dresser in the center of the room against the wall and a couple of milk crates to hold whatever couldn't fit in the drawers. Nina took the left side of the room while Jimmy took the right.

The room was painted a neutral off-white color. Nina's side of the wall was covered with pictures of flowers that she had painted, posters of LL Cool J, Kris Kross, Snoop Doggy Dog, De La Soul and a picture that her brother had made for her. It was mystifying to walk into her room. Walking into her room could make anybody forget that they were a poor family. She brought life to that room because she was such a peaceful and happy child. Jimmy's side of the wall was covered with pictures of his favorite wrestlers and an unusual picture of Michelangelo's sculpture David. For some odd reason, Jimmy liked the picture of David more than any of his favorite wrestlers. Perhaps, he saw in himself the strength of David. There were toys all around his space, mostly action figures of G. I. Joe.

Jimmy was usually idle in front of the television for hours, so his sister didn't have to worry about him disturbing her in the bedroom. Nina was caring and very protective of her younger brother. She was like a second mother to Jimmy even though they were only a couple of years apart. She had grown accustomed to taking care of Jimmy because they were left in the house alone, most of the time. Nina and Jimmy bonded in a way that only the constraint of their space would allow. They were very close and they looked out for each other.

Nina was overly developed for her age, so she looked like she was a few years older than her brother and Jimmy acted like he was light years younger than her. There was a sharp contrast in their maturity level. Nina was calculated, domesticated, careful and motherly while Jimmy was childish, artistic and careless. Nina made sure Jimmy went to bed on time and woke up on time for school in the morning because their mother was usually asleep when they got ready for school. She had become the caretaker for everyone in the house and did not show any resentment.

A Mother's Secret Revealed

The type of hours that Katrina worked kept her from her family every night. The children had grown accustomed to being alone at night while their mother worked. Jimmy was probably the most observant of Katrina's kids. He always noticed that his mother wore revealing clothes to go to work and wondered what kind of place she was working that she had to wear her skirt so short that if she sneezed it would roll up past her thighs to reveal that she was never wearing any underwear.

Actually, one day while Jimmy was running up the stairs to the apartment after his mother, he noticed that she wasn't wearing any panties. He exclaimed " Mommy where's your underwear?!" His mother was embarrassed as she and the neighbor from the apartment on the second floor crossed paths on his way out of the building. Not that the neighbor didn't know she was a prostitute, but she didn't want to confirm it. She quickly yelled for Jimmy to go in the house. She hurried Jimmy into the house and scolded him for what he had done. Jimmy started screaming at her and wondered why she was blaming him when she was the one not wearing any underwear in the first place.

Katrina and Jimmy usually went at it like two kids and most of the time, she wouldn't let up until she got Jimmy to see things her way. Jimmy had grown to be defiant of his mother, a trait that he must've inherited from her. All the signs of neglect were prevalent in the household. Katrina could only console herself by believing she was trying to do her best to provide for her children. Katrina went upstairs and fell asleep while Jimmy was glued to the television in the living room.

The sun was beaming around noon and the house was getting hot. Nina was outside playing with the neighborhood kids in front of the house while Jimmy was still inside watching television. Katrina had finally woken up and wanted to watch her favorite soap opera, but Jimmy was already in front of the TV taking in his daily dose of cartoons. He especially liked Tom & Jerry, Mighty Mouse, Casper, Sylvester and Tweety Bird. Katrina wanted to get Jimmy away from the television, she asked him to go outside and play with his friends and his sister. Jimmy told his mother he didn't want to go outside and would never go outside again. When his mother asked, why? He explained that the kids outside were stupid and they kept calling his mother a whore and would get into arguments with them.

Katrina wanted to refute those allegations and she tried her best to, but she couldn't honestly look Jimmy in the eyes to tell him that she wasn't a whore. Jimmy also told his mother that she'd rather be a whore than a mother to him and his sister. Those words brought tears to his mother's eyes. Jimmy also asked his mother how come his dad never came around like the other dads on the street. His mother also didn't have an answer to that question. He became angry and started crying and said to his mother "I wish I was never born to a whore like you. I hate you! When I grow up I'm not gonna marry a ho like you".

All Jimmy ever wanted was for his mother to stop working the streets. The secret was out and she couldn't conceal it any more. He would beg his mother everyday to quit working the streets as a prostitute, and she would explain to him that she had to provide for them and if she stopped working they would go without. Jimmy offered to take a job delivering newspapers to help his household so his mother could quit working the streets, but the reality of it was that he was too young to have a job and his mother knew it. It was a big gesture on his part to offer to take on a job so that his mother could be around. Katrina fell into a deep depression not too long after Jimmy made it known to her that he knew she was a prostitute. She knew that if Jimmy knew Nina did also. She told her kids that it was just a temporary situation and she would quit soon. The more she lied to her kids, the more depressed she became. Nina never wanted to confront her mother's prostitution, but she was well aware of it.

Discovering a New Struggle

Tyrone was an avid marijuana user. He used to be high twenty-four hours a day, everyday. One day he came to Katrina's house with an ounce of weed in his pocket and decided to roll a big joint in Katrina's house. When Katrina was in the right state of mind, she would not allow Tyrone to smoke marijuana in her house. However, on that particular day, she not only allowed him to smoke in the house, she smoked along with him. In all her years on the streets, Katrina had never done any drugs. She smoked weed for the first time with Tyrone and she liked it. Marijuana gave her the temporary relief she needed to escape her reality. For the first couple of months, she was sharing Tyrone's weed with him and he was happy to have a new smoking partner, he didn't mind sharing. As time went by, Katrina developed an insatiable appetite for weed and started smoking on a daily basis just like Tyrone. She even started buying her own stash and Katrina would smoke in her room with Tyrone while the kids were in the house trying to cover it up with air freshener like her children were too stupid to know.

There was a change in Katrina's attitude after she started smoking. If it were at all possible, she became more nonchalant and more negligent towards her children. The children took notice as well and decided that they had to become more self-sufficient. Nina and Jimmy started to rely less on their mother when she became addicted to marijuana. She couldn't stay sober; she had to be high all the time in order to function. It was straining the family emotionally and financially.

The little money she used to spend on groceries now was being spent on weed. She was even selling her food stamps at half the price so she could get weed when she didn't make enough money from prostitution. Sometimes the kids would only have what they could get with the food stamps they received from the Welfare Department. And most of the time they only provided the generic brand cereal and milk which they ate for breakfast; they would eat lunch at school and cereal again for dinner at home. It was pitiful and sad to see the deterioration of the family.

The situation would get worse for the Johnson family. Katrina had started to act like one of those crack head prostitutes on the street. Most of the time, she was so desperate for money to get high, she started to lower her prices on the streets for services. The more she smoked, the more her stock went down and the less attention she paid to her hygiene. She was no longer the glamorous prostitute amongst the crack heads. She was already a weed head on her way to becoming a crack head. All the small time drug dealers on her block had gotten a piece of Katrina for weed and she became known as the blowjob queen for a joint. Sometimes, guys used to set it up so that they could watch each other getting blowjobs from Katrina for weed.

Tyrone and Katrina remained an item despite the reputation she had built on the streets. He was still active in her life and would come by the house very often. Somewhere along the way, weed had become too weak a drug to satisfy Tyrone's high. After being addicted to marijuana for so long, Tyrone was not feeling its effect anymore. Katrina was not too far behind him in her addictions. A local drug dealer introduced him to crack cocaine in 1995 where he lived. His first taste of it was free and that's all it took for him to become an addict. Tyrone was a functioning crack head for the better part of three months; he would get up and go to work without any complications as long as he was high.

One day on his way to Katrina's house, he bought a small rock for ten dollars and placed it in his pocket. Tyrone had never revealed to Katrina that he was smoking crack for some reason. He must've felt that she would not want anything to do with him if she knew he was a crack head. But, on this particular day, Tyrone's urges got the best of him while he was over Katrina's house. He excused himself to the bathroom to go smoke his rock and while he was in there he was making all kinds of noise. He wanted his fix so badly he had forgotten to lock the door behind him. When Katrina opened the door to see what all the commotion was about, she found Tyrone smoking a crack pipe in her bathroom. He told her she should try it and it was the best of all highs. He handed the pipe to her, and against her better judgment, she took one whiff of it and didn't stop until he had to pull it out of her hand to get the last hit.

Katrina discovered crack that unfortunate day when Tyrone negligently bought a rock on the way to her house. It almost seemed like destiny doomed her from the beginning. A wonderful and excellent student's life had turned south all because her parents turned their backs on her. If Katrina still believed in God, she had better start praying because crack was the worst kind of evil that could ever hit the ghetto in which she lived. Whoever invented crack knew the ramifications of it. Crack would cause so much distress to the Johnson family; one can only fathom the idea that it was specifically created for the destruction of that family. Nina and Jimmy may or may not have realized it, but crack would affect them in the most severe way. They would end up losing the fiber from which their family was created to crack.

Most of the people who lived on Katrina's street had encountered crack heads one way or another, whether through a break-in into their homes or through a robbery on the street. Crack had directly or indirectly affected all of them in a negative way. They all developed new fears and stereotypes in their neighborhood that never existed prior to crack. As if their community needed another form of prejudice to use against their people. There were so many churches in the neighborhood, and maybe their eyes were watching God so much they were blinded by the reality of drugs in their community when it first started.

Katrina and her family were victimized because the local government cared nothing about their lives. People in their neighborhoods had access to guns, but there wasn't one single gun manufacturer within fifty miles of their neighborhood. Tons of kilos of cocaine were distributed daily in their ghetto, but no one in their ghetto had access to private boats or planes to make their way to Columbia to buy the drugs. The government had managed to fool most of the ignorant folks in Katrina's neighborhood by initiating a War on Drugs, were they at war with themselves? The war on drugs was reminiscent of the war on terrorism during the 80's; the only victims were the innocent folks who knew nothing about drugs, but fell victim to the circumstance.

For every drug dealer arrested in Katrina's neighborhood and sentenced to a long time in prison by the district attorney everyday, they created an additional ten new dealers. The drug dealers in the hood were sprouting like wild weeds on every corner thanks to the high demand for drugs. Katrina and her family and other future generations of people in the ghetto will continue to be the victims of circumstances as the cycle of life in the ghetto will never change because the status quo will forever remain.

Growing Up

It had been two years since Katrina had started using crack. She had fallen into the same trap as the other prostitutes on her street. Katrina was now serving up the goods in the back alleys and bushes for a mere ten dollars a pop. Her teeth started to decay and developed that permanent brown stain that looked so disgusting, just the sight of it could cause a person to vomit. She no longer restricted her prostitution activities to the night; she was a prostitute all-day everyday. The most important thing in Katrina's life had become her next fix and as a result, the demand for her personal product had drastically run low. No one was interested in her pussy anymore because it was being sold for pennies on the dollar. The regular customers had become her fellow addicts who were able to sometimes, steal, rob or even turn tricks to get a hit themselves. It was definitely a sad situation, but actually seeing it happened was even worse.

Nina and Jimmy were fourteen and twelve years old respectively. They had become completely self-sufficient and were now watching after their mother as much as they could whenever she was around. It broke their hearts to see their mother waste her life like that, but there was nothing they could do. There was no extended family to reach out to and the surrounding neighborhoods had the same problems. All Jimmy and Nina had were each other now. They pledged to look after each other until their last day on earth. Nina was always the caretaker for them, but Jimmy had grown to be the man of the house. Katrina had arranged for welfare to take care of her apartment directly with the landlord, so the kids didn't have to worry about becoming homeless. Nina was able to secure a part-time job at the local Burger King after school, while Jimmy joined the Boys and Girls club not too far from Nina's job. The children tried their best to stay out of the neighborhood for as long as they could. They practically lived their lives away from Kentworth Street.

Nina had become the provider for the household; she took all her earnings from her part-time job and spent it on food every week. She knew that her mother was in no state to care for her and her brother. Nina had always been a good student and having watched her mom deteriorate to nothing raised her awareness to some of the cancerous ills of the neighborhood. She stayed away from drugs, drug dealers, prostitution and all other negative influences in her neighborhood. She kept her younger brother away from the negativity and made sure he attended the Boys and Girls Club everyday until she got off work. Most of the time, after work, they would go to the local library and work on their homework until 9:00 pm.

Fall of 1996 was the turning point in the kids' lives. Nina had worked the allowable thirty hours a week for kids under sixteen years old all summer long to save enough money to buy school clothes for herself and her brother for the new school year. She wanted to make sure that he didn't' go without, but it was an even harder battle trying to hide money from her mother. Katrina had sold every possession she could possibly sell in the house. She would occasionally sell the food that Nina bought for the house to the dealers for a hit. Nina was fighting quite a few battles; however, her biggest battle was against her mother. She was trying to find ways to keep her mother alive until she became old enough to admit her into a drug treatment program, but it was hard to keep track of her mother.

Every time Nina found her mother passed out in the crack house down the street and brought her home to clean her up, she would go right back to the crack house after she got her hand on some money. She stole the clothes Nina bought for school for herself and her brother and sold them for crack. It was a futile battle and there were no winners. The more Katrina stole from her kids, the more they resented her. It got to a point where Nina started locking her mother out of the house. She wanted to protect her brother from all the shit that her mother was doing on the streets, but somehow she felt that Jimmy knew all along what was going on.

Jimmy was only twelve years old when he told Nina he wanted to help support the family. He believed it was his job as a man to find a way to help. Nina knew that Jimmy couldn't get a job, so she was wondering where exactly he was trying to go with the conversation. Jimmy came out and told Nina he wanted to start selling drugs to help the family. Nina gave Jimmy the coldest look she could possibly form with her face and yelled at the top of her lungs " there's no fucking way in this world I'm gonna let you get caught up in drugs". She told him she would kill him before she allowed him to go out there and sell drugs. She asked if he's been too blind to see what drugs had done to their mother and told him she didn't need any help and they were doing just fine. She even went as far as telling Jimmy she'd report him to the cops if he even thought about selling drugs. Jimmy was surprised that his sister reacted so harshly, he told her it was just a thought and she told him it was a thought he needed to erase out of his mind. She hugged her little brother and told him that they'd be fine as long as she was alive. She also told her brother that they could not allow drugs to influence their lives because it had already destroyed a greater part of their family- their mother.

Struggling with the Demons

Katrina pretty much abandoned her children when she became a full-blown crack addict. She spent most of her time on the street fighting with other crack heads over tricks so she could get money for drugs. The vacant building, located a block from her house had become her new permanent residence along with all the other crack heads in the neighborhood. Katrina's mind was gone and she rarely was sober enough to even remember that she had a family.

Nina had no choice but to give up on helping her mom because her Katrina had reached a point of no return. Instead, she focused on her younger brother, Jimmy. She tried her best to discover new routes to get home late at night so they could avoid running into their mother. She knew that seeing their mom out there on the street rummaging through trash cans looking for aluminum soda cans could affect Jimmy in the worst way. Jimmy loved his mother dearly, but hated the life she had created for herself. Katrina was so high sometimes Nina had to help her remember who her own daughter was. It was sad and disastrous to the morale of her kids but the kids knew they had to find a way to survive together. They couldn't alert the authorities because the Department of Social Services had a reputation of separating kids from their siblings when placing them in foster care. Nina's strength was Jimmy and Jimmy's strength was Nina, if they were ever separated, it would have been tragic for either of them.

One night, when Nina and Jimmy were coming home from school through one of their new discovered back roads, out of the blue, this lady came out of the bushes with a knife in hand and demanded their money. At first, the person was not recognizable to them, but after taking a long second look, Nina realized it was her mother who was robbing them at knife point. She didn't want Jimmy to figure out what she had just discovered, so she quickly gave her ten dollars and Katrina ran away. Sadly, Katrina never realized that she had robbed her own children. It was a good thing that Jimmy was still a young boy because Katrina would have certainly sunk as low as to try to solicit money from him for a blowjob like she did all the other males on the street. It was amazing how the use of crack made its users lose their memory or sense of who they were once they got addicted.

The incident with her mother only intensified Nina's desire to move out of the neighborhood, but she couldn't. Who was going to rent an apartment to a fifteen year old girl and her thirteen-year-old brother? They had to endure the painstaking abashment that their mother was putting them through. Nina was a very strong child, but every night after her brother fell asleep she would lie in bed and cry for hours. She wanted to know why their situation was so bad and why God wasn't protecting them. She would pray and ask God what sin had they committed for them to be going through such an ordeal. It was painstakingly hard for her to continue on, but she had to be the strength for her brother too. She couldn't show weakness in the face of adversity as her brother looked to her as a source of strength and comfort. Somehow Nina felt that there would one day be light at the end of the tunnel.

A Deadly Revelation

Another night, while Katrina and Tyrone were in the crack house getting ready to get high, Tyrone, for a quick moment while he and Katrina were still slightly sober, revealed to Katrina that he had molested both of her children. He wanted to tell Katrina how sorry he was for raping her daughter Nina one night while he was high. He also went on about how he had sodomized her son Jimmy as well. The guilt had gotten the best of him and he needed to tell her. Katrina, for a brief moment recalled having two children that she loved and would protect under any circumstances and it was at that time that something came over her. She picked up a big rock that was on the dirty ground and hit Tyrone as hard as she could over the head with it. He fell to the ground bleeding profusely from his wound. All the other incoherent crack heads gathered around Katrina and Tyrone's body lying on the ground like he was having a seizure. After a few minutes of fighting to breathe Tyrone's body finally gave up and he died from the blunt force that Katrina exerted with the rock.

Katrina knew that she had just killed Tyrone, but everyone around her was too high to notice or say anything. She sat down next to the body and lit up the pipe they had planned to smoke together and continued smoking on it until she got high enough and passed out. When she hit Tyrone over the head, his blood gushed out all over her face and body. She woke up the next day handcuffed to a hospital bed with a police officer standing guard.

The police routinely raided the crack house on Kentworth Street hoping to find a few of the drug dealers inside. On this day, however, when they raided the building, they found Tyrone's body lying on the ground, Katrina passed out next to him and the murder weapon covered in blood not too far from both of them. The police couldn't get an account of what happened so they took Katrina into custody. The police didn't have to look far for a suspect. Murder was murder, it didn't matter if it involved two crack heads, and somebody had to be arrested.

Some of the crack heads tried to keep the police from arresting Katrina, as she was a fellow crack head. However, the threat of a gun barrel down their throats quickly forced them into submission to the police. The cops were taking Katrina out to the patrol car as her daughter and son were going inside their house. Jimmy was a couple of steps inside of the house ahead of Nina when the cops brought their mother out of the crack house in handcuffs. Nina could recognize her mother's clothing from a mile away and she knew it was her mother the police had in custody. She quickly yelled for Jimmy to run upstairs as she hurried inside to shield him from the situation.

Nina didn't need any more obstacles in her life. She was trying her best to offer a better life to her younger brother; she didn't have the energy to worry about her mother too. Deep inside, Nina was somewhat relieved that her mother had been arrested. She knew that her mother would at least be safe from the streets and drugs in prison. Nina at the time didn't know why her mother was taken into custody, but whatever the reason was, it might've been a blessing from above. Maybe jail was the best thing that could've happened to Katrina at the time. The amount of stress and worry that her children were going through was starting to take a toll on Nina. She was the bridge that held the pieces together and that bridge would've crumbled if Katrina had stayed on the streets longer.

A Lifetime Away

It had been two months since Katrina was jailed. A grand jury had convened and found her to be criminally responsible for the death of Tyrone. Katrina had two months of forced sobriety and while incarcerated she thought long and hard about how she could protect her children from The Department of Social Services. She knew she couldn't reveal to the authorities that she had two minor children as they would have picked them up and taken them to a foster home. Instead, she lied about her name and gave the cops a phony address. Katrina used the name that Candy had given to her. During her trial she was known as Star Bright.

Katrina's defense attorney had advised her to cop a plea of manslaughter so her sentence could be commuted to twenty-five years in prison with the possibility of parole after half the sentence is served. She really had no defense because the murder weapon had her prints all over it and the victim's blood was splattered all over her when she was arrested. Katrina accepted a plea in order to protect her family. She didn't want to bother going through a trial because she didn't want her real identity to be revealed during the trial. It hurt that Katrina was not be able to stand before the judge and explain to him that she was defending the honor and safety of her children because of a drug addiction. Katrina had to keep the fact that she had children a secret from the court.

There was a sad and desperate look on Katrina's face the morning of her sentencing. She had so much to say, but she remained silent because her silence was more important than any words she could have uttered in front of the judge. The judge had made it clear to Katrina that she would serve at least twelve and half years before she would see the outside world again. She stood there in her bright orange jumpsuit with shackles around her ankles and wrists with tears rolling down her face, but said absolutely nothing. After the judge read the conditions of her sentence she was ushered away by two court officers to the waiting van outside the courthouse to be taken to the maximum-security prison for women in Framingham, Massachusetts.

During the van ride on the way to jail, Katrina took inventory of the other women around her. She was silently wondering if she was the only mother in that van who had neglected her kids because of drugs. Katrina knew it would be a long time before she would ever see her kids again. She also knew that she had messed up real bad and by the time she got out of jail, her kids would have raised themselves into adulthood. She had no connection to the outside world and the last thing she wanted to do was to contact her kids to tell them that she was doing time for murder. She made a decision before she got to the prison that she would stay out of her kids' life until she could talk to them about the circumstances that brought her to where she was.

Katrina's decision to keep away from her kids was the hardest thing she ever had to do as a mother. Being sober made her realize that she loved her kids as any mother would, but forces beyond her control had taken over her life and ability to make good decisions. Katrina found jail to be degrading and demeaning the entire time she was locked up. She decided to write a long letter to her children to explain her situation, but she couldn't muster the courage to mail it. She tore the letter and flushed it down the toilet. She had failed as a mother and it was time to let go of that guilt. Katrina woke up in jail everyday praying that her kids would one day forgive her. She only wished that she had the courage to ask her kids for the forgiveness that she yearned so much.

Coping With Life

Two years had passed since Nina and Jimmy saw their mother. Nina knew that her mother was taken to jail but she never bothered to learn the reason why. She had heard the rumors on the street that her mother had killed Tyrone, but she never made it a priority to confirm the rumors. She was seventeen years old and trying to complete her last year in high school without any complications. She wanted to see the year through in the most positive way that she could. She was an honor student at Hyde Park High School, which offered an after school work-study program to the best and brightest students during their senior year.

Because Nina was an honor student and overloaded on classes throughout her high school years, she only had to take three classes per semester in her senior year. She only attended school for half a day in her last year of high school. Her work-study placement was at the local police station where she worked as a receptionist for about twenty hours a week, depending on needs. Sometimes, she was able to work as much as thirty hours in one week to earn extra money. Everyone at the police station liked Nina, but she was very introverted, so no one really got to know her well enough to find out anything about her personal life and she made sure of that.

Nina really enjoyed working at the police station. She saw, firsthand, the effect of drugs on people and their families. Sixty percent of the criminals arrested at the station were brought in on drug related offenses. One lady in particular who was brought in for breaking and entering for the fifth time to the station, brought out some old emotions in Nina as the lady was facing some serious time as a repeat offender. Nina sat there and eavesdropped on the lady's conversation with the cops pleading for the cops to not charge her because she was going to go away for a long time.

The lady had five children all under the age of eleven years old. She had allowed drugs to take over her life instead of focusing on raising them and The Department of Social Services had been alerted when she was brought down to the station. She knew that she wasn't going to see her kids for a long time and The Department of Social Services was a not parent friendly agency. After Nina heard the lady's story, tears ran down her face because all she could think about at the time was the way she and her brother were neglected by her own mother. It was the first time that Nina had heard from another mother who was a drug abuser, how hard it was to cope with a drug addiction. The disease had taken over the neighborhood and every day a new family was falling victim to it. Nina wished there was a way she could have helped the lady, but more importantly, she wished she had put more effort into helping her own mother.

Jimmy was a loner who never tried to fit in with his peers and was just happy to be by himself most of the time. The teachers at the high school liked Jimmy because he was a good student academically, but they wished that he would open up more in class and get more involved in some of the class discussions. He wasn't the type to speak out loud or ask questions when he didn't understand something. When Jimmy had questions about anything regarding his homework or life in general, he waited until he got home to ask his big sister, Nina, for an explanation. He could have been just as great a student as Nina if he was just a bit more outspoken. As a result, his timidity kept him from maximizing his potential during the first couple of years in high school.

Jimmy was a freshman in high school when he was fifteen years old. He definitely had issues adjusting in school and he was involved in at least one fistfight a week through no fault of his own. One of the reasons he was always fighting was because the kids teased him about wearing clothes from Bradlees, an inexpensive department store frequented by low-income families. Nina couldn't afford to buy Jimmy the brand name clothes and sneakers that were in fashion. He didn't have a problem wearing the clean and neat clothes Nina bought him; it was the other children at the school whose families were probably on welfare themselves that had a problem with him. Sometimes they would pick on Jimmy all day for no reason. Jimmy was a pretty big kid, at fifteen years old he stood about six feet two inches tall and one hundred and sixty five pounds. He had developed great fighting skills from watching his favorite Kung Fu master, Bruce Lee, on television all the time.

Jimmy spent most of his time in front of the old television set watching VHS tapes of Bruce Lee films and other great kung Fu masters. Jimmy always wanted to take karate lessons as a kid, but the financial burden on his sister didn't allow them enough money for extracurricular activities. He had started taking lessons at the Boys and Girls club, but the class was short-lived due to budget cut at the center.

The first time Jimmy got suspended for fighting he was very upset that he had allowed someone to push him to the brink of near disaster. He was suspended for a week after pummeling another kid's face for teasing him. Jimmy was required to bring in a parent to the school at the end of the suspension period in order to be allowed back in school. The problem, however, was that Jimmy had no parent to bring back to the school with him. He and Nina had to figure out a way to get him back to school without the authorities finding out that they were two under aged kids living alone. It was a close call for them. Nina decided she was going to go to the school to present herself as Jimmy's twenty five year-old sister.

Jimmy attended English high school, which was on the opposite side of town and away from Nina's school. Nina had to miss school in order to bring Jimmy back to his school. That day Nina woke up early to try on different outfits from her mother's closet and wore enough make up-to try to look as mature as possible. She finally settled on a business suit that her mother had bought years ago when she had to go to court for prostitution. Nina's outfit and make-up was just enough to make her look about twenty five years old.

As Nina and Jimmy arrived at the school that morning, they were nervous. The seriousness of what they were about to do didn't kick in until they set foot inside the school building and was greeted by the six feet five inches tall and two hundred and ninety pound security guard. The child in Nina came out, as she was very intimidated by the security guard. It almost seemed like the much older sister act in her disappeared. She couldn't even look at the security guard with a straight face and Jimmy was just uncomfortable all together. Nina asked to see the principal and the guard offered to walk them over to the principal's office. As they were being led to the principal's office, Nina and Jimmy felt like they were both in trouble and were about to be scolded by the principal.

After they finally made it to the principal's office, Nina was relieved to find a short but stern man with presence in the office. They sat down and discussed the ramifications of the fights that Jimmy had been involved in all year and that if Jimmy was to get into another fight, he might be expelled from school. The principal knew that Jimmy wasn't a troublemaker, but he couldn't allow him to continue fighting even though the other kids instigated the fights. Nina and Jimmy were both nervous but they agreed that the principal was right and that it was in Jimmy's best interest to make sure that the fights didn't happen again. Nina firmly shook hands with the principal, thanked him for his time and told Jimmy that she would deal with him at home because she had to go to work. They didn't over act the situation; they kept it short, mature and brief.

When Jimmy and Nina got home that evening, Nina made it clear to Jimmy that he couldn't afford to get into fights with the other kids because she didn't know how many times she was gonna be able to pull off that adult sister stunt. Jimmy always listened to his sister because he knew she always wanted what was best for both of them. Jimmy finished the school year without any complications and no more fights.

The Worse News

It had now been two years since Katrina was incarcerated for murder and Nina wanted to see her mother. Jimmy had also been asking about his mother, but Nina always found a way to get around giving him a straight answer. She managed to change the subject most of the time without any fuss from Jimmy. However, this time, Nina was just as curious as Jimmy. She had missed her mother too and wanted to see her for old time sake. She had heard the rumor in the neighborhood that her mother was sent to the maximum-security prison in Framingham, Massachusetts for life. Back then, anyone from the neighborhood who went to jail, went to jail for life according to the rumors. Nina knew it wouldn't be too hard to find her mother so she made plans to go to the prison the upcoming Saturday, on her day off from school and work.

Nina had made the decision to go visit her mother alone. She wanted to make sure everything was fine before she took Jimmy to see their mother in jail. It was a decision that Nina never regretted to this day. She left her house early that morning for the trek to Framingham from Dorchester. She wanted to make sure that her brother went to the Boys and Girls club, so she accompanied him there and told him to wait for her until she got back from where she was going. She didn't tell Jimmy that she was going to see their mother; she told him that they needed her to do some extra work at the police station. After dropping Jimmy off at the Boys and Girls club, Nina hopped on a bus to go catch the Orange Line train, then to the Green line trolley to North Station where she caught the Commuter Rail to Framingham. It was quite a trek for Nina. She finally arrived at the prison around 10:30 that morning. When Nina arrived at the prison, she stood outside for about fifteen minutes before making up her mind that she had actually wanted to see her mother. Something in her gut told her that she was not going to be happy with what she was about to find out, but it was either then or never.

Nina walked up to the counter; the prison officer asked her whom she was there to see. She hesitated at first, but she told him her mother's name Katrina Johnson. The guard went through the list of inmates and he found another Katrina Johnson who was being held at the prison. Since there were no pictures of the inmates at the front desk, Nina had no idea that the Katrina Johnson they were going to show her wasn't her mother. She went to a booth to wait for the prison folks to bring out Ms. Johnson, but unfortunately, it was a different lady. When she told them that the lady they brought out wasn't the person she was looking for, the guard told her there was only one Katrina Johnson at the prison and that lady was she. Nina didn't know what to do, she had traveled all this way to see her mother and her mother wasn't there. Nina decided she was gonna leave and go back home because the guard couldn't help her anymore.

As Nina made her way out of the prison, she thought long and hard about some of the conversations she overheard from her mother. She recalled that her mother used to refer to herself as Star Bright around her boyfriend Tyrone. Nina quickly ran back to the prison and asked if there was a lady named Star Bright being held there. The prison guard recalled there was once somebody named Star Bright who resided at the prison, but she was no longer with them. When Nina asked where she was transferred to, the guard told her she wasn't transferred. Nina then asked, "What happened?" And that's when the guard let out the worse news possible. He told Nina that Star Bright had committed suicide and she was buried by the state because no family members ever came forward to claim the body. Nina wanted to make sure that the guard was talking about the right woman, so she asked to see a photo.

It was customary for the prison department to keep pictures of all the inmates who died while in their custody on file. In case a family member ever wanted to come forward, they could always access the pictures for identification. The guard reached under his desk and pulled out a book full of pictures of the resident inmates, unfortunately Star Bright and Katrina Johnson were the same people, Nina's mom.

Nina thanked the guard for all her help then ran outside of the prison crying hysterically. She was devastated that she didn't get a chance to say goodbye to her mom. She wanted to take some of the blame for her mother's suicide. She started thinking to herself if she had gone to see her mother on a regular basis maybe she would still be alive. Not that Katrina was ever a cornerstone for Nina, but now the reality of being left alone with Jimmy as her only kin was now a fact. On the train and bus ride back to the Boys and Girls Club to pick up her brother, Nina did her best to reminisce about the good times that she shared with her mother, though they were few. She blocked out all the negativity and made up her mind that her mother was a good person in her own way. Nina blamed the drugs for turning a good mother to a careless stranger. She knew if the drugs hadn't taken over her mother's life things would've been different. Nina wanted to find a way to cope with the loss and worst, she had to figure out a way to tell Jimmy that they no longer had a mother.

Nina arrived at the Boys and Girls club a couple of hours later. She was trying her best to look normal and happy, but her brother knew her too well. He knew that something was wrong with his sister and he wanted to talk about it so he could make her feel better. Jimmy always felt that he was the source of comfort, laughter and strength for his sister. He had his own little ways of making her feel good about anything. He had become the kind of brother that Nina wanted him to be. Because he was so big for his age, he acted as her protector. But on this day, even big Jimmy couldn't protect Nina from the pain she was feeling. This was a different kind of pain and she needed a different kind of comfort. Jimmy pleaded with his sister to tell him what was wrong and she kept telling him that nothing was wrong. Jimmy knew his sister well enough to leave her alone after pestering her for so long. He knew she would come around sooner or later to tell him what was wrong with her.

Nina said nothing to her brother during the whole ride home. Jimmy tried his best to give her space to deal with whatever it was that she was dealing with. When they finally got home it was still early in the day and Nina wanted to go back to bed. Jimmy found it strange that his sister would go to bed on a nice sunny afternoon. They had their little routine schedule that they followed on the weekends. They hung out downtown and went to McDonald's every Saturday for lunch. Downtown and McDonald's wasn't on Nina's mind that particular Saturday. All she kept thinking about was how she could've prevented her mother's death.

After a little while, Jimmy felt it had to be something very serious she was trying to keep from him, so he barged in on her and demanded that she told him what was going on. He told her he was no longer a child and she couldn't keep acting like his mother because she wasn't. Nina didn't feel the need to protect her brother any longer after hearing what he just said. She turned to him in a moment of rage and blurted out that their mother was dead. Jimmy was shocked and asked what she meant. Nina explained to Jimmy that she lied about going to work that morning, instead she went to see their mother in jail and she found out that their mother had committed suicide.

Jimmy and Nina drowned in their sorrows for the rest of the day and with each passing; they hugged each other for comfort. Jimmy spent the rest of the afternoon watching his favorite Kung Fu tapes while Nina stayed in her bedroom. They both knew that they were all they had and Nina had to become her brother's keeper. Jimmy knew that it would be much sooner rather than later that he would have to start helping out his sister financially. The day they found out that their mother had passed brought them closer than ever. They both realized their survival was more important than ever.

A Mother's Guilt

Katrina finally had to face her demons while in jail. She was no longer able to perform sexual favors for a quick high the way she did when she was on the streets. There was tight supervision at the prison where she was locked up. Occasionally, some people were able to sneak in the leisure drugs, but Katrina realized that drugs had taken her life on the outside and didn't want it to ruin her life while she was locked up in prison. For the most part, she isolated herself in prison. She never made a friend and rarely talked when she was spoken to. She had built a wall around her that no one was able to break down. Only the lord knows what went through her mind when she was alive in prison.

Katrina was trying her best to count the days as they went by, but somewhere along the way she lost her patience and decided to throw in the towel to let God deal with her. The guilt of neglecting her children had overtaken Katrina on the second anniversary of her prison sentence. She was the most sober that she had ever been in years when the reality of her actions hit her. Jimmy especially weighed heavily on Katrina's mind because he was the youngest and her dearest. She loved Nina, but Jimmy was special to her because he was her son.

She started thinking about all the special occasions in their lives that she had missed and was going to miss and she just broke down and cried. She knew that she would never see the day when Nina would ask to go on her first date, she knew that she would never watch her daughter get ready for the prom, she knew she wouldn't have the opportunity to talk to her daughter and son about sex, she knew she couldn't teach Jimmy to respect women because she didn't respect herself, she knew she couldn't attend her kids' graduation and she knew that she couldn't be the kind of mother to her children they wanted her to be.

Because there was so much that Katrina was thinking about, she decided she was doing too much thinking and it was eating away at her heart. Rather than looking for the light at the end of the tunnel, she made the decision to follow the dark path that she'd always followed. As tears flowed down her cheeks, Katrina pushed her bed closer to the metal bars in front of her cell. She jumped on the bed, took one of her long-sleeved prison shirts and tied the body of the shirt around the top of the metal bars about seven feet from the floor as tight as she could, then she took the sleeves and wrapped them around her neck. She stood on the bed for about one minute to pray to God for forgiveness, then she pushed the bed away from underneath her, leaving her suspended in the air with the shirt wrapped tight around her neck cutting off the oxygen flowing to her brain. By the time the prison guard found Katrina hanging in her cell, she was already on her way to judgment day. Katrina decided to end her life out of guilt and gave in to the demons that have traumatized her for most of her life. She was pronounced dead on arrival to the hospital.

Katrina never had that conversation she wanted to have with her children. She never had a chance to explain her circumstances to her children. She never even had a chance to say goodbye. No note was left to explain the reason of her suicide. She left her kids in a questionable state of mind.

Revealing the Pain and Abuse

Nina was only a little girl when Tyrone raped her, but the act stayed in her mind vividly as if it happened yesterday. She was angry that her innocence had been unjustly taken from her and she couldn't do anything about it. She had heard from the people on the streets that her Mother had killed Tyrone, but she didn't know the reason why. She just wished Tyrone were still around so she could confront him herself and made sure that she dealt with him the right way. She had many sleepless nightmarish nights over the incident. Sometimes she would wake up in a cold sweat fighting off a man in her dreams who was trying to rape her. There was one night when Nina was calling for her brother to come to her rescue from a rapist in her sleep. She screamed so loud that Jimmy jumped out of his bed and went to the kitchen and grabbed a butcher knife. When Jimmy got to his sister's room, he found her in a cold sweat terrified of what just took place in her sleep. Jimmy jumped in the bed with his sister for comfort.

As the two drifted into sleep Nina started telling Jimmy how Tyrone and another man who used to come by the house to see their mother raped her numerous times. Since they were both groggy neither of them really grasped the reality of what they were telling each other. Jimmy also revealed to Nina that Tyrone had raped him as well and he would have looked for him if Tyrone were still alive. They finally fell asleep vaguely revealing to each other the details of what happened to them. Jimmy held his sister like he was her father for the rest of the night and Nina held on to him like he was her protector.

The next day when Jimmy and Nina awoke from their sleep they weren't sure about the conversation that took place the previous night. Jimmy vaguely remembered his sister telling him that she had been raped by a couple of people but he couldn't remember who. Nina had also remembered that her brother mentioned that a couple of her mother's friends had raped him, but it was too sensitive a subject to talk about, especially to a boy who had been raped. Jimmy and Nina didn't want to have that kind of discussion when they were fully awake. However, they were now both aware of the fact that they both had been molested at one point or another in their lives. There was almost a sense of relief when the siblings finally revealed to each other their ordeal. There was light shed on the parallel in their lives as a result of their small talk. Coping with the abuse was often hard, but they tried to manage as best they could every day.

Divine Intervention

It was at the end of basketball practice at the Boys and Girls club that Pastor Jacobs from The Church of God of Boston stopped by to talk to Mike, who was the basketball coach at the center. He asked coach if he had a minute to discuss the workshop that they were planning to have for the boys and girls at the club regarding sex. Mike was excited about the workshop and the wealth of knowledge that Pastor Jacobs was bringing to his program. Pastor Jacobs was known as an enigmatic man with an infectious personality that people seemed to gravitate toward. The prospect was great and things were looking up for the Boys and Girls club. Having the kids get involved with Pastor Jacobs was going to bring excitement, energy, high enrollment and a positive voice to the center. Pastor Jacobs was a young minister who was well liked by most of the neighborhood teens for his innovative approach to subjects pertaining to their lives. Pastor Jacobs was indeed a crowd pleaser and a motivator who inspired many in the Roxbury community. He was always a breath of fresh air everywhere he went.

It was also a well-known fact in the community that Pastor Jacobs was an ex-convict who discovered a new way of life while he was in jail serving a sentence for drug distribution. He was always considered to be a diamond in the rough who hadn't discovered the right way yet. Pastor Jacobs had the ability to revive the deadest of the dead with his sermons. People were on their feet whenever this young pastor preached. Because he used to be a known drug dealer in the community, his sermons were always close to heart. He preached about his past and the change in his future.

Young pastor Jacobs had an insatiable appetite for the bible and a determination that forced him to visit centers around the Boston area on a daily basis. When he first got out of jail, he went to the only place that embraced him, his mother's church. Pastor Jacobs grew up in the church, but after his father died at the hand of a robber when he was a teenager, his life took a turn for the worst. He started hanging around with the wrong crowd, which ultimately landed him in jail. The church blamed the devil for trying to take away the soul of a good young man and baptized young pastor Jacob the day he was released from jail. His interest in the church had resurfaced while he was still in jail. The day his mother brought him a bible during a visit changed his life forever. Pastor Jacobs developed into the gem that he was after just a couple of years as a member in his church. Pastor Jacobs went to jail as a high school drop out, but came out with a master's degree in religion and ethics through a program offered at a local college in Boston.

It wasn't too long after pastor Jacobs started visiting the Boys and Girls club that he developed a close relationship with Jimmy. Pastor Jacobs' infectious smile and personality had gotten Jimmy to open up and they became good friends. He made sure that he and Jimmy spent one on one time together every time he visited the center. Pastor Jacobs was a man of substance who could see a troubled kid from a mile away. Having been there in the past, Pastor Jacobs knew the signs to look for and he knew that all these kids needed were for someone to reach out to them.

Jimmy was withdrawn most of the time and he only listened to the instructions of the coach when he was on the basketball court and nothing else. Jimmy isolated himself from his peers and teammates, he rarely engaged in any type of conversation with anyone at the center. Pastor Jacobs took notice of Jimmy's personality almost immediately and he set out to get him to open up and talk about it. Jimmy seemed like the protégé that Pastor Jacobs had been looking for. There was something familiar about the two of them. Pastor Jacobs saw in Jimmy a struggling young man reminiscent of himself when he was that age. Jimmy had a lot of presence and was developing into a great basketball player. Pastor

Jacobs took notice of Jimmy's skills and he wanted to guide him to earn a scholarship to college.

After a few months of getting to know each other, Pastor Jacobs and Jimmy were spending more and more time together. Jimmy visited his church a few times and enjoyed what the pastor had to say every time. He told his sister about pastor Jacobs and invited her to come to church with him one morning. When Nina went to church with Jimmy she discovered the reasons why her brother and the pastor had developed such a special relationship. She was enthralled by his presence and his sermon that morning as she and Jimmy decided to become members of Pastor Jacobs' church.

Pastor Jacobs had become the role model and father figure that Jimmy yearned for all his life. Over time, they became inseparable. Jimmy was also becoming a force on the basketball court. At the age of seventeen he stood six ft six inches tall and weighed two hundred and thirty lbs. He was a premiere forward at the Boys and Girls club as well as his high school. Jimmy averaged twenty points and ten rebounds a game. He was a star in high school that never acted like he was above anybody because pastor Jacobs kept him grounded. Pastor Jacobs counseled Jimmy once a week and had casual chats with him as often as possible regarding his life. He was on the right track to become a great person and a superstar on the basketball court. Jimmy's second love was still Karate and he spent the rest of his time practicing on his own through the books that he's read about Karate.

It seemed like there was no secret between Jimmy and his mentor. On the day that Pastor Jacobs came to the club to do his workshop on sex prevention, Jimmy didn't show up. Pastor Jacobs and Jimmy never really discussed his sexual life because it appeared to be nonexistent to the pastor since Jimmy was so busy. Whenever the pastor tried to bring up the subject of sex Jimmy clammed up and didn't want to engage in that kind of conversation with him. The level of comfort always disappeared when the subject was brought up. However, Pastor Jacobs became especially concerned on the day of the workshop because it was an opportunity for the kids to discuss sex amongst themselves and Jimmy was nowhere to be found. Throughout the whole time he was doing his workshop, he was looking for his favorite kid in the crowd and his favorite kid never showed.

Pastor Jacobs offered Jimmy a part-time job at the church so he would have spending money every week. Jimmy was delighted in accepting the Pastor's offer. Since Jimmy started working at the church, he and Nina had decided to get a home phone, so immediately after the workshop Pastor Jacobs got on the phone to find out why Jimmy didn't show up for his important workshop. He called the house and Jimmy picked up the phone with an attitude. Pastor Jacobs asked Jimmy if he was alone and he said "yes". He wanted to get an explanation from Jimmy as to why he missed the workshop and Jimmy couldn't give him one, instead Jimmy broke down on the phone and told pastor Jacobs that he didn't want to talk about it. Pastor Jacobs asked him if he could come by to talk about it in person and Jimmy told him not to bother. They both hung up the phone leaving pastor Jacobs bewildered.

Pastor Jacobs could always sense when there was a crisis with someone he knew. He ignored Jimmy's request about not seeing him in person. Pastor Jacobs got in his car and drove to Jimmy's house to see him promptly. When Pastor Jacobs arrived at Jimmy's house, he knocked on the door for about fifteen minutes and there was no answer. He knew Jimmy was inside and he didn't want to turn back and leave him in there alone. Pastor Jacobs decided to break down the door to get in.

Once Pastor Jacobs got in the apartment, he found Jimmy lying on the bathroom floor with both his wrist cut lying in a bloody mess. Pastor Jacobs checked for Jimmy's pulse and he was still alive. He quickly picked up Jimmy, placed him over his shoulder and drove to the nearest hospital. Pastor Jacob arrived at the hospital just in the nick of time because the doctors told him if he had gotten there a second later Jimmy wouldn't have made it. Jimmy had lost too much blood and it was pertinent that he was operated on and given a blood transfusion. However, in order to operate on Jimmy the hospital needed parental consent. Pastor Jacobs decided to take full responsibility for Jimmy and told the hospital he was his father. He signed all the papers as Jimmy was being operated on.

While Pastor Jacobs was at the Hospital he asked the nurse at the front desk if he could use her phone to make a phone call. Although he was known for having a gift to relate to children, he didn't really know how to tell Nina that her brother had attempted suicide without creating a state of panic on her part. He called the house and she hadn't gotten home yet. He waited a few minutes later and called again and still Nina wasn't home. He called a third time and left a message for Nina to come to the hospital because Jimmy had been in an accident and it wasn't that serious. With Nina, everything that involved her brother was serious. There was no way of downplaying an attempted suicide.

When Nina got home and heard the message, she immediately rushed to Boston Medical Center to meet Pastor Jacobs and to see her brother. Nina arrived at the hospital in a frantic state screaming at the nurse sitting at the front desk demanding to see her brother. When pastor Jacobs who was sitting down the hall heard the commotion, he rushed to the front to calm Nina down and explain the situation. He grabbed Nina and held her tightly in a hug and told her that everything was going to be all right. He tried his best to calm her down before he went into any detail of what happened.

After Nina was finally calm, Pastor Jacobs had to explain to her that she couldn't see Jimmy just yet because he was still in the operating room; however, the doctor came out earlier to tell him that Jimmy was going to pull through. There was a sigh of relief from both of them when he told her the good news. They both walked down to the waiting area and sat down next to each other. Pastor Jacobs explained to Nina that he was waiting for Jimmy to show up at the Boys and Girls club for his workshop on sexual prevention, and when he didn't show up as expected, he called the house and spoke with Jimmy. He sensed distress in Jimmy's voice so he rushed to the house to check up on him right after the workshop. When he got to the house, Jimmy wouldn't open the door, so he kicked the door in and found Jimmy on the bathroom floor with his wrists slit. She couldn't believe what she was hearing; she screamed out loud "I can't afford to lose my whole family". Pastor Jacobs asked what she meant, but she told him she didn't want to talk about it.

A Friendly Ear

As Nina and Pastor Jacobs waited for Jimmy to come out of the operating room, they started talking and trying to get to know each other better. Pastor Jacobs was more familiar with Jimmy than he was with Nina. In fact, he and Nina had never talked for more than five minutes before, but now the moment they had while they were waiting for Jimmy seemed like a lifetime opportunity. Pastor Jacobs was not an intrusive man who liked to probe for information. His approach with the younger people was a little different. He allowed them to get comfortable enough to open up to him when they were ready, and nothing was forced. Pastor Jacobs learned the importance of patience when he was in jail and recognized that in due time everyone needed a friendly ear just to listen without judgment.

At first, Nina just stared at Pastor Jacobs like she was trying to read his mind. This young thirty something preacher was handsome and had a baby face that even a thief would trust. If Nina had a camera that day she would have taken a close up of every fine line and blemish on Pastor Jacobs' face, but she didn't have a camera. She was taking mental notes and just reading the lines the best she could before she decided to open up to him about her home situation. It took a few minutes before Nina finally asked Pastor Jacobs how he felt about Jimmy. Without hesitation, Pastor Jacobs told Nina that he thought Jimmy was a promising young man who was going through the motions of adolescence and he would recover in no time. Pastor Jacobs also assured Nina that from then on he'd always make himself available to Jimmy for anything. Even though Pastor Jacobs had a way with words, that day he just couldn't find the proper words to describe the way he felt about Jimmy. Jimmy was like the son he always wanted and his personality reminded Pastor Jacobs of himself when he was young. There was a determination in Pastor Jacobs' voice to protect Jimmy.

After hearing Pastor Jacobs' kind words about her brother, Nina decided it was time to let Pastor Jacobs in on their little home secret. With tears running down her face, Nina told Pastor Jacobs they were all that they had. She went on "We've been taking care of each other ever since we were kids. My mother was a drug addicted prostitute who paid very little attention to us at home and when she went to jail, I tried my best to keep it from Jimmy. Sometimes, I think he just blocks her out of his mind in order to have some kind of sanity. I didn't want to tell him that our mother died in prison because I just didn't know if he could handle it, but I told him anyway and I'm not sure if that had any affect on him". Nina had run down most of the important parts of her life to Pastor Jacobs in a matter of minutes. Pastor Jacobs couldn't believe what he was hearing. He had no idea that the kids had gone through so much trauma and lost their mother in the process. He sympathized with them even more than ever. He pulled Nina close to him and held her tightly until she felt comforted enough to let out a sigh of relief.

Pastor Jacobs was still holding Nina's hand for comfort when the doctor came out of the operating room to tell them that Jimmy would recover completely and that it might be a good idea to sign him up for counseling with a therapist immediately after release. Pastor Jacobs shook his head in agreement, but he knew he was the unofficial counselor to most of the kids he came in contact with. The fact that most Black people from the hood didn't believe that a psychologist would have their best interest at heart, made it harder for Pastor Jacobs to persuade Jimmy to see one. Most of these psychologists were the reason why so many young black boys and girls ended up in Special Education at school for most of their lives. And the uneducated parents were too ignorant to recognize that the disability checks that they received from the government for these kids every month would end up being a lifetime handicap for their children who shouldn't have been in Special Education from the start. The doctor also told them that Jimmy would be kept overnight for observation and he'd be released the next morning. They wanted to know if they could see him. The doctor told him that Jimmy was still sedated, but they were welcome to see him.

Nina and Pastor Jacobs walked in the room and stood by Jimmy's bed to watch him sleep for about five minutes before they said anything. Nina walked closer to him and gave him a kiss on the forehead. Pastor Jacobs could feel the closeness between Nina and her brother. She was really hurt that she almost lost her brother, whom she considered her lifeline. It would be a few hours before the anesthesia wore off. Nina thanked pastor Jacobs for everything and the time that he took out of his busy schedule to stay with her family at the hospital.

She told him if he needed to go tend to his business he could. He told her Jimmy was more important than anything and he didn't mind staying. She insisted that he goes because he had been at the hospital for over six hours. He finally agreed to leave, but promised that he would be back in the morning to take Jimmy home. Before pastor Jacobs left the room, he asked Nina to bow her head to pray with him. The two of them prayed for Jimmy and then he left. Nina stayed by her brother's bedside all night until he woke up early the next day to find her sleeping in the chair next to his bed. He looked at his sister wearing a bright smile on his face.

A Father Figure at Last

The next morning Pastor Jacobs showed up at the hospital bright and early to drive Jimmy and Nina home. When he came in the room, they both were already up chatting away. Pastor Jacobs took one look at Jimmy and said "You're going to be fine, champ". Jimmy was very happy to see Pastor Jacobs, but there was still a sense of uneasiness on his part for what he had done. Pastor Jacobs instantly became a soother when he noticed the embarrassment in Jimmy's face. He told Jimmy that he shouldn't feel ashamed for what he had done because God would forgive him in his time of struggle. He told Jimmy that he was struggling with his demons and he won and that the lord is stronger than the devil. Jimmy was in a rush to leave the hospital, but before they could make their way out, Pastor Jacobs asked everyone to bow their heads in prayer. He thanked the Lord for giving Jimmy a second chance and he promised that he'd look after Jimmy and his sister in the name of the Lord then said "Amen".

As pastor Jacobs discovered more about Nina and Jimmy, they were discovering a father figure in him. Pastor Jacobs became a part of their daily lives. He talked to Nina about her future after high school whenever possible and he helped Jimmy with his schoolwork as well as his extracurricular activities. Jimmy was fast becoming a dominant basketball player in high school and the scouts were gazing at him. Pastor Jacobs wanted to make sure that Jimmy stayed on a straight and narrow path. He saw Jimmy and Nina everyday from then on.

Pastor Jacobs had become comfortable enough with the kids to talk to them about anything. So one day he suggested that they move in with him so he could be closer to them. He also felt that the street where the kids lived was just too dangerous and the temptations of drugs and prostitution were at their doorstep every time they walked out of their house. Nina was seventeen years old and Jimmy was an overdeveloped fifteen year-old who had grown accustomed to being on their own.

They thought about how the changes would affect their lives positively and negatively and they politely declined Pastor Jacobs' offer. It would just be too hard for them to re-acclimate themselves to a new environment and an adult parent. They felt the relationship they had with pastor Jacobs was better away from him. They feared if he discovered everything about them he might not like them as much. Pastor Jacobs didn't feel rejected at all as he told the kids that he understood their position. Nina and Jimmy didn't spend much time in their neighborhood to begin with. They were always busy with some extracurricular activity or work.

Nina had developed into a gorgeous young lady with long curly hair with a caramel complexion, deep brown eyes, high cheekbones and the sweetness of an angel. She had inherited most of her mother's aesthetic assets. Nina was personable and liked by everyone. She was definitely a threat to the other overzealous women at her school, but even more of a threat to the guys who were too afraid to ask her out. Nina had never shown any interest in boys as she didn't want anybody at her school to get too close to her so she wouldn't have to reveal much about herself. However, prom season had arrived and Nina wanted to go to her senior prom.

At first, she considered asking her brother to escort her to the prom, but that thought faded away because she felt it to be pathetic. She turned to the only person who could help her land a date for her prom; it was a job for Pastor Jacobs. Nina figured that pastor Jacobs could make a suggestion to one of the nice boys in the church and he was more than pleased to do it. Pastor Jacobs suggested that she went to the prom with the youth ministry leader, Kwame Jordan. Pastor Jacobs was a very observant man and he noticed how Kwame and Nina were always flirting with each other without saying a word. They were both too shy to say anything to each other. He talked to each one individually and told them each that they both wanted to go out with each other. Pastor Jacobs was always paying attention to the youths at the church, so he was well aware of the attraction between the couple. He set the whole thing up.

Pastor Jacobs knew that Nina didn't want Kwame in her business at home, so he suggested that she should come to his house to get ready and Kwame could pick her up from there. Nina agreed and she made arrangements with Kwame to pick her up from Pastor Jacobs' house on prom night. Jimmy stayed at Pastor Jacobs' house that night as well.

While Nina was upstairs getting ready, Jimmy and Pastor Jacobs talked in the living room about basketball and Pastor Jacobs gave him a few pointers on how he could improve his game. Jimmy was delighted to learn that Pastor Jacobs was also a basketball star back when he was in high school. Because he was a pastor, Jimmy never envisioned that he was a basketball player even though they were about the same height. Jimmy enjoyed the conversation he had with Pastor Jacobs about his greatness on the basketball court while they waited for Kwame to pick up Nina.

It was six o'clock in the evening when Kwame showed up at Pastor Jacobs' house. He rang the bell and Jimmy answered the door. Kwame already knew Jimmy at the church so they exchanged greetings. Jimmy called for Nina to come downstairs because her date had arrived. The moment of truth finally came. Nina walked down the stairs in a beautiful cream-colored gown that accentuated her every curve; she wore her hair up in a pinned style that exposed all her beautiful features.

The men couldn't believe how gorgeous she looked. For the first time, the men in her life saw Nina as a sexy woman. The sensual woman in Nina was brought to light on prom day. Jimmy, Pastor Jacobs and Kwame couldn't believe their eyes when Nina emerged from the bedroom upstairs. She applied just enough make up to bring about the glamour that was hidden in a poor little ghetto girl. It was almost like a Cinderella story, but she looked better than the book described. Just like the Cinderella story, her brother playfully gave her a midnight curfew. Pastor Jacobs snapped a few pictures of Nina with Kwame and her brother then they went to the waiting limousine outside to take them to the prom.

As expected, Nina didn't want to disappoint her brother so she came back home at midnight. She described the evening to him as they stayed up late that night to have a brother and sister chat. They felt like they were in a family home while they were at Pastor Jacobs' house. The only thing missing was their mother. They felt very comfortable with Pastor Jacobs and he made sure that they felt at home.

It was getting late; Pastor Jacobs came out of his room and suggested that they go to bed because they still had to wake up for school the next day. They both looked at each other and remembered why they decided they didn't want to move in with Pastor Jacobs. They weren't used to a parent telling them what to do. They were responsible kids who tried their best to do what was right most of the time. Even though it felt good to have someone that cared about them, it would be a hard adjustment on their part and they didn't want to create any drama between them and Pastor Jacobs. They valued him too much as a person and a friend to have any disagreements with him. They both went to sleep in their separate rooms.

It was June 22, 1997 when seventeen year-old Nina graduated from high school. Nina had made it past the point of the statistics. She didn't fall victim to the statistic and the low expectations set for her neighborhood and her future was looking brighter. Nina felt a sense of pride because she had surpassed a point that her mother never reached when she was alive. Jimmy was even more proud of his sister and he couldn't wait to get to her graduation.

Without notice, Pastor Jacobs showed up at the house in a limousine to take them to the graduation, it was the sweetest thing that anyone had ever done for them. Nina and Jimmy's eyes lit up like Christmas trees. They couldn't believe it. Pastor Jacobs had gone out of his way to make a special day feel even more special for them. That day sealed his faith with the kids. They knew they had a gem in Pastor Jacobs and it was by the grace of god that he was sent to them. All the sorrow and absentee feelings that were beginning to draw up inside of them just left. They were no longer thinking about their mother not being there as they rejoiced in the presence of Pastor Jacobs.

Nina graduated top of her class that year. She received many commendations and awards from the school and local businesses. Everyone was proud of Nina's achievements, but no one was more proud than her brother Jimmy. After the graduation ceremony, Pastor Jacobs surprised Nina and Jimmy by bringing them to this Chinese restaurant in Saugus called Weylu's for dinner. Nina and Jimmy had never been out to a nice restaurant before, so they tried to live the moment. Everybody had a great time throughout the whole night. It was an experience that the kids would cherish for the rest for their lives.

New Beginnings

Nina never really showed any interest in applying to college even with the persistence of Pastor Jacobs. Pastor Jacobs had discussed with Nina on many occasions the endless possibilities and the opportunities that a college degree would offer, but Nina wasn't convinced. She had made up her mind that she wanted to become a police officer. Nina's connection with the police department while working as an intern influenced her decision to become a cop. She wanted to fight the very element that landed her mother in jail and ruin her family's life as a result. After she graduated from high school, Nina was presented with the opportunity to work full-time as an administrative assistant with the police department.

The day her supervisor came to her with the offer was also her birthday. She turned eighteen years old that day and she still remembers that day as the happiest day of her life. Nina was looking at a five thousand dollar increase in salary and the opportunity to become a part of her local police department. Though she hadn't fully reached her dream of becoming a police officer, Nina was very grateful for the opportunity to get her foot in the door. Nina's immediate plans were to work for the department for a year until she would become available for their cadet program. The police department had set an age requirement of nineteen years old for cadets and twenty one years old for police officers. Nina had mapped out her three-year plan and she was looking forward to accomplishing her goals.

With the help of Pastor Jacobs, Jimmy had obtained a summer job working thirty hours a week earning enough money to buy his clothes for the following school year. Jimmy was developing into a responsible young man with a bright future. The ever kind hearted Pastor Jacobs offered Jimmy the opportunity to attend basketball camp for two weeks at the end of the summer to improve his basketball skills and he accepted. Jimmy went off to camp for two weeks and came back as an even more dominant player. He had adjusted better to his overgrown body. The clumsiness was eased out of him and his posture exuded more confidence. Pastor Jacobs knew that in order to keep Jimmy away from the bad elements of his neighborhood, he had to keep him busy. So, in addition to his basketball practice, Pastor Jacobs offered him a more responsible job at the church as Assistant Director of youth ministry during the school year. Jimmy's time was much more occupied than any of the kids he knew, but he also wanted it that way.

Nina dated Kwame after the prom and they became inseparable in the church for a little while. Unfortunately, all good things had to come to an end. Kwame who was also a football player in high school, and decided to attend school away from Boston at the University of Miami in Florida on a football scholarship. He and Nina parted ways amicably. Kwame knew that he needed to concentrate on school as well as football and that wouldn't leave him much time to see Nina. Kwame was a realist; he knew he would never reach the heights of a great football star, so he never aspired to become a professional athlete. He wanted to use his scholarship solely to get a free education.

On rare occasions, he would call Nina to check up on her and try to convince her to join him at the University of Miami instead of waiting for a job at the police station. After a while, Nina grew tired of his relentless comments on how a college education was more important than the career she had set her eyes on. She eventually stopped answering his calls, but he still held a special place in her heart.

All seemed to be going well in the kids' lives. They had a surrogate parent who loved them dearly; they were busy and weren't struggling financially. That year marked the first year that the kids didn't have to deal with any adversity. Pastor

Jacobs was very satisfied with their characters and was even more pleased with how well mannered Nina and Jimmy were.

They were leaders in the youth ministry and Jimmy was having a great year in school and on the basketball court. Jimmy was starting to become such a high profile high school basketball player that kids would sometimes stop him on the street to ask for autographs. His games were shown on the local television stations in full length. Pastor Jacobs helped to make sure Jimmy was a well-adjusted individual and the sudden star status didn't go to his head. Jimmy could always count on Pastor Jacobs to be honest and blunt with him. Pastor Jacobs was his source for constructive criticism. While most people thought he had a perfect game, Pastor Jacobs would always try to point out a weakness that he needed to work on and that made him a much better player.

There is Light at the End of the Tunnel

A year had passed and Nina was selected as one of the cadets for the police academy after successfully taking the police exam. She was no longer an administrative assistant in the office even though she still had administrative duties. Nina was just happy to wear the blue pants and white shirt uniform that cadets were required to wear everyday to work. The police station celebrated her selection as a cadet by throwing her a small party in the office. Nina was getting closer to realizing a goal that she had set for herself since high school. Each step closer she took towards her dream also brought her more money.

Nina was now 19 years old and working a decent job. She was getting tired of the long wait for the bus every morning and she decided it would be more beneficial to her to buy a car so she could get to work quicker and run her errands when she needed. Although her job was just a couple of miles away from her home, she had to take a tour of Boston just to get to work because of the way the buses were routed. Two miles may not have been that far, but the New England winter weather was almost as fierce as Iceland. A person could take a beating walking a couple of miles in subzero degree weather.

Nina was excited about the idea of owning a car but she didn't have a license yet. Naturally, she went to her surrogate father, Pastor Jacobs and told him that she would like to learn how to drive. He encouraged her to get her license because she would be more independent and self-sufficient. Pastor Jacobs took her down to the registry of motor vehicles and signed her up for a permit. It took Nina all but three months to get her license. Pastor Jacobs had also suggested to Jimmy that he should also get his license because he was 17 years old. Jimmy didn't see a need for a license at first, but when Nina told him she was going to buy a car after she got her license, he decided to sign up to get his license too. Jimmy wasn't as fast a learner as Nina behind the wheel. He almost wore out Pastor Jacobs' patience, but he eventually pulled it together and got his license a couple of months after his sister.

Pastor Jacobs had become a spiritual advisor, confidant, parent, friend and financial advisor to Nina and Jimmy. When it was time for Nina to buy a car, she asked Pastor Jacobs' advice regarding what kind of car she should buy. Sometimes the kids thought Pastor Jacobs was wise beyond his years, and he had become a valuable source of knowledge for them. The fact that Pastor Jacobs' track record with the kids was so perfect also helped keep things in perspective with them. Nina was thinking about financing a new car, but she didn't know which car manufacturer she should go with. When pastor Jacobs advised her to get a used car the first time around, she didn't totally agree with him. He wanted her to become more experienced before she invested in a brand new car. The fact that Jimmy was also going to be driving this car reinforced Pastor Jacobs' reasoning. Nina finally agreed with pastor Jacobs and saw that he was just making sure they went through the process of life.

He wanted them to learn patience and acquire the better things in life in due time. Pastor Jacobs also offered to pay half of the price of the car that Nina would buy if she came up with the other half. Nina worked her pretty bottom off and was able to save fifteen hundred dollars in six months for a car. As promised, Pastor Jacobs matched the money and she was able to shop around for a car with a budget of three thousand dollars. All three of them went to a local used car dealership and they settled on a five year old Toyota Camry. Pastor Jacobs also made sure Nina got her plates and insurance. Pastor Jacobs had made Nina feel once again like a little princess and she and her brother were very happy and grateful. She thanked Pastor Jacobs as she and her brother took off for a joy ride after picking up the car from the dealership. She also cooked Pastor Jacobs one of the best meals that he ever ate later that night.

Let's Talk About Sex

Jimmy developed into a handsome, popular young athlete in his last year of high school. He was a great college prospect and the young ladies knew it. Being a popular athlete in high school had its perks, but the peer pressure of being one of the guys was starting to get to Jimmy. Half the young ladies were throwing themselves at Jimmy most of the time, while the other half admired his strong character. Jimmy was not a jock; he was more refined than his teammates.

While most of Jimmy's teammates' first interests were sex and basketball second, he however, spent most of his time concentrating on his books and figuring out a way to make life better for himself and his sister. He didn't take advantage of people because he was a great athlete. Somewhere along the way through his life's journey, Jimmy learned that integrity was one of the most important characteristics in a man. It could've been Pastor Jacobs who instilled those values in him; nevertheless, he walked around with his head high and with a lot of integrity. Jimmy was overly sincere for a high school student. After practice in the shower, most of the other players on the team would brag about the women they slept with and who was going to be their next victim, but Jimmy was never interested in talking about women. He was not one to divulge more information than necessary.

Because of his intimidating size, Jimmy didn't really get into too many fistfights with the kids at school anymore. He was a fearless guy who knew how to manage and control his temper and his strength. Sometimes, the guys would try to rank on him in the locker room about his lack of desire for women, but Jimmy never allowed their jokes to get to him. One day he made it known to all his teammates that he was a virgin and he didn't have a problem with it. When one of the players who always second guessed Jimmy's honesty confronted him about really being a virgin in front of the team, Jimmy responded "Maybe that's why I'm the best player on this team; I don't waste my time and energy chasing skirts. Unlike you, I spend most of my time improving my game, which is something you need to do because even the bench is tired of your behind sitting on it". The whole team blew their top laughing at the other player. Jimmy had his own way to deal with his peers. He had a sense of humor that he rarely exposed, but when he unleashed a little bit of it, it was always legendary.

Jimmy may have played the nonchalant role at school when it came to sex, but deep down inside, it really bothered him as a teenager that he didn't know anything about it. Jimmy wanted so much to talk to someone about sex, but he didn't know how to approach the subject without the embarrassment. The entire dirty stigma attached to sex in the Christian world made it hard for Jimmy to try discussing the subject with Pastor Jacobs. The fact that Pastor Jacobs didn't even have a girlfriend forced Jimmy to believe that the Pastor was practicing celibacy and he would want Jimmy to do the same.

Enough was enough! Jimmy wanted to discuss sex with someone-anyone. He decided to go to the only person whom he felt comfortable with. Jimmy waited for Nina to come home so they could discuss sex, but not necessarily their sex lives. Earlier in the day, Jimmy had gone to the library to pick up a few books on the subject of sex just so he would know what types of questions to discuss with his sister. When Nina got home that night, she found Jimmy waiting in the living room on the couch with a couple of books on the table with sex headings plastered all over them.

They exchanged greetings then Nina walked to her room. Nina seemed like she was beat and was in no mood to talk about anything that night because she'd had a rough day at work. However, Jimmy had made up his mind that he wanted to talk to someone about sex and if he didn't do it soon, he was going to lose his mind. Nina sensed the urgency in her brother's face and decided that no matter how bad a day she had, her brother was always more important. She knew if her brother was at home waiting for her, it was something important. Nina was especially sensitive to Jimmy's needs after his suicide attempt. She didn't handle him with gloves or anything, but she was careful not to bring on another attempt.

A few minutes later, Nina emerged from her room wearing a comfortable oversized t-shirt and shorts. She went and sat next to her brother and asked what was on his mind. She knew it had something to do with sex because of the obvious titles of the books that were sitting on the table. Jimmy was anxiously waiting for his sister to ask that question. He told her that he wanted to know everything she knew about sex and if she could clarify a few things for him in the process, it would be helpful. He told his sister that the guys in the locker room made it seem like sex was the best thing in the world that he was missing out on and what was so great about it. Nina had a dumbfounded look on her face after her brother's statement.

This was the one area where Nina didn't have the experience or the maturity to discuss with her brother. She had originally thought that he was going to be asking about the human body. He caught her off guard with his statement and she felt that she could only be fair and honest with him. She told her brother that she had never had sex with anyone and she was just as ignorant about sex as he was. Jimmy then asked "Didn't you and Kwame get it on?" Nina couldn't believe that Jimmy thought she had slept with Kwame. She told him that Kwame was the youth ministry director and there was no way they were going to engage in any sexual activities. Jimmy then asked "If not Kwame, who have you had sex with?" Nina still couldn't believe that her brother was grilling her. She flat out denied ever having sex and told

Jimmy that she couldn't help him. She told him it would be unfair to give him misinformation about something she knew nothing about. Nina suggested that he should talk to Pastor Jacobs about it.

Since Nina made the suggestion for Jimmy to talk to Pastor Jacobs about sex, he left it up to her to bring up the subject to him. It had been a couple of days since Pastor Jacobs had come by the house to check up on Jimmy and Nina. It was just a coincidence that he decided that he wanted to see them on the night they were dealing with the sex issue. It was 9:00 PM when Pastor Jacobs knocked on the door. Nina opened the door and told him that they were just talking about him.

Pastor Jacobs had a sense of crisis when it came to Nina and Jimmy. He always seemed to show up at the appropriate time of need. Nina greeted pastor Jacobs with a hug and a kiss on the cheek. Jimmy walked across the room to the front door to greet Pastor Jacobs with a handshake. Nina asked "What brings you to our neck of the woods tonight?" Pastor Jacobs answered, "I wanted to see my two favorite people. I haven't seen you guys since church on Sunday, I wanted to check up on you and make sure everything is well". Jimmy echoed with "We always appreciate a visit from our favorite Pastor. Especially when we have certain subjects that we'd like to discuss and learn about from our favorite Pastor". Pastor Jacobs asked if they had something particular in mind. Jimmy told him " I'm sure Nina will have no problem telling you what it is we'd like to discuss while I get you guys something to drink in the kitchen". Jimmy left Nina vulnerable with no choice but to bring up the subject to Pastor Jacobs while Jimmy was out of sight.

Pastor Jacobs asked Nina what it was that they wanted to discuss, and the look on his face when she mentioned the three-letter word S-E-X, revealed discomfort. Pastor Jacobs had always anticipated that one day Jimmy would be curious about sex, but he never imagined that he would be talking to Nina about it as well. There was some limitation on his fatherly role, so he thought. Pastor Jacobs wished Nina and Jimmy had attended his workshop on sexual prevention at the center a few years back because he wouldn't have to do this now. This was just too personal and close to home for him.

Jimmy returned five minutes later with a pitcher of lemonade and three glasses for the long discussion he had planned on having with Pastor Jacobs and his sister about sex. The look on Pastor Jacobs' face seemed a little bit uneasy to Jimmy as he was trying to loosen his collar and a little bit of sweat dropping from his forehead when Jimmy walked in. After Jimmy set the pitcher and the glasses on the table, he asked, "So, are you guys ready to talk about this sex thing yet?" Pastor Jacobs hesitantly responded "Sure, whenever you're ready". Jimmy exclaimed, "I'm ready! I'll never be more ready".

The words came out of Jimmy's mouth as if he was planning to have sex the following day after learning about it. Pastor Jacobs looked at him with a surprised grin then quietly whispered "We shall start then". Nina asked "What is it that you'd like to know about sex, Jimmy?" He answered "Everything! How it feels? Why people do it? Am I missing out? How do I know I'm ready for it? And how do I make sure I do it right and well? You know all the basics". Pastor Jacobs answered, "I see...How about we start with the basics?" Jimmy said "Like what?" Pastor Jacobs started explaining to Jimmy and Nina that sex was more than just physical pleasure. He said, "Commitment is one of the most important aspects of sex and before two people should even consider sleeping with each other they should be committed to each other in the eyes of god". Jimmy answered, "So, as long as God knows that two people are committed, they can have sex?" Pastor Jacobs shook his head in agreement as to say yes.

Jimmy went on to say "Since God is the creator and knows what's going on in all our lives, he should know when two people are committed to each other. Those two people should be able to have sex then, right?" Pastor Jacobs quickly interjected by saying "No, no, that's not the kind of commitment I'm talking about. I'm talking about the kind of commitment that two people make to each other when they come before God in a marriage". Jimmy listened carefully to Pastor Jacobs then said, "In other words, a person should be married before they have sex". Pastor Jacobs answered, "Right". Jimmy then asked pastor Jacobs if he was married the first time he had sex. Pastor Jacobs told Jimmy that when he first had sex he was a sinner who hadn't yet found God and the rules didn't apply to him then because he was ignorant.

Jimmy and Nina stared at each other as Pastor Jacobs was trying to make sense of sexual relations. Jimmy had heard enough about premarital sex being a sin. He knew that from reading the bible but he only wanted to know the logic behind the whole thing. Jimmy wanted to know what the fascination with sex was. Nina sat quietly through the whole conversation between Pastor Jacobs and Jimmy. It was as if she allowed her brother to be her mouthpiece. Pastor Jacobs had no idea what he was in for that night.

The questions were coming out of Jimmy's mouth like a machine gun unloading on Iraqi soldiers. Pastor Jacobs wanted to regain control of the conversation, but Jimmy had led him astray and he was forced to answer the questions for general purposes. Pastor Jacobs explained that "when a woman and a man have sex they're not just sharing their bodies, there's also a spiritual connection associated with sex that many people fail to realize". Jimmy wanted to know what he meant by spiritual. Pastor Jacobs explained that sex could have stronger affects spiritually on a couple than physically. He went on to say that sex sometimes could take people where they've never imagined going. A man or woman can become possessive and obsessed after sex and that can be devastating to a person spiritually.

Jimmy had heard enough of the moral gibber from Pastor Jacobs, he wanted to know if sex really felt as good as his friends described. Jimmy bluntly asked pastor Jacobs "How does it feel to have intercourse with a woman?" Pastor Jacobs tried his best to give Jimmy an honest and direct answer without going around the question. He told Jimmy that,"It does feel good to have intercourse with a woman, but that feeling is only instant gratification". He also said "It feels even better when two people are in love and committed". At the end of Pastor Jacobs' statement, Jimmy looked at him straight in the eyes and told him that he only wanted to know about it, he didn't plan on having sex anytime soon. Pastor Jacobs released a sigh of relief then asked Nina, how about you? Nina timidly answered that she was not interested in sleeping with anybody before she walked down the aisle.

First Love

Jimmy only had eyes for this one special girl named Lisa at school. She was a studious young lady who wasn't part of any click at the school. She was one of a few individuals at the school who spent most of her spare time studying at the library. Jimmy met her one day during lunch period when he was at the library searching for a book on Stokely Carmichael for his "Black History Month" research paper. He started to explain to her his interest in the Black Liberation Movement of the sixties and they ended up spending the whole period talking about everything else. Lisa had no idea that Jimmy was the star of the basketball team; she was only interested in his views about the movement and the approach he planned on taking to write his paper.

Jimmy was fascinated with Lisa not because of her beauty, but her intelligence. She was not really a standout in the looks department because she didn't accessorized like the other "too hot to trot" women who threw themselves at Jimmy daily. Lisa's beauty was more subtle and natural; she avoided wearing skimpy outfits to school everyday like the other girls. Jimmy enjoyed the fact that she was able to remain anonymous among the students at the school.

Throughout their whole conversation, Lisa and Jimmy never realized that they didn't introduce themselves to each other. The conversation was flowing so well, neither of them wanted to stop the flow. When Jimmy invited Lisa to his church, it was like putting the seal on the coffin. She found it refreshing that one of her peers enjoyed going to church. Her face lit up as Jimmy demonstrated his knowledge of the bible. Jimmy was a proud Christian and perhaps Christ was the cornerstone of his strength. The bell finally rang, Jimmy asked Lisa if he could walk her to class and she agreed.

As the two were walking down the hall, all the hoochie mamas wearing nothing more than what the school considered inappropriate were giving dirty stares to Lisa. Jimmy and Lisa were totally oblivious to their stares as the two talked and laughed on the way to her class. It was when they arrived to her classroom that they realized that they hadn't exchanged names. They finally introduced themselves properly to each other as Jimmy rushed to get to class on time.

He and Lisa became an item soon after and she finally realized how important a person Jimmy was at the school. She was dating the basketball superstar, not just at her school, but the whole city of Boston. Their relationship was strong because it wasn't based on the superficial and idealized views that other people had of Jimmy. Lisa was genuine and she really was attracted to Jimmy's intelligence more than his popularity and athletic skills. For the first time in his life, Jimmy found a woman who was willing to love him for who he was.

They were both making plans to attend college the following year, but not together. Jimmy was interested in getting a good education as well as the best possibility to showcase his talent to the NBA scouts. Jimmy's top choice of school to attend at the time was University of Massachusetts at Amherst because he wanted to be close to his sister and Pastor Jacobs. University of North Carolina was his second choice because of the great basketball tradition there. Lisa was focusing on the Boston area; she was already accepted to the school of her choice, which was Boston University. Lisa was offered a full academic scholarship through the Upward Bound Program at Boston University and there was no way she was going to turn down a full scholarship. She couldn't afford to turn it down anyway; not too many students from English High School were presented with those opportunities. They both understood that they had to make the best of their situations and since they were both

Christians they hoped that their faith could keep them together while they went away to their separate schools the following year.

While Jimmy was head over heels for one of the regular girls at his high school, his sister Nina was head over heels for the highly respected officer at her precinct. From the time Nina started working her internship at the police station; Officer Brown had always made himself available to assist her with questions regarding her tasks and other job related issues. She grew fond of him in no time, but she was too young to let her feelings be known. The fact that Officer Brown saw in her, a respectable little sister, only helped to suppress her feelings even more. Nina looked forward to going to work everyday just to see Officer Brown. It was infatuation at first, but it grew to something more as she got older and became more mature. Nina was never into people her own age; she enjoyed the company and wisdom of older people. Nina and Kwame didn't work out because he acted immaturely whenever she'd discuss her goals with him. He was fixated on college and he had wanted her to do the same.

After Nina graduated from high school, Officer Collin Brown bought her a nice coffee mug as a graduation gift that she kept on her desk. He was very attentive, caring and protective of her. He didn't allow anyone to walk all over her because she was just an intern when she started at the station. He would occasionally offer her rides home when she was leaving work, but she always declined. He respected her decisions and didn't press the issue. Day by day, Nina's feelings for Officer Collin Brown were growing stronger and she fought harder and harder to suppress them. On her eighteenth birthday, Officer Collin Brown bought her flowers and a card. He hadn't yet become a detective when she turned eighteen years old. He was still a uniform officer with the desire, the drive, aspiration and ambition that any woman would admire in a man. The five year difference in age between Officer Brown and Nina didn't matter much to her, she saw it as more wisdom and experience that he could pass on to her.

Officer Brown was not like most police officers. He wasn't the womanizer that most police officers are perceived to be and he didn't get so many calls at the office from women like the other officers did. Officer Brown also held his mother in high regards, a quality which Nina really appreciated in him. Poor Nina fought her feelings and waited until she became a cadet to reveal to Officer Brown that she was interested in him. She wanted to show him that she was a woman of substance and determination.

Once Nina became a cadet, it basically validated to her that she was worthy of dating a police officer. The thought of her being less than him had never even crossed Officer Brown's mind. He couldn't deny the fact that she was a beautiful and smart woman, so he treated her like a little sister to keep from developing any strong romantic feelings for her. The day that Nina asked him if he'd be interested in going to see a movie with her, was the day that changed their relationship. Officer Brown wanted so much to date Nina openly at work, but he was afraid that people would start accusing him of favoritism. So he kept it quiet and flirted with her every chance he got.

Soon after Officer Brown and Nina went out on their movie date, they decided to become an item and immediately began dating each other seriously. The two were very inconspicuous at work, but inseparable out of work. Nina had finally gotten the man of her dreams and Officer Brown tried everything in his power to remain the man of her dreams. They catered to each other's needs like an old perfect couple still in love after twenty five years of marriage. It was wonderful that Nina had finally found some happiness in her life. Nina and Officer Brown were a match made in heaven. They had similar interests and hobbies. They were both movie buffs who didn't mind spending their Saturday nights in front of the television watching comedy movies all night.

Officer Brown found in Nina a caring, intelligent, beautiful, domesticated, goal oriented woman and a wonderful caretaker. They both provided physical as well as intellectual stimulation to each other.

Facing the Challenge Ahead

In June 2001, Jimmy graduated with honors from English high school. Pastor Jacobs decided to throw a graduation party for Jimmy where his friends could come together one last time before he left for college. Jimmy may have been a popular guy in high school, but he didn't have a lot of friends. Most of the people at the party were his teammates and people from the youth ministry at the church. He was happy just to graduate from high school and headed to a good college, but he appreciated the gesture from Pastor Jacobs. The party was more like a cook-out than a party that ended when the food ran out.

Jimmy had decided that he was going to attend University of Massachusetts at Amherst. Attending University of Massachusetts at Amherst would allow him the opportunity to study accounting, play for a big Division I basketball program as well as give him the opportunity to visit his sister during the off-season, on the weekends. Pastor Jacobs, Jimmy and Nina took a trip up to Amherst to visit the campus and Jimmy fell in love with the rural setting of the school. Because they visited the school in the summer time, there were hardly any students around on campus, which gave the campus a sense of serenity. Jimmy enjoyed the fact that there were about five or six other colleges in the surrounding towns. He was also impressed with the basketball coach there who assured him a starting spot on the team as long as he worked hard and kept his grades up.

The dormitories at University of Massachusetts weren't the best, but Jimmy was not use to any kind of luxury to begin with, so he didn't mind the dorms. Pastor Jacobs was impressed as well with the student life the university had to offer. There was a small African American community of about three to five hundred undergraduate and graduate students on campus, which represented approximately five percent of the student population at U-Mass. Nina was very excited for her brother and she was glad that he was staying close to home because she could always drive up to visit him on the weekends.

During the summer before leaving for college, Jimmy continued to work his job at the church to save money for the school year. He also played in the basketball tournament at Washington Park in Roxbury. Washington Park was a place where anyone who thought they had basketball skills and talent could showcase their talent on the weekends. It was the official gathering place for all the young people of Boston who enjoyed a good game of basketball. It was also the best place to check out some of the finest around the way girls.

In Washington Park, you could find a big time hustler maxing and relaxing behind the wheels of a hooked up Mercedes Benz. You could also find a Harvard student basking in the essence of their community while enjoying a great game of basketball. It was a place where people came together to have fun; eat some of the best bar-b-q chicken and ribs that the local merchants had to offer. You might run into an old classmate, an off-duty police officer, a pastor from the local church, a city counselor or a state representative trying to solicit votes from their constituents. You might also have to disperse when the local knucklehead decided that he wanted to show people he knew how to pull a trigger of a gun. The same people usually came back the following week as if the incident never took place. The sounds of gunshots couldn't keep folks away from Washington Park. Washington Park is a legendary place in Boston.

It was early August, when Jimmy, Nina and Pastor Jacobs packed up the car to take Jimmy to school. For the first time in her life, Nina was going to be without her younger brother. Although she was excited that her brother was going to be pursuing his dream of attending college with a chance to play basketball for a big school, she was also sad that her best friend wasn't going to be at her reach anymore. Jimmy was sad as well but he knew that he had to do what he needed to do to secure a better future.

When they arrived at the school, the campus was relatively dead except for the few players on the soccer and basketball teams who were around. Jimmy's room was located on the tenth floor on the southwest side of campus. They unloaded the car and one by one the boxes found their way in Jimmy's room. It seemed like the final box took forever to get to the room. Tears welled up in Nina's eyes as she carried the last box into Jimmy's room. The time to say, "See you later" had arrived and it was an emotional one for everybody. Even Pastor Jacobs got in the act of shedding tears as they all embraced until the next time they would see each other again. Pastor Jacobs and Nina wished Jimmy good luck and told him to stay clear of the women and other distractions that could possibly keep him from having a successful year in school. The final words out of Pastor Jacobs' mouth were "Remember that you can enjoy many things in moderation. Don't over indulge in any one thing". Jimmy thanked them and promised to call as soon as he got a phone in his room.

On the ride back to Boston, Nina said very little to Pastor Jacobs as he drove. Nina was missing her brother already, but she had her boyfriend Collin Brown who had now become a Detective with the Police Department back home waiting to console and comfort her. Since Jimmy was going to be out of the house, Nina would get the opportunity to get closer to Det. Brown. Pastor Jacobs assured Nina that he'd always be there for her if she ever wanted to talk him or if she just didn't want to be alone. They looked at each other and smiled. Pastor Jacobs told Nina how proud he was of her and Jimmy and that they both turned out to be the kind of children that every parent dream of.

Re-gentrification and the Hood

Nina and Jimmy saw their neighborhood change from having prostitutes roaming the streets in the dead of night, gunshot ridden streets, drug dealing and robbery to one of the hottest sought-after properties that white people wanted to buy. Re-gentrification had changed the neighborhood drastically. Sometimes it's weird to understand the psyche of some folks. It seemed as though the white people suddenly came to the conclusion that they were tired of the long commute that they faced everyday on the way to work. They no longer wanted to run to the suburbs in search of safety and peace of mind. Convenience took precedence over safety. Or perhaps they came to the realization that safety and peace of mind is up to the individual and that the suburbs didn't necessarily shield anybody from an unforeseen act of violence. White people forced property values in Boston to quadruple during the late nineties and Nina took notice.

It was funny how the Boston Police department helped clean up the neighborhood the instant that white people decided the neighborhood was worth investing in. It seemed like black folks always allowed white people to determine their value and worth without actually realizing it themselves. The drug pushers, pimps, prostitutes, thieves and other delinquents were removed from Nina's neighborhood in no time. The one good lesson that Nina learned from white folks was that a home could be her biggest mean of income in times of need.

Nina's landlord was an old man who wanted to retire down south and didn't want to be bothered with his house anymore. The re-gentrification that was taking place in the neighborhood had also taken a toll on the older homeowners. They were faced with new assessments on their homes and their taxes went up as a result. Most of them were living on fixed incomes in the first place and couldn't afford to hold on to their houses. Nina's landlord offered to sell Nina the house without even contacting a realtor to find out the market value for the house. He didn't want to come out on the losing end of the deal because he'd lost his other homes due to the excess taxes that the city charged him. The landlord figured he could save a lot on the commission if he sold his house himself. His decision to sell it himself was Nina's gain because if he'd called a realtor, he would've gotten almost three times the selling price for his house.

Since Nina was now a cadet earning enough money to be qualified for a loan, she figured, why not buy the house she'd been living in most of her life. Nina had the opportunity to buy the three-family home from the old man for less than one hundred and fifty thousand dollars, which was a steal in 2001. The house needed a lot of renovation that the old man didn't want to deal with nor did he have the money to put into it and Nina saw it as a chance for her to become a homeowner. Nina talked to Det. Brown and Pastor Jacobs about the old man's asking price and they both advised her to buy the house. Det. Brown himself was a homeowner who took advantage of the real estate boom in Boston through a special program for Boston police officers and teachers. Pastor Jacobs and Det. Brown both promised that they would help with renovating the place. Nina did the math and figured that she wouldn't be paying anything out of pocket for the mortgage once the house was renovated and rented. As a matter of fact, she would be pocketing about five hundred dollars a month after paying her mortgage, taxes and insurance. She was very money conscious, so she tried to save money every chance she had.

Nina became a homeowner in October of 2001 at the young age of twenty years old. Nina took out a home improvement loan and fixed the house like it was new. Another reason Nina wanted to buy the house was to ensure that her brother always had a place to stay when he came home from school. Jimmy had a permanent place to stay in

Nina's house. It was the best financial decision she ever made.

Nina was able to adjust to the fact that Jimmy was no longer around all the time, but they talked to each other every night on the telephone. She wanted to maintain the closeness that she shared with her brother. They were both still involved in each other's lives even while away from each other. When Jimmy decided to sleep with Lisa even though they weren't married, Nina was the first to know. She didn't pass any judgment because she knew in the near future she was going to sleep with Det. Brown as well. They were Christians, but they were not saints. They always included each other in all their decisions before they made them.

A Memorable Night

Nina and Det. Brown had been dating for a couple of years and everything was going great between them. Det. Brown finally took Nina to meet his family and they loved her. During a conversation at Collin's parents' house, his parents said they were looking forward to meeting Nina's parents, Collin protected his woman as any good man would; he told his parents that Nina's parents passed when she was young and that she had an uncle named Pastor Jacobs who helped take care of her and her brother since they were young and he was going to be person that they would meet. Nina had this look of admiration on her face for her man. She knew then that Collin was her knight in shining armor and he was the man she wanted to spend the rest of her life with. The expression on Collin's face made it obvious that he shared the same sentiments as Nina. It was like the decision to be with each other forever had been made right then and there.

Nina and Collin had the affectionate pet names of Sunshine and Heart respectively for each other. He called her his sunshine because she brightened his days and she referred to him as her heart because he was the heartbeat that lived within her. When Collin asked Nina to come by his house for a special dinner on February 14, 2002, she had no idea what he had planned for her. Normally, they celebrated Valentine's Day at their local favorite restaurant, which was called No Name, a reasonably priced seafood restaurant located on the water by the Boston pier. They both loved seafood and No Name was very convenient and offered great food.

On the evening of Valentine's Day when Nina arrived at Collin's house, there was a note taped to his door telling her to come in and follow the roses. She opened the door to find rose petals on the floor from the front door leading to the bathroom. When she got to the bathroom there were lit scented candles surrounding the tub and a bathtub nicely filled with warm water and her favorite raspberry scented bubble bath. There was another note taped to the bathroom mirror telling her to take off her clothes and get in for no longer than an hour. She didn't want to stop following the directives of her Heart, so she obliged and took off her clothes and got in the tub.

It was the most soothing bath that she had ever taken. While she was in the bathroom enjoying the warmth of the bubble bath, Collin showed up with her favorite shrimp dish that he had especially ordered and picked up from No Name. He set up the table in the dining room with his best china, candlelight, a bottle of Dom Perignon and a new arrangement of flowers in a crystal vase. The Best of Luther Vandross was on cue in the CD changer in the bedroom.

It was getting close to the allotted hour that Nina was supposed to spend in the bathroom and she'd have to get out of the tub soon. Nina had her eyes closed the entire time she was laying in the tub. Collin snuck in and left a box on the sink counter with yet another note for her to wear what was in the box. When she got out of the tub she dried herself with the fresh towel that he'd left for her on the towel holder located above the tub. She opened the box as directed and found a nice black-laced teddy from Victoria's Secret. She put it on as instructed; she went to the mirror to check herself and made sure she was looking good. To her liking, there was a bottle of Chanel #5 placed below the mirror on the soap holder. She lightly sprayed the perfume all over her body, put on the high heel shoes that she was wearing when she came in. She stepped out of the bathroom to find Collin wearing nothing but a pair of silk boxers, a matching silk robe with a rose in his mouth. He grabbed her hand and led her to the table in the dining room where he had dinner waiting for her.

Collin and Nina had great conversation over dinner and the champagne made them a bit tipsy, as they didn't have a high tolerance for alcohol. Neither of them were regular drinkers. After dinner, Collin carried his woman to the bedroom where she found more rose petals all over the bed. As she rolled around on the bed over the rose petals, she felt a hard object underneath her. She reached around and grabbed what appeared to be a small jewelry box from Tiffany's, after she closely examined the box, she determined that it was definitely a jewelry box from Tiffany's and didn't know what to expect. By the time she opened the box, Collin was already on one knee beside the bed waiting to ask her to marry him. When she saw the sparkling two-carat solitaire diamond, she knew that she had found the man of her dreams. She didn't hesitate to tell him "Yes, I'll marry you". They hugged and kissed more passionately than they ever had in the past. The kisses were wet, with more tongue and a lot more tugging from lip to lip than they had done in the past. They verbally confessed to each other how much they loved each other and how much they meant to one another.

Collin was in the mood to make love to his woman, but he didn't want to force it on her. He was very pleasantly surprised when she started to slowly kiss him all around his face and down to his chest. She gently sucked on his nipples until they became erect and as she was slowly wandering his body with her tongue, she effortlessly took her left hand and reached in front of him for his boxers. He lay there watching blissfully as she reached around his ass with her right hand to pull off his boxers.

He sensed Nina was inexperienced, but it just felt good to him because she was the woman he loved. Before she could go down and give him the royal treatment that he longed for, he pulled her up to his face and started kissing her very gently again. He wanted her to feel the passion of his touch and kisses, so he gently started rubbing her breast with his hand. She was moaning softly with every stroke of his hand. He slowly went up to the back of her neck kissing it and slowly blowing it creating a frigidly sensitive effect that she enjoyed very much.

Collin had Nina so turned on, she was on fire. She wanted him to take her the same way she saw the romantic scenes on her favorite soap opera. Nina's romantic fantasies only came from television; she had never been in a romantic setting with a man before, much less had sex. As Collin licked his way down to her nipples, she grabbed hold of his head pressing it against her chest, moaning and anticipating the kind of pleasure that she's always dreamed about. He slowly caressed her breasts with his mouth and hands until her nipples stood erect. Nina was hotter than ever and Collin hadn't even begun to fully please her. He wanted to take his time with her and made sure that he treated her as gently as possible. He continued to lick his way down to her naval while rubbing her clit with his finger. Nina was screaming like she couldn't bear the guilty pleasure that Collin was whipping on her.

Nina became very vocal when Collin finally made his way down to her cookie; eating her gently like she was his favorite lobster dish and his tongue was the butter. Nina reached not just one, but multiple orgasms for the first time in her life. She couldn't believe how great an orgasm felt. Her clitoris became so sensitive and she had to tell Collin to stop because she couldn't endure his pleasure any more and that she needed a break to regain herself. He simply moved up to the pillow and held her in his arms for about a half hour.

They talked and she revealed to him that it was the first time that she had ever been with a man sexually and she was glad that it was him. She asked him if he wanted to have intercourse with her, he told her it was up to her and only if she felt comfortable with it. She told Collin she was willing to at least try it with him and if it felt anything like what he just did to her, she couldn't wait to marry him and have it all the time.

Collin slowly kissed his way back down to Nina's cookie, licking her sensually to get her stimulated enough so he could slide inside her. The minute he touched her, she was as wet as a river. He attempted to penetrate her and Collin immediately noticed that Nina was very uncomfortable with his penetration and seemed a bit apprehensive and scared about going through with 'it. It was as if she was having a flashback to when she was raped. He quickly stopped, held her tight in his arms until she calmed down. The two of them fell asleep in each other's arms and slept until the next morning.

Nina and Collin woke up the next morning; they talked about their future and looked forward to a great life together. Collin and Nina didn't want a long engagement, so they decided to get married seven months later in September. Nina waited till the following day to call Jimmy to tell him the good news. A part of Jimmy was very happy for his sister, but the rest of him felt like he was about to lose her to another man like he lost his mother to the streets. Jimmy knew that he couldn't be selfish and Nina would remain his sister no matter what her status was. He congratulated her and told her he was happy for her. She also asked Pastor Jacobs if he would give her away and he was honored by her request.

The Idiomatic Encounter

Jimmy had just completed his sophomore year in college and he was talked up to be one of the high prospects of the upcoming NBA draft that upcoming June. Many experts predicted he could be a first round pick if he so chose to make himself available for the draft. Jimmy wrestled with the idea of not completing his college degree. He talked to Pastor Jacobs and Det. Brown about what he should do, but he knew that the decision was ultimately up to him. There were also the detractors who doubted that he was good enough to make the jump from college to the NBA. Those doubters were more attacking the fact that another talented, young African American man was about to become a multi-millionaire without a college degree. Jimmy was a very mature young man who earned the respect of his peers in college as well as the college and NBA coaches across the nation. He still had a few weeks to think about his decision.

Meanwhile, Jimmy came home for the summer to help with the preparations for his sister's wedding. He was very excited for her and he knew she was happy by the glow in her face whenever she talked about Collin. Jimmy was also looking forward to having Collin as a brother in law as he would gain a buddy and a hang out partner. He was just happy that his sister found her soul mate that she could settle down and have a family with him. Jimmy was still seeing Lisa and was hoping that one day they could walk down the aisle as well.

During his summer vacation, Jimmy dropped his sister off at work every morning and kept her car during the day to run the necessary errands that she needed him to run and some of his own as well. Jimmy picked up his sister from work on a Friday afternoon at about 3:30 to take her to one of her appointments downtown with the seamstress. They were driving down on Congress Street when Nina noticed this familiar face coming out of the Creep Bank building in Boston. Something came over Nina and she shouted, "There goes the asshole!" Jimmy was wondering what the hell was wrong with his sister. She pointed to the guy and said, "There he goes". Jimmy didn't initially make the connection because she was about to bring back something that he'd buried in the back of his mind for years. She turned to him and said, "Don't you remember, Jimmy?" He looked at her and said "Remember what?" She said "That's the asshole who raped me and you as children".

He pulled the car over and stared at the man like he was rewinding an old VHS tape in the back of his mind. All the abuse was suddenly vivid in his mind. He started to recall how the man used to come by his house when his mother was working as a hooker and he'd sneak into their rooms and raped them while their mother was passed out on drugs in her room.

Jimmy tried to get out of the car to chase the man to put a beat down on him, but his sister pulled him back because she felt the guy was not worth Jimmy going to jail. Jimmy asked his sister if they were just going to let the guy walk away and she shook her head saying yes with disgust and tears running down her face. Jimmy was flying off the handle beating his fist on the dashboard of the car saying " I'm gonna get that bastard!" It was the first time Nina had ever heard her brother used such foul language. She begged Jimmy to leave it alone and they drove off. Jimmy was pissed but he kept quiet the whole ride home.

He and Nina had nightmares for weeks after seeing the guy. All the sick memories they buried deep inside resurfaced and they had a hard time coping again. It brought them back to square one. Nina became very jumpy and agitated very easily with her Collin. She didn't know how to explain to him that she had run into the man who made her life miserable as a child. She never even told Collin that she had been raped as a child. He assumed she was wincing and grimacing the first time they tried to have sex because she was a virgin.

Jimmy had an even harder time as a man dealing with the rape. The man took away his manhood and childhood before he even had a chance to develop as a young man. He tried blocking it out of his mind for years, but he couldn't suppress it anymore. Jimmy became angrier as time went by and promised that he would do something about it, not just for his sake, but also for the sake of his sister. Jimmy walked inside the bank one day as the man was coming out; he went to the security desk and asked if they knew the man's name. The security guard told him that the gentleman's name was Mr. Patrick Ferry, one of the executives at the bank and that was all the information he needed.

With that information, Jimmy followed the man for days and became very acquainted with the man's schedule. He also did a background check on the man via the Internet on a GOOGLE search. He knew where the man lived, what hours he worked, his hobbies, his name, his favorite food, his wife's name, his kids' names and his favorite prostitute pick-up location. He was like an FBI agent working relentlessly to familiarize himself with the man. Jimmy used the Internet to do a thorough background check on the man whose life happened to be very public because of his status. Jimmy was so preoccupied with the man, the deadline to declare himself available for the draft in June had come and gone and he didn't even realize it. People were calling him about representation for the draft, but he never got back to them. He was too obsessed with the man to think or do anything else.

Nina started to notice a dramatic change in her brother's behavior, so she tried her best to talk to him whenever possible and she'd always tell him that they could get through this ordeal together. Jimmy understood that his sister was planning her wedding and he didn't want to be a burden on her. She suggested that maybe he should go back to Amherst to regain control of his life. And perhaps he could come back in the fall for the wedding. He wrestled with the idea at first, but he decided it was better if he went back to Amherst.

Nina dropped off Jimmy at the Greyhound bus stop at South Station in Boston so he could catch the bus to Amherst. They hugged and said their goodbyes. Nina made him promise that he'd come back for the wedding. He told her that he wouldn't miss it for the world. Nina told him not to hesitate to call her whenever he felt like he needed to talk to someone. He promised that she'd be the first person he'd call during any time of crisis.

She only made the suggestion to her brother to go back to Amherst because Amherst had become more of his element. He was a well-known guy in Amherst who was loved by everyone, not just as a basketball player, but also as a person. Amherst had become a sanctuary for Jimmy; everybody knew his name there.

Lisa also had a hard time dealing with Jimmy's departure. He didn't feel comfortable enough with Lisa to tell her about the tragic ordeal he went through as a child. First of all, he didn't want Lisa to know that his mother was a prostitute and a drug abuser. He simply told her that he had to go back to Amherst because of basketball. He told her he was sorry that they weren't going to be spending much time together during the summer but she was welcomed to visit him anytime she wanted to at Amherst. Jimmy was also not ready to talk about the rape with Pastor Jacobs. Jimmy's pride got in the way. He was too proud to allow anyone in his life to share his pains and sufferings.

Marital Bliss

A month before the wedding, Nina finally took her brother and Pastor Jacobs to meet Collin's family at a special invitation dinner that Collin's parent had arranged at their house. Nina felt a little awkward not having her mother there with her, but Jimmy and Pastor Jacobs almost made her feel like they were all the family she needed and that took away the awkward feeling for the most part. Collin's mother was a beautiful dark skinned woman from Haiti who was in her early fifties and his father was a brown skinned African American man in his late fifties. They had been together for close to thirty years and had two children, Collin and Stephanie.

Mrs. Brown had been working as a registered nurse at Massachusetts General Hospital for over twenty five years and was looking forward to having some grandchildren who could occupy her time after she retired. Mr. Brown was a high school teacher and football coach who had been working for the Boston Public Schools department for close to thirty years. A mutual friend introduced them in the early seventies.

Through dinner, Nina was enjoying the loving tales of Collin's parents about him. They both seemed to be still in love with each other and they connected on every subject. All Nina could think about at the dinner table was her own life with Collin. She wanted a piece of what his parents had. She knew that Collin had a great foundation, but it might be a struggle for her to learn to be a good wife because she didn't have any good examples in her life. She was relying on God to guide her through it all. Pastor Jacobs didn't have to reveal too much about himself because the Browns were already familiar with his good work in the neighborhood. They were happy that he could share in the blessings of the happy couple. Jimmy was still in college and didn't have much to say during dinner.

They briefly touched upon the fact that he might become a professional athlete in the near future and how he planned on spending his millions. Jimmy was too shy to participate in that conversation. He allowed everyone to talk up his life while he listened. Stephanie was the only person in the room who could relate to Jimmy. She was entering her senior year at Boston College in the fall. Stephanie could sense how uncomfortable Jimmy was when his name came up in the conversation. She helped out by changing the subject and redirecting the focus to the honored couple.

Nina and Collin felt like time just flew by while they were planning their wedding. There was never enough time to do anything. The wedding really tested their patience for each other. Collin's parents were very helpful in lending a hand with the preparations, but it was still taking a toll on his relationship with Nina. Nina and Collin worked the same 8:00AM to 4:00PM shift at the police station, so it was hard for them to keep appointments because most of the places they were dealing with closed at 5:00PM. They were always rushing from one appointment to the next. Jimmy had helped to alleviate some of the burdens for the couple when he was around, but he unfortunately had to return to U-Mass. to regain his sanity.

Other disagreements about the wedding also existed. Collin wanted to have his friends be the groomsmen in the wedding, while Nina didn't have any girlfriends to ask to be her bridesmaids. Nina never really took the time to make friends when she was younger, so there was no special female friend in her life. She didn't like the idea of anybody probing into her private life. They were at a crossroad for relatively a short period, but Collin offered a solution that satisfied both of them. He asked his sister and a couple of cousins to walk with three of his closest friends. Collin also asked John O'Malley, his former partner to be his best man.

When Collin asked O'Malley to be his best man, it was the first time that he had ever referred to O'Malley by his first name, John, since they had known each other. O'Malley always wished that he and Collin could share a closer civilian relationship. He was surprised that Collin thought that highly of him to ask him to be his best man. Collin always kept his professional relationship with O'Malley separate from his personal relationship.

Nina never really envisioned any particular type of wedding. She had never been to a wedding before and she only watched the big lavish weddings on television. Nina and Collin acted miserly with their spending, so they wanted to keep the wedding as moderate as possible. They had decided on a budget of ten thousand dollars, but Pastor Jacobs and Collin's family offered an additional five thousand dollars to go towards the wedding. Nina also broke wedding traditions when she asked her brother to be her best man. Their wedding was the only wedding that Collin's church had ever seen with two best men.

Choosing the right color for the wedding forced Nina and Collin to be at odds with each other, so they allowed the bridesmaids to choose the color of their choice. The bridesmaids all agreed on a pale green color because it was a fall wedding. Most of the decision-making regarding the wedding went to their supporting cast when they couldn't agree on something. There were times when they both disagreed with the supporting cast and they had to compromise their own choices in order to please each other. When it was time to choose a ring bearer and a flower girl, Pastor Jacobs offered the children of a nice married couple in his church. The couple was very fond of Nina and Jimmy and they wanted to help in any way possible.

Since Nina didn't have any friends or family to help with the wedding, Mr. and Mrs. Brown offered to help them with the invitations and other minor arrangements that she and Collin couldn't make. Stephanie also helped out when she came home from college. Nina's invitations included a picture of the bride and the groom in a warm embrace on the front of the card. On the back, there was the time, church, place of the reception and the directions to the reception. They had planned on having no more than one hundred guests at the wedding. Nina didn't have too many to people to invite, but the groom had a large extended family who flew in from all over the country. The accommodations for hotels were left up to the groom's family to make and it almost drained them trying to get the best rates for their cheap relatives. No rate was cheap enough for them, and after a while, Mr. and Mrs. Brown settled on the best offer they received from the Holiday Inn in Dedham where the reception was taking place.

The wedding ceremony would have taken place at Pastor Jacobs' church, but he couldn't do two things at once. He was giving the bride away and Nina placed more importance on that task than having him perform the ceremony. They decided to have the wedding at Mr. and Mrs. Brown's church located on Blue Hill Avenue for convenience. The whole wedding was planned and the day was fast approaching. Nina and Collin couldn't wait for their big day. They were living in their separate homes at the time, but they agreed that once they were married Nina was going to move into Collin's first floor apartment. They factored in their decision the fact that Jimmy would still need a place to come home to from school when he was on break. Jimmy was going to live in Nina's apartment until he was ready to move into his own house.

The day before the wedding, a rehearsal dinner was scheduled for the wedding party at Mr. and Mrs. Brown's house immediately after rehearsal. Rehearsal was scheduled to start at 6:00PM, but the wedding party seemed to have been operating on (CPT) colored people time. No one was there on time except for the reverend, bride, groom and the best man who was a white man. There wasn't a soul in sight at the church until quarter to seven. Everybody had an excuse as to why they showed up late. The couple was frustrated with the whole situation, but they had to regain their composure in order to get through rehearsal and the wedding. Rehearsal went well and everybody was on cue as to what they were supposed to do the next day. Right after rehearsal, everyone drove to Mr. Mrs. Brown's house as planned. Though they arrived late to the dinner, everyone had a great time and they all got to know each other a little more. At the end of dinner, Nina and Collin could only beg the wedding party to be ready on time the next day to be picked up by the limousine drivers.

The moment of truth had finally arrived; it was the second Saturday of September 2002. That marked the beginning of a new life for Nina and Collin. Most of the people arrived at the church at the scheduled time of five o'clock in the evening. They were seated according to their arrival time. The seating arrangement was not planned like most weddings. Collin knew that Nina didn't have many friends and family members, so he suggested that guests from both sides sit together. Otherwise, there would have been a great disparity in the number of people from the bride's side. Collin always put his wife to be first in everything he did. It was a good habit to form because putting his wife first would ensure that he'd have a lasting marriage.

It was time for the wedding party to walk into church. One by one, the couples, consisting of bridesmaid and a groomsman, walked in harmony step by step and arm in arm pacing themselves to the traditional wedding song playing on the piano by the church's piano player. The flower girl walked a few steps faster than the ring bearer who was also her younger brother. She kept screaming at him telling him to keep up. She also ran out of flowers half way to the center of the podium. Then finally, the moment that everyone had been waiting for. The groom walked in escorted by his mother. He was wearing a black tuxedo, white shirt, a white satin bow tie to match his wife's dress, and black shoes. The groom was already a handsome man, but something about a man wearing a tux just placed him way above the handsome category.

The expression on Collin's face only confirmed his love for his wife to be. The bride walked in escorted by Pastor Jacobs. The bride wore a traditional, simply designed white satin dress with the long train flowing behind her. She wore matching satin shoes, a white pearl necklace and a white veil covering her face. Her face was filled with joy and happiness. It was as if her childhood dream had come true. She couldn't wait to get to the altar to meet her prince charming.

When the bride's face was unveiled, her make-up was flawless, her face was radiant, and she wore a beautiful bright smile that lit up the whole church and the most beautiful eyes that her husband had looked into. She was the most beautiful bride that Collin had ever seen. The ceremony was traditional, and the reverend tried his best to keep it simple and quick. The bride and groom exchanged their traditional vows and in no time the ceremony was near the end.

It was a thrilling moment for them when the pastor announced them as Mr. and Mrs. Collin Brown. Collin wanted to give his wife a fat juicy kiss, but he didn't want to mess up her make up before they took their pictures, so he settled for a long peck on the lips. Immediately after the ceremony, the wedding party headed for the waiting limousines outside of the church. They were driven to the Boston Arboretum to take pictures for about an hour while the guests drove to the Holiday Inn for the reception.

The guests arrived at the hotel before the wedding party arrived; they were directed to a table where the names of the parties and their table assignments cards were placed.

Everyone was asked to take the card with their name and their assigned table number. The festivities at the reception were wonderful. The party began with hors d'oeuvre being served in the front lounge where the bar was located. The hors d'oeuvres included shrimp cocktail, freshly cooked glazed ham, scallops wrapped in bacon, fruits and vegetables and oysters. The DJ played the latest R&B and soul music that were hot at the time. There was also an open bar all night for all the guests to enjoy. The bartenders and the waiters were very cordial and friendly. Everyone mingled for about an hour until the wedding party arrived for the reception.

The wedding party arrived an hour after the guests, everyone was asked to report to the main reception room and take a seat at their assigned table. One by one the DJ introduced the wedding party and the crowd applauded for each couple. It was time for the couple du jour to make their grand entrance, the DJ asked everyone to stand up and put their hands together to welcome the new Mr. and Mrs. Collin Brown. It was a long standing ovation and the couple savored every minute of it. The couple headed to their seats at the center of the wedding party table. Meanwhile, people took pictures of them and walked up to congratulate them. Some people had gift envelopes, others just wanted to make sure they were seen at the party.

Everyone finally settled in their seats with their drinks and was comfortable; it was time for the best man to toast the groom. He stood up with the champagne glass in one hand and a salad fork in the other hand tapping his glass to get everyone's attention. The crowd soon followed and everyone in the room was tapping their glasses.

After about five minutes of glass tapping, all the guests were on their feet to hear the toast of the best man. Det. O'Malley had everyone's attention as he addressed the bride and groom; his speech was short and to the point as he wished the happy couple all the luck in the world and offered an open door to them whenever they needed advice. O'Malley's wife was one of a few white people at the wedding. She was pointing to her husband and telling people at her table proudly she was the best man's wife.

Immediately after the toast, the couple danced their first dance to the song called "For You" by Kenny Lattimore. A couple of minutes into the song, the DJ asked everyone to join the couple in their song. Jimmy wanted so bad to dance with his girlfriend Lisa who was sitting at the same table as O'Malley's wife, so he jumped at the chance to reach for Lisa and share in the blessings of his sister and her new husband's wonderful day.

Everyone at the party had a great time. Lisa caught the bridal bouquet and Jimmy was able to reach over everyone and grabbed the garter belt from the groom. The party died down around 12:00AM even though they had the place booked till 1:00 AM. Only family members stuck around until the end to help out with the wedding gifts. It was the most treasured and beautiful moment in the couple's lives. Jimmy and Pastor Jacobs no longer felt the need to refer to Collin as Det. Brown after he became part of the family. However, it was hard for them to get used to calling him Collin.

Post-traumatic Stress Disorder

Since Jimmy had missed the draft, he decided to return to school for his junior year and to also devise a plan to deal with his nemesis. Jimmy always found basketball to be a good tool to release his stress. He came back to school as a man determined to dominate on the court. All the anger that was built inside him came out the minute he set foot on the basketball court. He was ferocious and fearless on the court. His scoring average went up along with every other statistics related to his game. Jimmy's coach couldn't believe how much his game had improved.

He spent a lot of time in the weight room getting stronger and bulking up on muscle. Jimmy gained ten pounds of muscle in a few months. Jimmy indulged himself in basketball and schoolwork. In his coach's eyes, he was a model athlete and student. The coach was very fond of Jimmy, but Jimmy never allowed their relationship to flourish beyond a professional level. He simply didn't want to make room in his life for another person. The coach tried to reach out to Jimmy by inviting him to his house on special holidays, but he always declined the coach's invitations.

Jimmy also dedicated his time to a Tae Kwon Do class that was offered on campus by one of the master students. He was fast becoming an expert in Martial arts. Jimmy always loved the martial arts. Ever since he was a kid, he was fascinated with the movements and the art itself. He tried his best to emulate his martial artist role model, Bruce Lee, when he was in Tae Kwon Do class. It didn't take Jimmy long to earn a brown belt in his class. He received training in Tae Kwon Do when he was a child, but the adult class was much different and more of his speed. He enjoyed the aggression and the sparring with other students in the class. He wasn't allowed to spar against other students when he took Tae Kwon Do as a kid.

A few months had gone by and Jimmy's team, as good as they were, didn't receive a number one seed at the NCAA tournament. He wanted to prove to the world that his team belonged in the tournament and they were going to earn everyone's respect. They easily won the first round of the tournament, but Jimmy became a selfish player and other teams took notice. Jimmy also became agitated with his teammates for their lackluster efforts on the court. He was very vocal at the end of game one; he blamed his teammates for every mistake that was made during the game. One of his teammates got up in his face during his rant and said, "I don't understand how you have the audacity to come in here and blame us for everything, when the ball was in your hands ninety percent of the time". Jimmy turned to the player and said, "The ball is in my hands ninety percent of the time because I make things happen. You all are just standing around waiting for things to happen for you". The coach intervened and put a stop to the arguments. He told them the bottom line was that they were moving on to the next round and they should be proud of themselves for doing a good job.

The coach knew Jimmy was his star player and a leader on the court, but he had never seen Jimmy come down so hard on his teammates before. He was not known as a tyrant motivator. Jimmy usually encouraged his teammates after every game. The change the coach saw in Jimmy disturbed him greatly and he wanted to address it with Jimmy. He asked to see Jimmy in his office after he showered. A few minutes after leaving the locker room, he showed up at the coach's office with a chip on his shoulder. The coach simply wanted to know what was going on in Jimmy's life, but Jimmy blew his top and told the coach that he was tired of letting people get the best of him and abuse him and he wasn't going to let that happen anymore. The coach couldn't understand how that was related to his teammates. Jimmy was in no mood to discuss it with his coach and the coach was in no mood to be around him. He quickly adjourned the meeting and told Jimmy he'd see him at practice the following day.

The team practiced for two days before their next game. Jimmy played well in practice and stayed a couple of hours longer each day after team practice to work on his shot. On game day, the Minute Men came out dominating the first quarter. They were leading the other team by ten points. Jimmy scored almost all the points for his team. The other team noticed that Jimmy was the only dominating player on the Minutemen squad, so they decided to double-team him whenever he touched the ball. Jimmy committed 6 turnovers by halftime and his team was down by six points. They went in the locker room and the coach told Jimmy that he was trying to do too much by himself. Jimmy felt like he was being used as the scapegoat for his team's weak performance, so he lashed out at his coach for not addressing his teammates' mistakes.

When the second half started, the Minutemen came back out hot again and grabbed 6 offensive rebounds. They went on a 6-0 run and the score was tied with five minutes left in the game. Jimmy decided it was time for him to take over the game. Jimmy was forcing shots, not making the necessary passes, committing offensive fouls and cursing out the players on the opposite team. With three and a half minutes left in the game, Jimmy drew a technical for elbowing a player. The referees were watching him closely. On the next possession, the same player was defending Jimmy and another player set a pick. Jimmy crossed over to his left leaving the first defender on his back then went up and over a second defender and dunked the ball on him. It was a dunk for the highlight reel. Unfortunately, after the dunk Jimmy taunted the defending player, and he received a second technical and was ejected from the game. His team went on to lose the second round game to their opponents.

After the game, all of Jimmy's teammates wanted to get a piece of him and he challenged them all to do something about it. Jimmy even cursed out his coach and told him that he would never play for him again. Jimmy had reached the point of no return with his teammates and coach. The media made him look worst than Dennis Rodman, Rasheed Wallace and Charles Barkley combined. His attitude made his stock plunge drastically for the upcoming NBA draft. Jimmy's demons were getting the best of him and he didn't want to open up to anybody about them. Jimmy knew that he couldn't return to the team the following year to complete the final year of his senior season. He immediately held a press conference a week after the NCAA championship and announced himself available for the upcoming NBA draft in June.

After making himself available for the draft, Jimmy focused much of his attention on his schoolwork and Tae Kwon Do. The obsession with his abuser kept resurfacing and Jimmy wanted to deal with it once and for all. He secluded himself from the media while he figured out a way to confront his former abuser. The buzz about Jimmy had subsided and other players from the national championship team were being talked up to be higher and better prospects for the NBA. Jimmy was too consumed by his schoolwork and his nemesis to allow what the press was saying about him to be a factor in his life. He wanted to face the man who had caused all this turmoil in his life.

Jimmy had become the poster child for post-traumatic stress disorder. He was suffering from depression, sleeplessness, lack of appetite, loss of energy and he was disconnected to everybody except Pastor Jacobs. Pastor Jacobs who had taken a few psychology and counseling courses while he was in prison noticed that Jimmy had all the symptoms of Post-traumatic stress disorder, so he urged him to take advantage of the free professional psychological assistance offered at U-Mass. Jimmy was a bit apprehensive at first, but after a while he realized if he didn't seek help he was going to self-destruct.

Jimmy saw the school psychologist for the rest of the year to help him deal with some of his issues. However, he never really got to the root of his problem because he purposely avoided mentioning the abuse in counseling. The psychologist was only able to offer a few exercises that could help him cope with his stressors and a better way to deal with his problems. The exercises helped tremendously and Jimmy was starting to become the nice person that he once was.

Uncalculated Murder

The motel room was dimly lit with a double bed in the center, a nightstand with a lamp in the right corner and a bureau at the bottom of the bed. There was a couple in there that appeared to be engaged in some kind of kinky sexual activity. They were totally unaware of the man trying to open the door. He first appeared like a blurry figure, but he was definitely a man dressed in black turning the door knob with his shirt wrapped around his hand to prevent finger prints. He made his way around to the right side of the bed where the lamp was sitting on the nightstand. He tapped the man on his shoulder, but the man just turned around and lunged at him with a ten-inch army knife that he picked up from the floor under the bed. The intruder defended himself like he was a professional fighter. He was able to grab the man's arm and pulled the man towards him and spun him around to get the knife away from him. Unfortunately, the man ended up stabbing himself accidentally once in the heart with his own knife as he fell to the floor.

The victim never stood a chance. It was quickly executed and it didn't last any more than a minute. The victim didn't even have time to address the killer. The victim acted like he was expecting someone to come after him. Maybe he had so many enemies; he carried a knife for protection. Within seconds after the stabbing, the man's fully naked lifeless body laid on the bed as the prostitute screamed mercilessly for help. She was begging, "Please don't kill me! You can take the money", but the man was not interested either in her money or her. The man coldly looked at Jean, the prostitute, and told her to "Shut up, bitch" then left the room leaving the knife in the victim's heart.

Once the man was out of the room, Jean was able to untie herself loose from the bedpost and quickly ran to the front desk to the clerk for help. Jean didn't even bother putting on any clothes. It was mid- April in 2002 and she didn't seem to be bothered by the chilly spring weather in Boston. She was standing in front of the clerk butt naked and screaming hysterically. The clerk was so overly occupied with the view of her naked body before him he took his time and very slowly watched her body before he responded to her plea for help.

Jean was an attractive twenty four-year-old prostitute who had fallen on hard times and had no way out of the ghetto. She hadn't been working as a prostitute for too long when she witnessed this murder. She had only been on the street for a few months, but the money was rolling in enough to keep her on the street every night. After standing in front of the door begging for the clerk to open it, she finally was able to scream loud enough through the glass door that someone was murdered in room twelve to the sixty-year-old perverted clerk. The clerk was taken aback. He asked, "What the hell are you talking about, lady?" Jean was so shaken, she tried her best to articulate to the clerk that a crazy man had broken into the room where she and this guy were and the crazy man killed the guy she was with.

The clerk who was also the owner of the place was looking forward to his retirement in a few weeks. He came from behind the front counter clutching a big forty-five shotgun. He quickly ushered her inside, locked the front door, picked up the phone and dialed the cops. The clerk started pacing back and forth looking through the glass door for the murderer while talking to Jean. He told Jean "Look, lady I don't know what you did to this guy or what's going on between you all, but I do not want you to come back to my motel ever again. By the way... is he still in there? You know what? I don't wanna know because I ain't going to look for him anyway and if he comes here I'm gonna hand you over to him to settle whatever dispute y'all got going on. My name's Bennett and I ain't in it".

It was a cool spring night, the sky was dark and somber very early that evening. In the distance, a barrage of headlights rose over the hills as police cars made their way to the motel in full speed. The police cars with siren lights on raced over the pothole filled roads of Blue Hill Avenue. The police finally arrived to the motel and when they got there, the woman who was in the room when the crime took place was standing at the front counter with the clerk. When the dust cleared, this tall, average looking white male who looked to be between forty to forty five years old emerged from his unmarked patrol car and headed to the front desk. He could see the clerk holding a shotgun standing next to the naked woman through the glass door. The detective drew his weapon, flashed his badge and ordered the clerk to lay down his weapon and open the door. The clerk apprehensively laid down his gun then opened the door to let him in. The detective introduced himself as John O'Malley then asked, "What happened here?" The clerk didn't want the detective to know that his motel was a prostitute haven, so he started telling the detective about Jean being in a room with her boyfriend when a man came and attacked them, then stabbed her boyfriend to death. Detective O'Malley asked for the room number and if anyone had been back to the room where the crime took place. The clerk and Jean both looked at each other and shook their heads in fear exclaiming "Hell no!"

Det. O'Malley and a couple of officers surveyed the crime scene to make sure the killer was not still in the area. After making sure the coast was clear, Det. O'Malley asked two officers, Joe Murphy, a uniformed officer who was relatively new to the department, to seal the area along with another officer. A few minutes later while Det. O'Malley was still gathering evidence from the crime scene, another detective arrived in an unmarked car.

This tall, dark and handsome African American man walked onto the crime scene and ordered everyone away. It was Detective Collin Brown; the case had been assigned to him because his specialty was hard to solve murders. Brown and O'Malley were former partners who were separated due to lack of funding from the police department. They were now assigned to different beats, but every now and then they would share an assignment with Brown as the lead detective on special cases. O'Malley pointed to a dildo that was found at the scene and expressed that maybe deviant sexual behavior might be a motive.

Brown asked O'Malley to brief him regarding the case. O' Malley explained to Brown how a young woman and her friend were in the room when an intruder suddenly attacked them. The intruder killed the man but left the woman untouched. Brown wanted to figure out a motive for the killing, so he went to the witness, Jean, to ask her a few questions regarding the killing. O' Malley quickly warned him that the woman is still shaken from the incident.

As Det. Brown approached Jean, he noticed she was still naked and shivering as if she were cold. He quickly ordered Murphy to get him a comforter. Murphy ran and got a comforter from the room and handed it to Det. Brown. He walked over to Jean and wrapped the comforter around her and told her to go back in the office to settle down and that everything was going to be all right. He told her he'd be back momentarily. He walked back over to the crime scene to gather evidence and investigate what happened. O'Malley was still standing in the room baffled by the way this crime was committed. He pointed out to Brown that the victim was only stabbed once and the person who stabbed him could have been a professional killer to kill him so easily. They could not immediately come to a conclusion; however, they knew the murder weapon was a knife because it was left in the man's heart.

Det. Brown told O'Malley to do a background check on the murder victim. He wanted to know the victim's name, address, his wife's name, children's name, favorite food, favorite color, criminal record if any, where he worked, and any foes in the victim's life. O'Malley assured him that he would get right on it. Brown also told O'Malley not to notify the victim's family just yet. He wanted to first gather more information on the case. Det. O'Malley had always felt that his relationship with Det. Brown was comfortable enough to call him by his first name, Collin. And as much as he would've liked the same in return, Det. Brown never addressed him by his first name during their entire relationship. On that particular day, O'Malley wanted to know what was up with Det. Brown and the formality all the time, so he asked him. He wanted to know why Det. Brown always called everyone by his or her last names. Brown made it clear to him that in his line of work it was always easier for him to remember people by their last names. O'Malley didn't buy it and told Brown that he should reserve the last names for the perpetrators and not his best man. Brown had grown accustomed to his ways since becoming a detective and there was no way of stopping it.

The fact that Brown kept his relationship with O'Malley professional bothered O'Malley. Det. Brown had to reiterate to O'Malley it was a matter of formality on the job. He also told O'Malley that he thought when he asked him to be his best man at his wedding, validated the significance of their relationship. Det. Brown didn't want his friendship with O'Malley to interfere with his work and for the first time he revealed to Det. O'Malley that he always thought of him as a role model from the time he joined the police force. Det. Brown also had to deal with the issue that he wasn't cut out to be a detective because he was black. It was very unusual for a young black officer to move through the ranks so quickly in Boston. Even though Det. Brown earned a reputation as one of the best detectives in Boston, some of the white cops still had a problem with his promotion. He didn't want his friendship with O'Malley to overshadow his accomplishments.

After doing some investigative work at the crime scene, Det. Brown went back to the front desk to speak with Jean about what she saw. She felt a little uneasy at first with detective Brown. As a matter of fact, she was uncomfortable around him and Det. Brown sensed it. He told her to relax and that everything would be all right. Det. Brown asked the clerk to go outside for a few minutes because he needed to talk to Jean alone. Jean felt something in the pit of her stomach after Det. Brown said the word "alone". All she could think about was the fact that somebody had just been killed in that room when she was alone with him.

The clerk left and Det. Brown locked the door, Jean quickly asked Brown if he made sure that the killer was gone. Det. Brown assured her that the killer was gone and if he came back he would have to deal with him. When he asked her if she saw the killer, she told him she had in fact seen the killer. Det. Brown was shocked to hear that this woman saw the killer and he didn't kill her. Not that he wanted the woman killed.

He was trying to figure out the motive behind the killing and the reason why a witness was left unscathed. He knew he needed to become this woman's friend and gain her trust and confidence. A decorated cop who didn't enjoy the spotlight, but wanted to solve his cases at all cost, he made it clear to Jean that he was there to protect her. He knew there was a reason why the killer didn't harm Jean and he wanted to find out why.

Det. Brown still had more work to do with the witness. He needed to find out information about the perpetrator that was pertinent to solving the case. Besides the fact that the killer didn't harm her, he needed to know the killer's characteristics and his relationship with the victim. Det. Brown wanted to confirm the kind of relationship Jean and the victim shared and wondered if it was an on-going fee for service relationship or just a one-time thing for this unlucky guy. Det. Brown suspected that Jean might have been a prostitute from the time he arrived on the scene of the crime. Det. Brown asked Jean for her full name, she told him it was Jean Murray trying to sound convincing. Det. Brown asked her if she was sure that Murray was her last name and she answered with a confident "yes". He then proceeded to ask her about the basis of her relationship with the victim.

With tears running down her face in her most convincing tone, Jean told Det. Brown that the victim was her boyfriend and that they had been dating for a short period of time. Jean was trying to keep from going to jail for prostitution, so she lied about her relationship with the victim. Det. Brown knew she was lying but he went along with Jean's story at that moment. He told her the suit the guy was wearing easily cost about a thousand dollars and couldn't understand why they were in a cheap motel. She didn't really have an answer, he told her to cut to the chase, stop playing games and to be forthcoming with him. He continued to assure her that the only protection she had now was the police. He told her he could only help if she played ball and she had better start telling the truth.

After playing good cop for a little while, Det. Brown was able to get Jean to start opening up to him moments later. He told her his job was to protect the victim and make sure that this killer was caught before he could kill again. She felt a sense of sincerity in his voice so she let down her guard and started to tell him the truth. She told him that she was really tied up to the bedpost and blindfolded when the killer walked in the room. She told him that the killer must have been very swift and efficient in his tactics because the victim didn't even have time to warn her about what was going on.

She went on about how she was only able to identify his distinctive cologne and the sound of his voice and she said she was certain that he was a black man because of his tone and the way he spoke. She also told Det. Brown that by the time she managed to break loose from the bedpost, the killer had already left the room and the only thing he said to her was "Shut up, bitch!" and that was how she heard his voice. Jean was trying to save her ass, so she embellished the situation at first.

The man had a deep voice and from where he stood in the room when he told her to shut up, she figured he must've been a very tall man. She knew even less about the man she laid down with that night. She didn't get to chit-chat with the man prior to sleeping with him and the only conversation they had was about her price and what the victim wanted to do to her. Det. Brown was probing for more information from Jean about the victim, but she couldn't provide any. He kept probing and told her to think long and hard about any insignificant thing that the victim could have said or done that might have led to a clue. She started yapping about how the victim was a total freak looking to get his thrill in ways unimaginable. She said, at first, she was afraid to hook up with the guy because he was so weird but he made her an offer she couldn't refuse.

He offered her five hundred dollars to tie her up, blindfold her, pee on him while he performed oral sex on her, for her to beat him with a belt and insert a dildo in her anus while having sex with her. She said they were just beginning when the killer walked in; the guy had only tied her up and was licking her ass while she was lying on her stomach at the time. She said she felt helpless and feared that the killer was going to kill her too after he was done with her customer. She explained it was like a nightmare happening before her eyes but she couldn't see it. She also told Det. Brown she and the victim took a cab back to the motel from downtown where he picked her up.

Det. Brown by now had figured that the victim must have had his head literally up Jean's ass when the killer walked in. It appeared as if he didn't have time to react to the attack. Det. Brown didn't want to take any chances, knowing that the killer might want to come back to finish Jean off, he ordered Officer Murphy to place her under arrest. The arrest came out of nowhere and was a surprise to Jean. She was upset and started calling Det. Brown all kinds of demeaning names. She said, " You asshole! I can't believe I told you the truth and now you're placing me under arrest. You tricked me into opening up to you". Det. Brown assured Jean that it wasn't personal and that he was placing her under arrest for safekeeping more than anything, however, if she persisted with the name calling, ranting and raving, he could see to it that she spent a couple of years in jail for prostitution because he was sure she had a few priors. Det. Brown ordered Murphy to book Jean for prostitution while he tried to sort out the details of the case. Jean was the only available witness to the case. Even though she didn't see the killer, she was a valuable witness.

Det. Brown figured that Jean would be too accessible to the killer as a prostitute on the street and it was just too much of a risk. Det. Brown was confident that this wasn't the first time Jean was arrested for prostitution and he knew they could find a way to keep her in jail long enough to apprehend the killer and close the case.

Jean was angry and started to curse out all the cops very loudly as she was being led away in handcuffs to the cruiser by Officer Murphy. Det. Brown paid her no mind as he walked back to the front desk to speak with the clerk. The clerk was still in shock that someone had been killed in his motel. He was still in a state of paranoia, so he scooted behind the counter trembling. Det. Brown walked through the door and stood in front of the counter just as the clerk was getting up from behind the counter. He was startled and reached for his shotgun. Det. Brown had to calm him down and talked him into putting down his weapon.

The clerk figured Det. Brown was with the police department because his badge was dangling on a chain around his neck. Det. Brown wanted to know if the clerk had seen anything unusual earlier that night. The clerk was very quick to respond and told Det. Brown he hadn't seen anything remotely suspicious all night and that he had owned that motel for twenty five years and never had a murder taken place in his motel. They finally introduced themselves formally to each other after talking for five minutes. Det. Brown apologized for not properly introducing himself earlier. He extended his hand to the clerk and told him his name. The clerk told him that his name was Thomas Riley and he bought the place twenty-five years ago from its previous owner.

Det. Brown knew that he still had a job to do and he didn't want to be caught up in a conversation with this guy. He went right back to official business with Mr. Riley. He wanted to know if Mr. Riley habitually rented rooms to prostitutes. Mr. Riley quickly dismissed the question by telling Det. Brown that he had no idea who the lady was or what she did for living and nor did he care. Det. Brown sarcastically responded, "She looks so much like a school teacher, I'm sure you couldn't tell, right?" Mr. Riley got defensive and told Det. Brown "Hookers gotta sleep too, and who am I to turn away customers based on looks. As a business owner, I couldn't do that. I'm not gonna open myself up to a lawsuit". Det. continued to press on about the couple in the room.

He asked at what time was the room rented. Mr. Riley told them the lady came in around 10:30-11:00 PM to rent the room and that she was alone. Det. Brown asked if he saw or heard anything. Riley responded that he didn't hear or see a thing except for the butt naked woman who ran to the front desk screaming for help. Det. Brown then asked "What did you do when you saw the naked woman running to you for help?" Riley answered, "I grabbed my gun, locked the door and waited for you guys to get arrive. I'm no hero and my name ain't Schwarzenegger". In any case, Det. Brown handed him his card and asked him to call if anything came to mind.

Det. Brown went back to his office to get his investigation underway.

Her Final Statements

By the time Det. Brown arrived at the police station, Jean had already been booked for prostitution and held in one of the cells. He went and sat down in his office to go through some of the paperwork regarding the case for about fifteen minutes before he called for Officer Van Cleef to bring Jean to his office. Officer Van Cleef went to the cell, placed Jean in handcuffs then escorted her to Det. Brown's office. When Jean got to Det. Brown's office, the first words out of her mouth were "How long do you plan on keeping me here?" Det. Brown didn't hear what Jean said to him because his attention was focused on Officer Nina Brown who walked by his office and flirtatiously smiled at him. Brown and Brown always made time to flirt with each other. Jean felt like she was being ignored purposely, she got right up to Det. Brown's face and said "Hello! Can I get some attention here?" Det. Brown quickly redirected his attention back to Jean and told her that he was going to hold her for as long as it took to ensure her safety and capture the murderer.

Det. Brown asked Jean to sit in the empty chair across from his desk, while Officer Van Cleef made his way out. Jean stared straight into Det. Brown's face and told him that she could tell he was hard for Nina. Det. Brown dismissed her comment as none of her business. She kept on about how she could see the lust in Det. Brown's eyes when he looked at Nina and he would probably jump at the chance to get with her. He wanted to redirect the conversation back to the investigation, but Jean got smart with him and told him that he was frustrated because he hadn't had any pussy in a while. Det. Brown became defensive and asked her "Do I look like one your customers?" Jean responded " No, of course not. My customers don't usually put me in handcuffs just to ask me a few questions. I know your type; you're the kind of guy with a dick so small that you bury yourself in your work to avoid the embarrassment that you may face if a woman sees it". Det. Brown got pissed and told Jean that his dick was not to be discussed and who he chose to show it to, was none of her business. It got tensed between Jean and Det. Brown for about fifteen minutes. She was trying very hard to push his buttons.

A few minutes had passed since Det. Brown and Jean said anything to each other. As Nina walked her way back to her desk, Jean felt the need to tell her "Don't waste your time with him, he has a small dick". Brown gave Jean the coldest look ever while he smiled at Nina. He didn't have to say anything to Nina; she knew it was Jean's way of flirting with the attractive officer. Brown wanted to wrap things up with Jean before she really got out of hand. He wanted to make sure the description she gave of the killer's voice and cologne were accurate. She confirmed that she could smell a man from a mile away and as much as she had been blindfolded in her line of work, she only had her ears and her sense of smell to rely on most of the times and she could never forget a voice or a scent.

Jean wanted to know if she would be released from jail. Det. Brown agreed to release her on the condition that she kept herself out of harm's way. However, before she could be released Det. Brown asked her to look through a line-up of some of the perpetrators they had picked up the previous night to start the process of elimination. Five criminals were lined-up behind a two way mirror and each one was asked to step forward and say the words "Shut up bitch". After the last criminal stepped up, Jean couldn't connect any of them to the crime. She was let go and told by Det. Brown to keep in touch with him. He took her cell phone number and she took his card as she left. Jean wasn't as observant as she thought. If she were really observant, she would have noticed the wedding rings on Det. Brown's and his wife, Nina's fingers. Maybe she had chosen to ignore that fact all together.

After leaving the station, Jean ran into a fellow hooker and friend. As they stood there having a conversation to catch up on what had been going on in their lives, their conversation was abruptly cut short just a block from the police station when a speeding, drunk driver lost control of his car and headed toward Jean's friend. Jean pushed her friend out of the way just in the nick of time to save her, but unfortunately she wasn't able to save herself. She was hit so hard that the car sent her body flying up about ten feet off the ground. The driver continued on and hit a light pole one block away. He was pronounced dead at the scene and identified as Jose Ramirez, an ex-army veteran from the Gulf War who was battling alcoholism since his return from the war. Jean was rushed to the hospital where she remained in a permanent coma.

Same Old Reaction

The Boston Police Department wanted to put out an all point bulletin out on the killer, but they didn't have a description for this guy other than his voice and the cologne he wore. They were in a tight spot but they wanted to alert the public about the possibility of running into this criminal. The police department decided to call a news conference with the media to alert the public. The all out media blitz on the case was supposed to either force the killer to come forward or scare him out of hiding.

The press initially portrayed the murder victim as an innocent man who happened to be in the wrong place at the wrong time. It turned out that the victim was a man of notoriety and prestige from the suburb; with a lot of skeletons in his closet. Patrick Ferry, a Caucasian man who lived with his wife and two kids in Andover, Massachusetts. Mr. Ferry was an executive at the Creep Bank in Boston. The grieving widow and the Andover community blamed the whole Roxbury community where the motel was located for the murder of Patrick Ferry.

The cops went around the Roxbury community harassing every young black man over six feet tall with deep sounding voices for the murder. The terror and chaos they created in the Black community instilled so much fear in the people, the African American parents made sure that their sons didn't stay out after dark. They were rounding up black men for no reason. They were all suspects as long as they were black and tall. The terror went on for weeks because the police had no clue and no lead. Many young men were forced to write confessions that didn't hold up in court.

The Boston Police had put more effort in trying to catch the killer of a man who solicited prostitutes than they spent on trying to eradicate the drug problems and black on black crime going on in the hood. The murder of this

Caucasian man dominated the headline of every newspaper and television news stations in Boston and the surrounding towns. They painted a cynical picture of a black killer that was lower than scum. Most black folks in the Boston area just avoided the news all together because nothing positive was being said about the young black men of Boston for weeks. Black people were angry at the treatment their young sons, husbands and brothers were receiving at the hands of the police officers. White people were up in arms because the killer hadn't been caught. It was sad that the Boston Police Department had enough resources to allocate to their local precincts to investigate the murder of one man while the lives of many others were in jeopardy everyday.

Throughout the whole media hoopla that went on with this case, Nina had never once taken the time to read about it in the paper. She was just hoping that her brother didn't fall victim to the harassment that the young black men in Boston were subjected to. Nina was not oblivious to the existing racism prevalent within the Boston Police Department, she did however, know that the Black males were harassed and arrested more than their white counterparts. Most of the time, she found some of the trumped up charges that they had against these young men laughable. However, she knew it was no laughing matter because the judges were very quick to agree with the police version of whatever incident they presented in court.

Nina's desire to become a police officer was not solely to get the bad guys; she also wanted to help the young kids in her neighborhood. She had witnessed so many young people destroy their lives, she grew sick of it. She wanted to commit herself to community policing. One of the characteristics she admired in Collin was the fact that he talked to the young people first and gave them the opportunity to choose the right way or the wrong way to do things. He was not gung ho about arresting a bunch of people for little or no reason at all.

Blessings

The NBA season was over in early June and the draft was slated to take place at the end of the month. Much of Jimmy's personal life was kept out of the limelight with the help of Pastor Jacobs. He made sure he shielded Jimmy from a ferocious media with a voracious appetite for negative press. Everything that was going on with Jimmy was dealt with behind closed doors and only with family. All the negative press that Jimmy received during the NCAA tournament had subsided and people almost forgot that he had a few bad moments. The fact that he had two great years in college and was a model citizen and athlete far outweighed the few minor outbursts he had during his junior year, but it could always be left to the press to scrutinize and focus more on the negativity while sweeping the positive under the rug.

On draft night, his sister, her husband and pastor Jacobs accompanied Jimmy. He wore the best blue pinstripe business suit, blue shirt and yellow tie that Pastor Jacobs' money could buy. Pastor Jacobs wanted to make sure he dressed Jimmy the same way he would dress his own son if he had one. This was the most important occasion in Jimmy's life. The buzz about Jimmy was still alive and quite a few teams were interested in him. All the experts had Jimmy pegged as a first round pick, but they didn't know how high or low a pick he would be. The whole family was nervous and happy at the same time. Everyone was hoping that Jimmy would be picked by one of the teams closer to Boston.

Their choices were the Knicks, the Nets, Seventy-Sixers and their number one choice, the Celtics of course. The Celtics had the fifteenth pick and there was a high probability that they could pick Jimmy, but the Knicks and Nets who had the twelfth and thirteenth pick respectively had shown high interest in Jimmy as well. Both teams had invited

Jimmy to work out at their camps prior to the draft and both teams were impressed with him. Jimmy was a power forward, which was the perfect fit that the Celtics needed. The Knicks already had too many forwards on their roster and the Nets were committed long-term to the two power forwards that they already had on their roster. If the Nets picked Jimmy, he wouldn't have seen any playing time for at least a year much less become a starter.

All the team executives knew what they needed and what they were looking for. But it was a game of who could psych whom out first. The Knicks knew they couldn't use Jimmy because they had too many forwards, but they didn't want the Celtics to get him because of the possible threat he would pose to the Eastern Conference. The Nets were doing the same thing; they were trying to advertise for a player that they wouldn't have much use for. All the forwards on the Nets' team were good and decent enough to keep. The Celtics knew what the other two teams were doing and they weren't going to be psyched out by neither team.

The Celtics played the best game of all. They never invited Jimmy to their camp; they weren't interested in watching him in a try-out. They had watched him enough as a college player to know what he was capable of and also had gotten hold of the tape of his try-out for the Knicks. They remained cool, calm and collected through the whole process. The fact that they had learned about Jimmy's work ethic helped out tremendously. When it was the Knicks' turn to select a player, they decided to go with a point guard that they desperately needed. They were hoping that the Nets and the Celtics would pass on Jimmy and their hope came true when they Nets opted to select a center that they badly needed.

The Nets had dominated the Eastern Conference for the past two years, but they were never able to go all the way because they didn't have a dominating center. Two more teams from the Western Conference had the opportunity to select Jimmy, but they chose to overlook one of the best prospects of that year's draft. And finally it was the Celtics' turn to pick and without hesitation they selected Jimmy.

Jimmy was a good fit for the Celtics in many ways. He was a local star who was born and raised in Boston and spent his entire basketball career attending school locally. He was the local hero the Celtics needed to help bring back the local interest in the team. They knew that he was going to make an impact on the team instantly. His style of play and his demeanor on the court was a perfect fit for the team.

Jimmy was elated that he was going to get the chance to stay close to his family and play for the team he grew up watching. Jimmy was a big fan of Dennis Johnson, Robert Parish, Gerald Henderson, Kevin McHale and Larry Bird and now he was going to get the chance to follow in their footsteps. Pastor Jacobs gave Jimmy a hug and congratulated him after the selection was announced. Nina and Collin were very happy that Jimmy was going to be around the Boston area. Jimmy had become a younger brother to Collin and he enjoyed spending time with him. Nina was just glad that her brother was staying close to home and she didn't have to travel too far to see him. The closeness they developed was not at all threatened by the possibility that he could've gone to the West, but she enjoyed the fact that he was only going to be a few minutes away from her.

A few months had passed since the draft and Jimmy's agent was able to secure a three-year deal, worth seven million dollars with the Celtics. In addition, he also managed to ink a deal with Adidas and Dr. Pepper worth close to twenty million dollars over a five-year period. Jimmy now had enough money to buy whatever he wanted for himself and his family. Jimmy was a selfless guy who always put other people's needs ahead of his. The day after he signed his contract he went to the BMW dealer in Norwood and picked up a brand new 745 IL for Pastor Jacobs, his mentor and guidance since he was fifteen years old.

Jimmy knew Pastor Jacobs didn't want to leave the hood; he didn't even bother offering to buy him a new house, he simply paid off Pastor Jacobs' mortgage. Nina had just graduated from the police academy and she was earning a decent salary. Collin was earning an even better salary than Nina and they were not hurting financially at all. They were both financially savvy individuals who had invested their money wisely. Since Nina and Collin each owned a multi-family house in Boston, Jimmy decided to offer them one hundred thousand dollars towards the purchase of a single-family house and their choice of a brand new car. Nina and Collin were grateful for the gesture. They always wanted an E Class Mercedes Benz, so Jimmy bought them an E 500 Benz. They each already had a car that they could still keep and use for everyday driving.

Jimmy went house shopping all over the Boston and South Shore area. He had a hard time making up his mind, until he went to Canton, Massachusetts and found this gorgeous house in a new development. The house offered ten thousand square feet of living space, four bedrooms, three full baths and a half bath, a large modern kitchen, formal living room, dining room, an office, television/family room and a library. The master bedroom alone was twice the size of the whole apartment Jimmy grew up in. The house also had a heated swimming pool, guesthouse, basketball and tennis courts on the secluded three acres lot. The other amenities included a sauna, game room, a screened porch, and weight room. The house was very private with an electric front gate and a circular driveway in the front. Jimmy fell in love with the house, but he couldn't buy it until the woman in his life approved of it.

He called Lisa on his cell phone and asked her to meet him at the house. He gave her directions and told her he would wait for her to get there. The selling agent was too eager to get the sale, the extra hour they had to spend waiting for Lisa was no inconvenience for him. His eyes lit up when he noticed the look of amazement in Jimmy's face; he knew this was a commission check that was sealed. He offered to take Jimmy to this local eatery to pass the time until Lisa arrived.

Forty-five minutes had passed and Jimmy and the realtor were done eating. They went back to the house and found Lisa in front of the gate of the house jumping for joy looking at the house from the outside. They pulled up to the gate and asked her to hop in the car. They drove up the circular driveway in front of the house so Lisa could get a better view of the whole property. Lisa was at a loss for words. She couldn't believe her eyes. The house was the most amazing and glamorous residence she had ever seen. She walked through the house checking out every room and taking inventory on how she would decorate each room. She was sold on the house way before she even saw the swimming pool and all the other amenities. It was a done deal, they both wanted the house and the realtor was more than willing to sell it to them. Canton offered one of the best school systems in Massachusetts and it was just minutes away from Boston.

Jimmy and his soon to be fiancée bought the home of their dreams and it was time to buy the vehicles that they wanted. Jimmy may have seemed a generous man to most but he was also miserly with his money when it came to spending. Jimmy watched every penny that he spent and knew exactly what was in his account. The days of eating bread and mayonnaise and sugar water kept him in check with his spending. Jimmy didn't need an accountant to balance his checkbook for him.

Jimmy wasn't the typical athlete. He may not have graduated from the University of Massachusetts, but he was an accounting major who absorbed every aspect of his accounting, management and economic classes. He knew a good deal when he saw one. Jimmy was all about spending less for more. When Jimmy walked into the car dealership, he was fixated on the demo models. He figured buying a car with just a couple of thousand miles on the odometer and saving five to ten thousand dollars is better than buying a brand new car and having the value drop five to ten thousand the minute he drove it off the lot. He did not want to absorb those kinds of losses. Jimmy bought the brand new demo models of the 500 S class Mercedes Benz for his fiancée and Range Rover for himself, saving him close to twenty thousand dollars.

Nina and her husband decided to rent out both houses they owned in Boston. They moved to a single-family house they bought in Hyde Park. They used half of the money they received from Jimmy as a down payment for their new four bedrooms and two and a half baths home. Nina and her husband wanted to move to Milton to be closer to Jimmy and to take advantage of the much better school system that the Milton School department offered, but the city residency requirement for Boston Police officers prohibited them from living out of the Boston City limits. The money Nina and her husband received monthly for the rent from their houses in Dorchester more than covered their mortgages for all three homes they owned. As a matter of fact, they pocketed an extra thousand dollars a month plus their salaries. They were financially sound and wanted to share their financial knowledge with Jimmy.

Nina and her husband wanted to make sure that Jimmy didn't rely solely on basketball as a mean of income. They knew that accidents could happen and they were not preventable, most of the time. They had seen too many black athletes go broke after their NBA career was over or because of injuries; Nina and Collin wanted to make sure Jimmy didn't become part of those statistics. They advised Jimmy to invest in real estate in the Boston area, as the soaring prices of real estate made it seem like a promising investment.

The plan was for Jimmy to buy a couple of brick buildings located on Massachusetts Avenue and hire a realty company to manage them. They were able to get in touch with a good realtor in Boston who secured a couple of foreclosed properties for Jimmy at a fraction of the value. The buildings needed minor renovations, so Jimmy hired a small minority owned construction firm in Boston to renovate all the buildings saving him a ton of money from what the bigger companies wanted to charge him. Jimmy invested close to two and half million dollars of his own personal money on rental properties in Boston. He was bringing in a net income of over half a million dollars a year from the three buildings he bought. He had hoped to convert them all to condominiums in the future. A three bedroom condo on Mass. Ave. could easily sell for half a million dollars. Each building contained 10 three-bedroom units and twenty percent of them were set-aside specifically for qualified low-income families. Jimmy always found a way to help other people in need as it was his nature.

The Confessions

Jimmy had wealth, status and respect, but he didn't have peace of mind. Something was bothering Jimmy and affected his entire life. He had achieved everything that he ever imagined he could. He was able to provide for his loved ones more than the average man could. Specifically, Jimmy had totally avoided becoming a statistic in terms of society's expectation of him. He did not end up dead or in jail and he was one in a million who made his dream become reality. Jimmy used to have nightmares of being hunted by a rapist as a child and as a young man, but this time his nightmares were different. The nightmares had changed, but Jimmy was still waking up in cold sweats and was becoming afraid to fall asleep at night. It was a losing situation because Jimmy couldn't fight off sleep and when sleep got a hold of him, he was awakened by his nightmares. The person in Jimmy's nightmare was of a holy nature and he wasn't out to hurt Jimmy this time around. Instead, the person was trying to chase the demon out of Jimmy and wanted to force him to confess something that only Jimmy and his God knew. Jimmy never imagined a person in white clothes and angel wings in his sleep could be a nightmare.

Although Jimmy was Baptist, he seriously considered walking into a confessional booth at a catholic church to confess to a priest. He would go to the local Catholic Church and paced back and forth in front of it for hours. Religious preference didn't seem to matter to Jimmy anymore. He would kneel down and pray in front of any church. It was as if he had gone mad in his mind. Something was controlling him and he needed to tell someone about it. Jimmy's suicidal ideation was once again looming around in his head. He wanted to straighten out his life and live in peace, but didn't know how.

Jimmy had gotten no more than four hours of sleep in four days and he knew he couldn't go on living like that anymore. He was going to end his life once and for all and this time he wanted to make certain it wasn't going to be a failed attempt like the last time. He wasn't planning on cutting his wrist; rather, he was planning on shooting himself in the head with a single bullet. Jimmy bought a gun three days earlier and asked for a single bullet from the merchant so he could take his life. But his angel, not the one in his dream, the one who came into his life when he was a teenager, always called in times of crisis. Pastor Jacobs was calling Jimmy to see if he wanted to go to a community center with him to talk to some kids. It was the second time that Pastor Jacobs had intervened just in the nick of time.

The phone rang at least five times before Jimmy finally answered. He was relieved to hear Pastor Jacobs' voice on the other line. He told Pastor Jacobs what he was about to do and if he didn't talk to someone soon, he would go through with it. Pastor Jacobs told Jimmy he was coming right over and to put down the gun at least until after they talked. He assured Jimmy that whatever it was that was bothering him could be worked out.

After Pastor Jacobs hung the phone up with Jimmy, he called his office to ask his secretary to cancel all of his appointments for the day because he had an emergency that he needed to tend to right away. Even the visit at the community center, which took a long time to put together, had to be cancelled. Pastor Jacobs always put Jimmy and Nina first in his life. He had seen them through the tough times and he wanted to see them through even tougher times if that was the case. Pastor Jacobs drove frantically and erratically to Jimmy's house in Canton. He had to be careful going through Milton and Canton as the police out there made the black people their primary targets. Those jerks would pull a black person over without a second thought for DWB (Driving While Black). Every Black man who drove an expensive Luxury or sports car through Milton and Canton was a suspect.

The black man was always guilty until proven innocent, according to those cops in Milton and Canton. As fast as Pastor Jacobs was driving, there was not one cop in sight that day. Maybe the Lord was watching over the whole situation and he wanted to make sure that Pastor Jacobs got to Jimmy's house quickly enough to save him from grace. As Pastor Jacobs drove to Jimmy's house, he was going out of his mind trying to figure out what it was that was bothering Jimmy so badly that he was contemplating suicide, again.

Jimmy was living in the house alone because Lisa was trying to finish her senior year at Boston University. Pastor Jacobs reached Jimmy's driveway about fifteen minutes later. He rang the buzzer and identified himself through the intercom and Jimmy pressed the button to open the front gate to let him in. Pastor Jacobs parked his car right in the circular driveway in front of the house. He ran inside the house looking for Jimmy anticipating the worst.

Because Jimmy told Pastor Jacobs he had a gun, Pastor Jacobs knew that there was imminent danger and he wanted to stop it. When he got to the house, he thought he was going to stop a suicide, just imagine how surprised he was when Jimmy blurted out to him that he had killed somebody. Pastor Jacobs couldn't believe what he'd just heard coming out of Jimmy's mouth. He wanted to make sure it was indeed a confession, so he asked, "Did you just say you've killed somebody?" Jimmy replied, "Yes" Pastor Jacobs asked "When? Where? How? Why? Jimmy told him it happened a few months back in April when he came home from school for a couple of days. Pastor Jacobs asked, "Is that why you have a gun?" Jimmy told him no and he just got the gun to kill himself to take away his pain. Pastor Jacobs then asked, "How did you kill the person?" Jimmy answered, "The man lunged at me with a knife and I was able to spin him around before he could stab me, and in the process the man ended up stabbing himself in the heart". Pastor Jacobs told Jimmy that he needed a glass of water to calm down. Pastor Jacobs was not ready for that kind of news.

After drinking a glass of cold water, Pastor Jacobs was calm and he wanted to know from Jimmy what happened from beginning to end. Jimmy went back to the first time when he tried to commit suicide. He told Pastor Jacobs that when he was a child, his mother used to work as a prostitute and one of her customers used to come by the house to see his mother for business and because she was also a drug user, she would pass out in her room, and the guy would come into their room and rape him and Nina. The man raped them repeatedly and they felt like it had gotten to the point when the man came over it wasn't to see their mother anymore, it was to see them.

He wasn't the only man who had raped them. There was another guy who raped them only once. He told Pastor Jacobs he had a hard time dealing with it and that's when he decided to take his life the first time. Pastor Jacobs alluded the fact that Nina had mentioned that their mother was a prostitute and drug abuser, but she didn't mention that the kids were sexually abused. Jimmy told Pastor Jacobs that Nina probably didn't tell him about the rape because at the time they didn't want the authorities involved in their lives and they didn't want to live with any foster families. Pastor Jacobs asked if their mother knew about the abuse. Jimmy told him that she didn't know and they couldn't tell her because she was never around or sober enough for them to talk to her. Jimmy also told Pastor Jacobs that his mother had killed the other guy who raped them as kids, which was the reason why he thought she went to jail, but he wasn't sure.

Pastor Jacobs for the first time since he met Jimmy asked him what his mother's name was. When Jimmy told him that his mother's real name was Katrina, but most people who came to the house called her Star, Pastor Jacobs' jaw almost hit the floor. Pastor Jacobs couldn't believe that he was talking to Katrina's kid after all of these years. Pastor Jacobs paused for a few minutes and tried to recall in his mind the conversation he had with Katrina when he was a street hustler named Leon.

Although Pastor Jacobs' full name was Leon Jacobs, he was known on the streets as Leon, "The Hustler" when he was younger. He recalled this woman named Star he used to see regularly; she came to him and told him that she was pregnant by him and he told her that there was no way that he was going to claim to be the father of a child by a street prostitute. The words kept echoing in his head over and over. Pastor Jacobs started looking deeper into Jimmy's face to see if there was any resemblance. He started to notice that Jimmy's mannerism favored his a little and the fact that Jimmy was very tall and was a good basketball player attributed to their blood relation. Pastor Jacobs couldn't believe he was talking to the son that he had turned his back on when he was a young man.

Pastor Jacobs knew he was a changed man and was a man of God, so he couldn't keep this secret from Jimmy. However, he didn't want to tell Jimmy that he was his father and ruined the relationship that he had developed with him. He didn't want any resentment to surface from Jimmy because he wasn't involved early enough in his life. He looked at Jimmy with admiration and smiled. He was lost for a few minutes just staring at his son. Pastor Jacobs finally shook out of his daydream and refocused on the fact that his son needed his help.

Pastor Jacobs wanted to know how the sexual abuse was related to the murder. Jimmy told Pastor Jacobs that one day he and Nina were driving through town to run an errand when Nina spotted the man who had raped them. Since that time Jimmy had been obsessed with the man. He didn't think about going to the police because of the statute of limitation and the fact that his mother was a prostitute at the time when they were raped. They felt that no one would believe their story and the police department was more likely to take the other guy's side because he was a white suburbanite.

Their story just wouldn't have stood a chance with most people. Pastor Jacobs wanted to know if Nina was in on the plan to confront the man. Jimmy told him that Nina had no idea that he had planned on confronting the man. Pastor Jacobs then asked "How did you kill this man when you were in school the whole time?" Jimmy reminded Pastor Jacobs the reason he didn't see him at all the previous summer was because he went back to U-Mass to try to alleviate the stress from the situation. He couldn't sleep or deal with the fact that this man who had ruined his life was walking around freely without confronting him. It was at Nina's suggestion that he moved away, but the urge to confront him didn't go away. Jimmy also told Pastor Jacobs that he did a little research on the man via the Internet and found out that he actually worked for the Creep Bank in Boston, the place from which he was coming from when they saw him. He knew the man lived in Andover and the man hadn't stopped the habit of sleeping with prostitutes.

Jimmy described to Pastor Jacobs his plan on how he followed the victim, Patrick Ferry and this prostitute to this motel in Roxbury. He said he sat in the car for about thirty minutes waiting for the guy to come out to confront him, but the guy never came out. He got out of the car and walked up to the window of the room, which was located on the first floor. He saw the prostitute laying flat on her stomach in the bed with blindfolds on and her hands tied up to the bedpost. The guy had his face buried in her ass and a dildo in his hand getting ready to stick it in the prostitute's butt.

Jimmy had lost his patience; he decided to open the door, which was left unlocked by the couple. When he walked in the room, he tapped the guy on the shoulder and wanted to ask the man out of the room to talk to him, but the man lunged at him with a knife that he picked up from under the bed. Jimmy didn't anticipate being attacked, but his Tae

Kwon Do training and instinct kicked in. As the man swung the knife attempting to stab Jimmy, he inadvertently grabbed the man's hand and swung him around and the man ended up stabbing himself in the heart. It happened so fast, Jimmy didn't even have a chance to react. Jimmy never even touched the knife, and only the man's print was on the knife. Jimmy left the knife in the guy's heart and ran out of the room leaving the prostitute on the bed.

After Jimmy had shed enough light on the situation, Pastor Jacobs started to put all the pieces together. Pastor Jacobs figured out it was the same high profile case that the Boston Police department was wreaking havoc in the community trying to solve. Pastor Jacobs also remembered that about twenty-five other victims had come forward, including the man's own children to say that he had molested or raped them as well. Pastor Jacobs told Jimmy that "perhaps I shouldn't be telling you this, but the Lord works in mysterious ways and sometimes people do reap what they sow. And, maybe, the man deserved what he got and it was up to you to ask God for forgiveness, but he couldn't erase a sin with another sin.

The sins were already committed and it was a matter of making up for the wrong that you have done". Pastor Jacobs was trying his best to comfort Jimmy in his time of need and told him that he had two choices, he could either go to the police to turn himself in and spends the rest of his life behind bars doing a disservice to the young victims everywhere or he could pray to God and ask for his forgiveness and do some good for other victims as a free man. He also told Jimmy that he was sure that he could find a number of organizations that could use his celebrity and/or financial support to help other deprived children and victims of sexual abuse.

Pastor Jacobs offered to counsel Jimmy as his minister if and when he needed it, but the ultimate choice was Jimmy's and he did not plan on revealing anything to anybody but God. He promised that he would pray for Jimmy and ask his congregation to keep him in their prayers.

While Jimmy and Pastor Jacobs were wrapping up their conversation, they heard something that sounded like footsteps in the house. When they ran to the hallway to check it out, they found Jimmy's cat in the kitchen and the front door closed. Pastor Jacobs asked Jimmy to hand him the gun so he could take it back to the store where it was bought. Jimmy handed him the gun and they hugged for about five minutes. Pastor Jacobs told Jimmy that everything was going to be all right and he would see to that. As he walked out the door, he told Jimmy that God chose him to be a victim because he was special and God had bigger plans for him in the world. He also told him to pray and that he would call him later to check up on him. When Pastor Jacobs got to the front gate out of Jimmy's house, he found the gate wide open and had to call Jimmy to remind him to close the gate. He also told Jimmy through the intercom as he drove out, " By the way: I'm your father and we need to talk later". Pastor Jacobs just couldn't keep that big happy news from his newfound son.

Dealing with Unresolved Issues

Jimmy never thought that he would feel so badly about taking the life of the man who abused him as a child, and after a while he started to realize that the solution to his problem was not that the man was gone. The man was dead and gone and Jimmy still didn't feel complete as a person. He also realized he had used the man as a scapegoat to deal with a problem that was deeper than he had originally thought. Those issues were still present in his life and he needed to deal with them once and for all.

He may have been a superstar athlete since he was an adolescent, but the insecurities that he developed as an adolescent never went away and they followed him into adulthood. Jimmy lacked nurturing from his mother and he never got a chance to talk to her before she died about any of the events that took place in his life and hers. Jimmy needed to find closure to some of the issues regarding his mother that bothered him. And the only way he could do that was to forgive his now dead mother as a man for all the bad experiences and emotions he had experienced in his life.

Jimmy was never interested in his mother's final resting place before, and he had never once asked his sister about his mother's burial ground. He just didn't care to know, he felt she didn't care enough about them to protect them from harm nor did she care about herself. She was never sober enough to seek help for her drug problem for the sake of the family when she was alive. Jimmy also knew that the animosity in his heart was the root of his problems. The animosity was eating away the love and kindness that he had in his heart like a cancerous virus eating away at his flesh. He needed to let go of it and free himself from the bondage that held him captive most of his life.

It was on a Sunday afternoon after church that Jimmy decided to finally ask his sister where the burial ground for his mother was located. She offered to take him to the site, but he told her that he didn't want her to go with him because it was something that he needed to do alone. Nina gave him the directions to the burial grounds as he requested. He decided to drive to the burial site alone to speak with his mother.

When Jimmy arrived at the burial site, he couldn't believe how the state department only fulfilled the basic requirements to only have his mother's name carved on the headstone. They didn't even have her correct name written on the stone because she had used an alias when she was arrested. Jimmy felt like his mother was a Jane Doe amongst the rest of the world's unwanted criminals. The prison never contacted any next of kin because she had never listed any. No one at the prison even knew she had a family.

He knelt down in front of his mother's grave to have a heart-to-heart with his mother. He wanted her to know that everything in his life turned out fine and that Nina did a great job raising him and he was a professional basketball player living a much better life than he ever imagined. He told her that he could sometimes feel her presence around him. She may not have been there physically, but he knew she was there in spirit guiding him. Jimmy wanted his mother to know that he forgave her for all the bad things that she had done to him. He told her it wasn't her fault that she was a teenage mother and he knew how big a burden it must've been on her to have to raise two kids on her own. He told his mother that he didn't blame her for getting hooked on drugs, working as a prostitute or for neglecting him and his sister. He knew that she was trying her best to provide for a struggling family, but he also knew now that she was very busy in her new role as his new guardian angel looking over him and Nina every time they're faced with obstacles.

He wanted his mother to know that he knew that she was the angel who sent Pastor Jacobs to them. He told her how great Pastor Jacobs had been to them and Pastor Jacobs was everything that he ever wanted in a father. Jimmy also told his mother that he loved her and knew that she loved him and his sister too even though she never took the time to tell them how she felt when she was alive. Jimmy emphasized to his mother that he also knew that she was in a better place and she should hold a place for him and his sister next to her in heaven.

Jimmy couldn't leave without informing his mother that Pastor Jacobs mentioned that he was his biological father. The news was just too thrilling not to share with his mother. He wanted his mother to know that he accepted Pastor Jacobs in his life without any judgment and he could do the same for her. He wanted her to know how lucky she was to have spent time with such a wonderful man. He also wanted her to know that he wasn't looking for a father, but he was happy to have found one in Pastor Jacobs. He felt that Pastor Jacobs had done more than made up for lost time. He wanted her to know that his life was going in a better direction, but he still needed her strength and guidance in his life to be a stronger man.

After visiting with his mother, Jimmy went to the prison authorities and requested that his mother's body exhumed from the ground. He wanted to give his mother a proper burial and funeral. Jimmy knew her body belonged in a regular cemetery surrounded by people who were loved. The authorities were more than eager to honor Jimmy's request, not because of his celebrity, but because it would free up another space from the state's already crowded cemetery. There was limited available space for their unclaimed rapidly dying prison population to begin with. The prison department and Jimmy were both happy with the arrangements. Jimmy also asked the prison officials to honor his request of keeping his mother's past situation from the media. He wanted her to be in peace.

Jimmy and Nina had a proper funeral and burial for their mother at the Longwood cemetery. Pastor Jacobs conducted the ceremony at the cemetery. Jimmy and his sister bought their mother a marble headstone and inscribed on it the words "Here lies the greatest woman that ever lived, a woman and a mother whose time on Earth ran out, but her legacy will live on forever" along with her real name and date of birth and date of death. It was the last thing the two of them could've done to honor their mother. Jimmy and his sister hugged as they descended the coffin in the ground. They both needed closure in their lives and this was the final step with their mother.

Making Amends

It was time for Pastor Jacobs to make amends for turning his back on his son as a child, and Jimmy needed him now more than ever. Pastor Jacobs and Jimmy sat down and had a long conversation. He explained to his son that when he was involved with his mother, it started out as a fee for service relationship that grew into something more special, but he wasn't looking to be a father at the time. He wanted Jimmy to know that he was a young seventeen year-old hustler who had put the streets first in his life and at the time he couldn't bear the responsibilities of a child. He also said the fact that he went to jail at the age of eighteen, clearly demonstrated his lack of maturity.

Pastor Jacobs wanted to focus on the present relationship with his son and find a way to form a closer relationship as father and son. Jimmy had never in his life called anyone dad and he didn't want to start then. Pastor Jacobs was okay with that and didn't want to put any additional pressure on Jimmy and their relationship. He missed out on the first fifteen years of Jimmy's life and he wanted to make sure Jimmy's life didn't go down the same path his life went when he was a young man.

Pastor Jacobs wanted Jimmy to make up for his sin and the crime he played a part in. He enlisted Jimmy to be part of many charitable functions and organizations around the Boston area and to be more of a public servant with his celebrity status. They chose to keep the fact that Pastor Jacobs was his father from the public. Pastor Jacobs was a local hero in the Boston area who was known and loved by all in a different way just like his son. Whenever Pastor Jacobs was asked to speak to young boys at the different Centers around Boston, Jimmy always accompanied him. Jimmy became a role model and a source of inspiration for many young boys and girls in the Boston area. He was never too busy to take the time to sign an autograph for anyone who asked. Everything that Jimmy did was therapeutic for him. It was almost like a cleansing of his soul whenever he helped make other people's situations better.

Jimmy established a few charitable scholarships of his own. One of the scholarships that he and his father created was a scholarship specifically designed to cater to the needs of neglected high school students whose parents were documented drug abusers or in jail for serious crimes. His scholarship fund was the first of its kind and many other similar scholarship programs followed around the country. Jimmy's foundation gave out ten scholarships a year to the ten best achieving student applicants selected. Jimmy wanted to keep his scholarship requirements simple. One of the reasons for the scholarship was to ease the burden on these kids in college, not to make them go through hoops in order to pay for it. Jimmy simply required that each applicant wrote an essay about their hardships and how they dealt with it. Jimmy inspired even the most underachieving kids to make the impossible possible.

A charitable trust fund was set up by the people in Andover to assist the widow of Patrick Ferry with her finances because her husband had left her and her children almost penniless. It was revealed that he was an alcoholic who also had a gambling problem along with his insatiable sexual appetite for hookers and young kids. All the abuse Mrs. Ferry suffered at the hands of her husband also came to light after his death. The dark side of Mr. Ferry was kept hidden by the entire family. A few notable psychologists and psychiatrists in her community offered counseling services to the family at no charge. The guilt that Jimmy had felt initially after he killed Mr. Ferry didn't disappear, but he felt better knowing that his run-in was with a menace to society. All the negative revelations about Patrick Ferry helped bring Jimmy out of a depressed funk. Jimmy was one of the first donors who anonymously donated a six-figure check to help out the family. He went to the fundraiser dinner that was held for the family in Andover and also donated some of his jerseys and college game balls to be auctioned.

Jimmy learned from his father the importance of a second chance and how it could help a person reincarnate himself into a new man with a purpose in life. Jimmy and his father were closer than ever. Jimmy was the person who introduced Pastor Jacobs to the love of his life and his future wife. Jimmy knew this great, single woman who had lost her husband to prostate cancer a few years earlier. He fell in love with her after meeting her at one of the charitable events he attended. He knew that she and Pastor Jacobs would like each other because of their devotion to help other people. Pastor Jacobs and the woman dated for a year and married three months after their engagement.

Jimmy and his dad developed a well-deserved loving relationship and whenever Pastor Jacobs was available, he attended Jimmy's games whether they were away or home. Nina was thrilled to find out that Pastor Jacobs was Jimmy's biological father. She didn't feel any void in her life because she'd long considered Pastor Jacobs to be her father as well. Pastor Jacobs was the first to hear from his son that he wanted to marry his longtime girlfriend Lisa and Pastor Jacobs along with Nina helped pick out the engagement ring for Lisa. They had a moderate wedding a year later and Collin was Jimmy's best man.

The Outcome

When Collin entered Jimmy's house unannounced on the day of his suicidal attempt, he didn't know he was about to find out some of the deepest secrets that his wife had kept from him. He always wanted to know why his wife was so petrified in the bedroom, and never opened up to him. He figured, perhaps, she was too ashamed of being a virgin to discuss sex with him. Collin and his wife would go for weeks without having sex because she was uncomfortable with sexual intercourse. She was always finding excuses not to have intercourse with him. She had become an oral expert over the period of time they were married, but never wanted to venture much into the intercourse department. Any effort from Collin to ease the process only created more tension and resentment on her part. She was overly uncomfortable with intercourse and it made no sense to him.

Collin and Jimmy had developed a close enough relationship where he would show up at Jimmy's house unannounced to check on him. On this particular day, however, Collin didn't have to go through the normal routine of pressing the buzzer for Jimmy to let him in. When he drove up to the gate at Jimmy's house, he found it wide open and thought that something might be wrong. He pulled his car up at the bottom of the hill and walked up the house just in case something was wrong. He drew his gun from its holster and walked slowly to the front door, which he found cracked open.

As Collin walked inside the house, he could hear the voices of two men and he also noticed Pastor Jacobs' car in the driveway. He was going to make himself known until he heard Jimmy confessing to killing the man in the murder case that he had been trying to solve for a long time. Collin stood there and eavesdropped on the whole conversation between Pastor Jacobs and Jimmy. As he was standing there, Jimmy's pet cat came up to him trying to lick his shoes. He picked up the cat and held it in his hand throughout Jimmy's whole confession.

Collin's police instincts wanted him to barge in and take Jimmy in for the murder of Patrick Ferry, but the love for his wife and devotion to his family prevented him from acting on instinct. The human being in him took over and the fact that Jimmy was actually defending himself against Patrick Ferry when he died made it easier for Collin to keep his dignity as a man and a police officer for not placing Jimmy under arrest. Collin was actually relieved to find out that he wasn't the cause of his wife's negative reaction to his sexual advances. At least, now he had an idea of what happened and he could make suggestions to his wife to see a therapist to make things better between them. Many loads were taken off many different shoulders in the living room on that day. Everyone seemed to have been carrying a burden of some sort.

As long as Jimmy and Pastor Jacobs didn't know that he knew that Jimmy was the murderer, Collin was not an accessory. All Collin wanted was to help his wife and as a husband and a police officer he understood that Jimmy was only defending himself and the honor of his sister. The reality was that Collin knew that he would probably have killed Patrick Ferry himself if his wife had let him in on her secret. Collin's conscience was clear because he knew that the bastard victim deserved his just punishment. He figured justice could come in many different forms and it wasn't always the police and the justice department that should be responsible to seek it.

Collin had heard enough and it was time for him to exit without being noticed. He used the cat to create a diversion to leave the house unnoticed. Collin tip toed to the front door, and then threw the cat towards the living room knowing she would land on her feet and would be held accountable for the noise that he made when he pulled the door behind him as he snuck out of the house. Collin raced down the hill to his car and left the premises before anyone could see him.

The medical examiner's office had determined that Mr. Ferry was killed during a physical struggle, at which time he might have stabbed himself in the heart. They also determined that Mr. Ferry could've easily initiated the struggle, which resulted in his death. A couple of years had passed and no one had been caught for the death of Patrick Ferry. The pressure on the Boston Police Department to solve the case had diminished significantly. There were many more allegations from many different children that Patrick Ferry had molested. He was no longer an honorable man when all his skeletons started coming out.

Mrs. Ferry was always suspicious of his deviant behavior but she never alerted the authorities out of fear. It was also later found out that her husband emotionally and physically abused Mrs. Ferry. While it was true that the man was dead and couldn't defend himself against these allegations, however, the overwhelming number of abused children who came forward to file reports against him may have added credence to their claims. The number of victims had amounted to more than fifty children a year after his death.

Det. Brown had never hit a roadblock in his career and this time would be no different. He solved every case that was assigned to him in the past, but somehow it was not hard for him to come to grip with the fact that this case didn't deserve to be solved, when it actually was already solved in its own special way.

After it was revealed that Mr. Ferry was in fact a child molester and abuser, Mrs. Ferry finally resonated with the fact that her husband was an evil person and she had contributed to his evilness by keeping quiet about the abuse she and her children suffered at his hand. She'd stopped putting pressure on the Boston Police Department to solve the case and one day, out of the blue, she called Det. Brown who still had the case open because of departmental procedures, she asked him if he could close the case because she wanted closure for her family and knowing that somebody took care of the scum was closure enough for her. Det. Brown was happy to honor her request without asking any questions.

Even though Nina was the closest relative and friend that Jimmy had, he and Pastor Jacobs decided not to reveal to her that Jimmy was partly responsible for Mr. Ferry's death. Nina was having a hard enough time dealing with the fact that she never had a chance to confront the man before he was killed. It was in the best interest of everyone to allow her to close that chapter in her life. She felt better knowing the man was no longer going to be able to molest more children. Also, Jimmy didn't want Nina to feel that she had failed him despite all the effort she had put into helping to raise and make a good man out of him.

Nina eventually discussed the abuse with her husband. He helped to strengthen their relationship by seeking counseling along with his wife. Their therapist was able to help her make the adjustment to her new role as a wife and a loving companion easier. The two of them had two children two years into their marriage, a boy and girl. The boy was named after his father, Collin, and the girl was named after Nina's mother, Katrina. Jimmy and Lisa were asked to be the godparents of the kids and they gladly accepted. The Boston Police Department promoted Det. Brown and his wife to lieutenant and sergeant respectively.

Jimmy had a great rookie season with the Celtics. He was given the opportunity to start when the veteran forward on the team went down with a calf injury halfway through the season. He shared rookie of the year honors with the overall number one pick from the past draft. Pastor Jacobs continued to support his son and attended every home game at the Fleet Center and always brought a group of kids from The Boys and Girls club with him to cheer Jimmy on.

The End.

Please enjoy this sample chapter from

Neglected No More, the very last part of the series.

Mr. & Mrs. Johnson

Since kicking Katrina out of the house, Mr. Johnson was trying his hardest to keep Karen under lock and key. Mr. Johnson didn't want, Karen, the only daughter he had left to end up pregnant or raped like Katrina did. The only place Karen was allowed to go without supervision was the tutoring program at the church. The fact that Mr. Johnson had turned his back on Katrina really bothered him, but he didn't want to show it to his family. His wife, Mrs. Johnson, had started to develop some resentments of her own. Her eldest child had been gone for a long time and she wondered everyday what became of her. The family never really expected for Katrina to be gone out of their lives forever. However, the stubborn Mr. Johnson allowed his pride to get in the way of finding his daughter.

At night, Mrs. Johnson would cry herself to sleep thinking about how Katrina just disappeared out of her life. She was so dependent on her husband; she never even learned how to drive a car. From the time she married her husband, he told her that he was the man of the house and whatever decisions he made regarding his family, she had to support him. She was a wonderful subservient wife for most of their marriage. That is until Katrina was kicked out of the house. Mrs. Johnson had missed her daughter so much; she started talking back to her husband after a while. She didn't want to always listen to his idiotic rants about how the family should be anymore.

Mr. Johnson's idea of a functional family was so out of line with time that he could easily be mistaken as someone from the Stone Age. At first, he didn't want to accept the fact that his daughter, Katrina, was a good person and he drove her away just like he was driving his younger daughter, Karen, to do bad things. He was constantly suspicious of Katrina for no reason. She had never failed any classes in school and didn't really do too many bad things at home for him to think that she was a bad child. Because Mrs. Johnson sat back and said nothing about what was going on, Mr. Johnson thought everything he was doing was correct. He drove Katrina out of the house.

Katrina's disappearance was never discussed in the Johnson household. Their silence about the whole situation was eating away at Mrs. Johnson's heart everyday. She would be driving with her husband in the car and she would suddenly see someone and thought it was her daughter. One day Mrs. Johnson chased this woman down because she walked a little like Katrina. When she saw the lady from behind, she was overcome with joy and ran after the lady hoping to give her a big hug. However, after reaching the woman and tapping her on her shoulder, she realized it wasn't her daughter when the woman turned around and looked significantly older. Mrs. Johnson was once again disappointed and had started to become a little delusional even. She wanted to see her daughter at all cost.

While her husband was away at work, she would go through the phone directory looking for Katrina's name. One day, she got on the phone and called about two hundred people whose first name started with a K and the last name Johnson. As a mother, she knew that she had not done right by her daughter. Mr. Johnson had never revealed to the church that he had kicked his daughter out of his house because she was pregnant. Instead, he told the congregation that Katrina was sent upstate New York to live with his mother. He felt that Katrina had brought shame to his family by getting pregnant and he didn't want the church to find out.

As much as it would've seemed like the First Baptist church was a place that was receptive and would accept everyone with open arms without prejudice, it was also a place where people talked about each other. That congregation could have a family's private business spread from Boston to Tallahassee in a matter of minutes. Rumors and gossips played a big role in that church. The women who held each other's hands and prayed together every Sunday were the same women who dogged other families behind their backs. It was understood by the Johnson family that the church was not always as welcoming as they liked people to believe. So, Mr. and Mrs. Johnson made sure that they got their story straight with their children, Karen and Eddy, as far as what they needed to tell the church about Katrina.

The pastor at the church found it weird that Katrina suddenly stopped coming to church with her family. And when he asked her father where she was, Mr. Johnson had to lie to maintain his good standing and reputation in the church. The commandment "Thou shall not lie" had been totally ignored by Mr. Johnson. In fact, Mr. Johnson was the biggest hypocrite there was in the church. He had kicked his daughter out of his family's life for lying, and he turned around and asked his family to lie to the church about Katrina's absence from the church.

Mrs. Johnson may have been passive and subservient in the past, but she was not stupid. She was the one who pointed out to Mr. Johnson how much of a hypocrite he was. She was getting tired of living for people whose opinions had no significance to her. Mrs. Johnson told her husband that he had allowed his faith to destroy their family and she was tired of it. She also reminded him that she was the one who introduced him to the life of Christ and now all of sudden he wanted to show her how much more of a Christian he was than her. She was furious when she realized that she had lost her daughter for good. The agony and the pain that Mrs. Johnson suffered over the years was all because her husband did not want to let go of his stubbornness.

As bright and honest Mr. Johnson wanted to appear to his family, they had lost respect for him because of his ignorance. The children stopped talking to him after a while and his wife vacated their bedroom all together. Mrs. Johnson moved into Katrina's bedroom years after she had left. She forbade the other children, Eddy and Karen to ever go into Katrina's room because she was hoping that her daughter would one day come back home to her family. For years, she went in that room every Saturday and cleaned it spotless. She never changed anything in the room, as she needed every little reminder when she thought about Katrina.

Moving to Katrina's room after close to fifteen years was the final step to Mrs. Johnson's declaration of independence in her household. She had grown tired of listening to her husband, her pastor and everyone at her church as far as the way she was supposed to live. It was because of them that she never set out to find her daughter to begin with. Mrs. Johnson had become bitter towards her husband and her church, but by the time she had decided to do something about it, it was a little too late. Katrina was long gone and she had missed out on the opportunity to see her daughter and grandchildren grow up. Mrs. Johnson prayed and wished everyday that her daughter was okay out there in the world.

Despite all the animosity she may have felt towards her husband and her church, she continued to attend the church with her family every Sunday and also continued to prepare her husband's favorite meals at home. Though she and her husband hardly spoke any words to each other, they had created a new way of communicating silently. They were both two miserable souls who hadn't yet connected to the modern world. Mrs. Johnson couldn't see herself leaving her husband and children at home. And the fact that she was also dependent on her husband financially weighed heavily on her mind.

A woman in her late forties, Mrs. Johnson was encouraged by Karen and Eddy to do more with her life. But first, she had to find a way to earn her GED. With the tutoring help of an adult education program in Boston, Mrs. Johnson earned her GED by the time her son entered high school. She wanted to be a role model for her children and she also wanted to show them that it was never too late to accomplish certain goals in life. Mr. Johnson, however, felt threatened by the fact that his wife was able to earn a GED. He had always made it seem like he was the most intelligent person in his household even though he only had a sixth grade education. It was his way of elevating himself while degrading his wife. As Mrs. Johnson started to learn more and more through reading and writing, she also discovered how the lack of an education kept her husband in total darkness.

She soon started to realize why her husband had been acting so ignorantly during their marriage. She wanted to teach him about her new discovery and love for reading, but he fought her every time. He even tried to belittle her achievements on a few occasions by telling her that she would never be more than a wife and a homemaker to him no matter how much she had learned through her readings. Though Mr. Johnson quit school in the sixth grade, his reading skill was at the third grade level and he never tried to improve it. When he went to church with his wife, he acted like he was reading from the bible, but most of the time he had memorized the scriptures after his wife had read them aloud to him at home. He had proven that most illiterate people are usually pretty smart in concealing their deficiencies to the rest of the world.

Mr. Johnson concealed a lot about his life and he wasn't open to any new changes unless it was directed by his pastor. In the process, he also created a barrier of communication between him and his wife. Because it was so important for Mr. Johnson to be the head of his household, he chose to stay ignorant so that he could lead by force instead of common sense and intelligence. Through no fault of his own that he never finished school, but he was too proud to allow people to know that he was deficient in any way.

Mrs. Johnson had decided that she wanted to become a counselor to help other families with their social adjustment and issues, and also to be an inspiration to her children in life. At the urging of her daughter and son, Mrs. Johnson enrolled at the University of Massachusetts in Boston to study counseling in the adult continued education program. She completed a Bachelor's Degree in just three years and after graduation, she accepted a position at a local center to help families on welfare.

It may not be Histeria Lane, but these desperate housewives are fed up with their neglecting husbands. Their sexual needs take precedence over the millions of dollars their husbands bring home every year to keep them happy in their affluent neighborhood. While their husbands claim to be hard at work, these wives are doing a little work of their own with the bedroom bandit. Is the bandit swift enough to evade these angry husbands?

In Stores!!

NEGLECTED SOULS
Motherhood and the trials of loving too hard and not enough frame this story...The realism of these characters will bring tears to your spirit as you discover the hero in the villain you never saw coming...
In Stores!!!

Jimmy and Nina continue to feel a void in their lives because they haven't a clue about their genealogical make-up. Jimmy falls victims to a life threatening illness and only the right organ donor can save his life. Will the donor be the bridge to reconnect Jimmy and Nina to their biological family? Will Nina be the strength for her brother in his time of need? Will they ever find out what really happened to their mother?

In Stores!!!

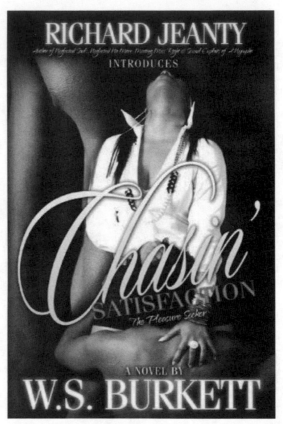

Betrayal, lust, lies, murder, deception, sex and tainted love frame this story... Julian Stevens lacks the ambition and freak ability that Miko looks for in a man, but she married him despite his flaws to spite an ex-boyfriend. When Miko least expects it, the old boyfriend shows up and ready to sweep her off her feet again. She wants to have her cake and eat it too. While Miko's doing her own thing, Julian is determined to become everything Miko ever wanted in a man and more, but will he go to extreme lengths to prove he's worthy of Miko's love? Julian Stevens soon finds out that he's capable of being more than he could ever imagine as he embarks on a journey that will change his life forever.

In Stores!!!

The police in New York and other major cities around the country are increasingly victimizing black men. The violence has escalated to deadly force, most of the time without justification. In this controversial book, noted author Richard Jeanty, tackles the problem of police brutality and the unfair treatment of Black men at the hands of police in New York City and the rest of the country.

In Stores!!!

Just when Darren thinks his relationship with Tina is flourishing, there is yet another hurdle on the road hindering their bliss. Tina saw a therapist for months to deal with her sexual addiction, but now Darren is wondering if she was ever treated completely. Darren has not been taking care of home and Tina's frustrated and agrees to a break-up with Darren. Will Darren lose Tina for good? Will Tina ever realize that Darren is the best man for her?

In Stores!!

Ronald Murphy was a player all his life until he and his best friend, Myles, met the women of their dreams during a brief vacation in South Beach, Florida. Sexual Jeopardy is story of trust, betrayal, forgiveness, friendship and hope.

In Stores!!!

Tina develops an insatiable sexual appetite very early in life. She only loves her boyfriend, Darren, but he's too far away in college to satisfy her sexual needs.
Tina decides to get buck wild away in college
Will her sexual trysts jeopardize the lives of the men in her life?

In Stores!!!

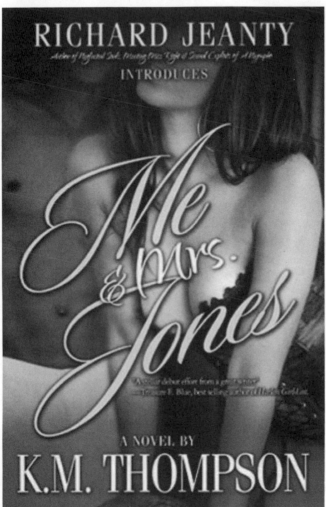

Faith Jones, a woman in her mid-thirties, has given up on ever finding love again until she met her son's best friend, Darius. Faith Jones is walking a thin line of betrayal against her son for the love of Darius. Will Faith allow her emotions to outweigh her common sense?

In Stores!!!

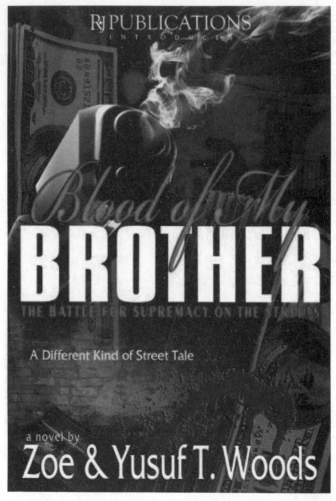

Roc was the man on the streets of Philadelphia, until his younger brother decided it was time to become his own man by wreaking havoc on Roc's crew without any regards for the blood relation they share. Drug, murder, mayhem and the pursuit of happiness can lead to deadly consequences. This story can only be told by a person who has lived it.

In Stores!!!

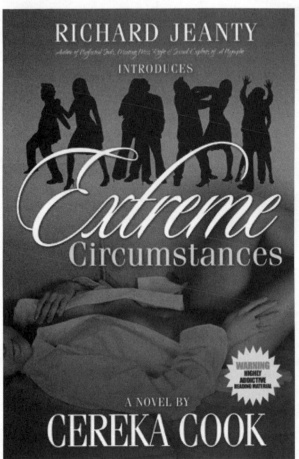

What happens when a devoted woman is betrayed? Come take a ride with Chanel as she takes her boyfriend, Donnell, to circumstances beyond belief after he betrays her trust with his endless infidelities. How long can Chanel's friend, Janai, use her looks to get what she wants from men before it catches up to her? Find out as Janai's gold-digging ways catch up with and she has to face the consequences of her extreme actions.
In Stores!!!

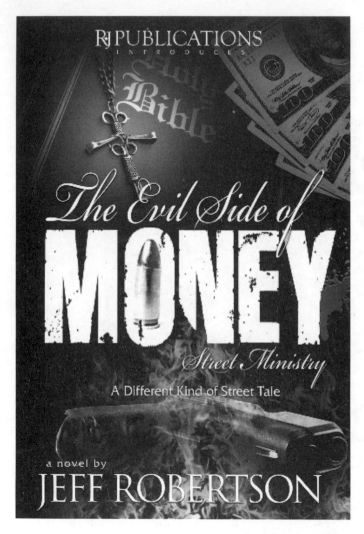

Violence, Intimidation and carnage are the order as Nathan and his brother set out to build the most powerful drug empires in Chicago. However, when God comes knocking, Nathan's conscience starts to surface. Will his haunted criminal past get the best of him?
In Stores!!

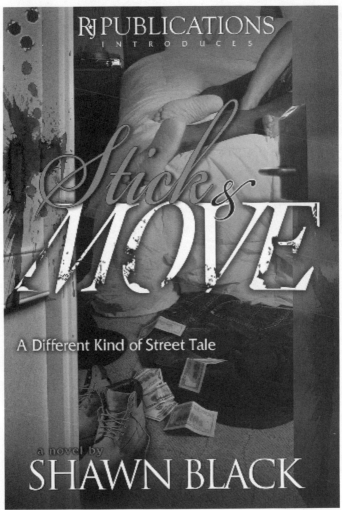

Yasmina witnessed the brutal murder of her parents at a young age at the hand of a drug dealer. This event stained her mind and upbringing as a result. Will Yamina's life come full circle with her past? Find out as Yasmina's crew, The Platinum Chicks, set out to make a name for themselves on the street.

In stores!!

Ashland's mother, Bianca, fights hard to suppress the truth from her daughter because she doesn't want her to marry Jordan, the grandson of an ex-lover she loathes. Ashland soon finds out how cruel and vengeful her mother can be, but what price will Bianca pay for redemption?

In stores!!

Malcolm is a wealthy virgin who decides to conceal his wealth
From the world until he meets the right woman. His wealthy best
friend, Dexter, hides his wealth from no one. Malcolm struggles to
find love in an environment where vanity and materialism are
rampant, while Dexter is getting more than enough of his share of
women. Malcolm needs develop self-esteem and confidence to
meet the right woman and Dexter's confidence is borderline
arrogance.
Will bad boys like Dexter continue to take women for a ride?

Or will nice guys like Malcolm continue to finish last?

In Stores!!!

What happens when a woman's devotion to her fiancee is tested weeks before she gets married? What if her fiancee is just hiding behind the veil of ministry to deceive her? Find out as Sean Mitchell takes you on a journey you'll never forget into the lives of Angelica, Titus and Aurelius.

In Stores!!

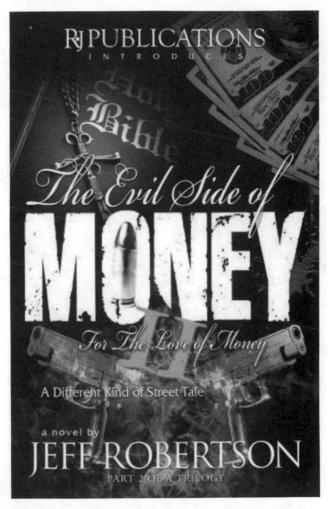

A beautigul woman from Bolivia threatens the existence of the drug empire that Nate and G have built. While Nate is head over heels for her, G can see right through her. As she brings on more conflict between the crew, G sets out to show Nate exactly who she is before she brings about their demise.

In Stores!!!

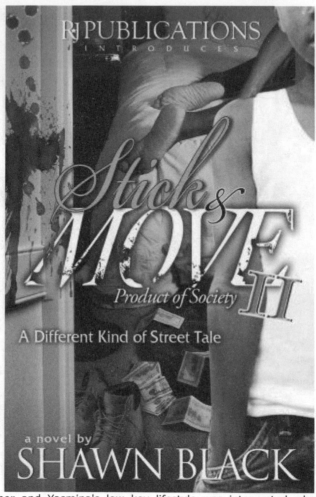

Scorcher and Yasmina's low key lifestyle was interrupted when they were taken down by the Feds, but their daughter, Serosa, was left to be raised by the foster care system. Will Serosa become a product of her environment or will she rise above it all? Her bloodline is undeniable, but will she be able to control it?

In Stores!!

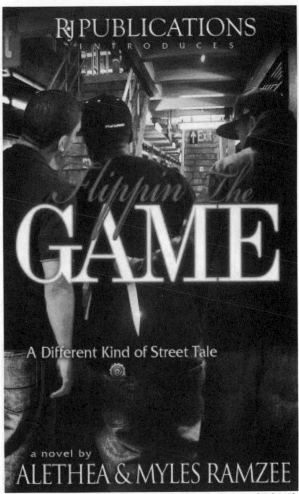

An ex-drug dealer finds himself in a bind after he's caught by the Feds. He has to decide which is more important, his family or his loyalty to the game. As he fights hard to make a decision, those who helped him to the top fear the worse from him. Will he get the chance to tell the govt. whole story, or will someone get to him before he becomes a snitch?

In Stores!!!

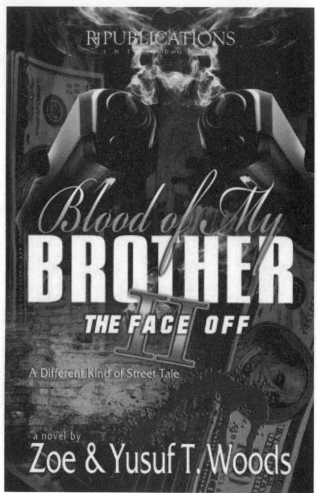

What will Roc do when he finds out the true identity of Solo? Will the blood shed come from his own brother Lil Mac? Will Roc and Solo take their beef to an explosive height on the street? Find out as Zoe and Yusuf bring the second installment to their hot street joint, Blood of My Brother.

In Stores!!!

Dave Richardson is enjoying success as his second book became a New York Times best-seller. He left the life of The Bedroom behind to settle with his family, but an obsessed fan has not had enough of Dave and she will go to great length to get a piece of him. How far will a woman go to get a man that doesn't belong to her?

Coming September 2010

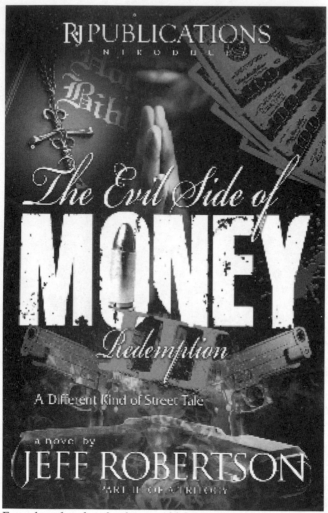

Forced to abandon the drug world for good, Nathan and G attempt to change their lives and move forward, but will their past come back to haunt them? This final installment will leave you speechless.

Coming November 2009

Nafys Muhammad managed to beat the charges in court, but will he beat them on the street? There will be many revelations in this story as betrayal, greed, sex scandal corruption and murder unravels throughout every page. Get ready for a rough ride.

Coming December 2009

Deon is at the mercy of a ruthless gang that kidnapped him. In a foreign land where he knows nothing about the culture, he has to use his survival instincts and his wit to outsmart his captors. Will the Hoodfellas show up in time to rescue Deon, or will Crazy D take over once again and fight an all out war by himself?

Coming March 2010

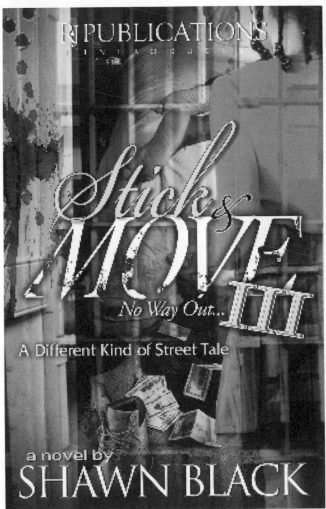

While Yasmina sits on death row awaiting her fate, her daughter, Serosa, is fighting the fight of her life on the outside. Her genetic structure that indirectly bins her to her parents could also be her downfall and force her to see that there's no way out!

Coming January 2010

The drama continues as Deshun is hunted by Angela who still feels that ex-girlfriend Kayla is still trying to win his heart, though he brutally raped her. Angela will kill anyone who gets in her way, but is DeShun worth all the aggravation?

Coming September 2009

Buck Johnson was forced to make the best out of worst situation. He has witnessed the most cruel events in his life and it is those events who the man that he has become. Was the Johnson family ignorant souls through no fault of their own?

Coming October 2009

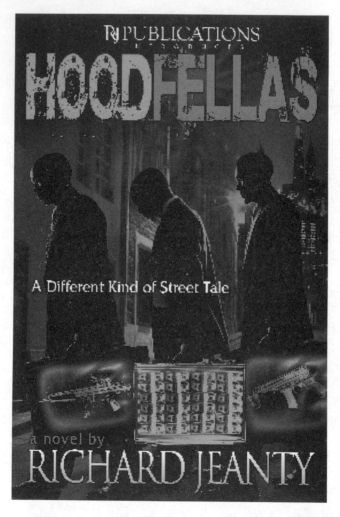

When an Ex-con finds himself destitute and in dire need of the basic necessities after he's released from prison, he turns to what he knows best, crime, but at what cost? Extortion, murder and mayhem drives him back to the top, but will he stay there?

In Stores !!!

What happens when someone falls insanely in love? Stalking is just the beginning.

In Stores!!!

Use this coupon to order by mail
1. Neglected Souls, Richard Jeanty $14.95
2. Neglected No More, Richard Jeanty $14.95
3. Ignorant Souls, Richard Jeanty $15.00, October 2009
4. Sexual Exploits of Nympho, Richard Jeanty $14.95
5. Meeting Ms. Right's Whip Appeal, Richard Jeanty $14.95
6. Me and Mrs. Jones, K.M Thompson $14.95
7. Chasin' Satisfaction, W.S Burkett $14.95
8. Extreme Circumstances, Cereka Cook $14.95
9. The Most Dangerous Gang In America, R. Jeanty $15.00
10. Sexual Exploits of a Nympho II, Richard Jeanty $15.00
11. Sexual Jeopardy, Richard Jeanty $14.95
12. Too Many Secrets, Too Many Lies, Sonya Sparks $15.00
13. Stick And Move, Shawn Black $15.00 Available
14. Evil Side Of Money, Jeff Robertson $15.00
15. Evil Side Of Money II, Jeff Robertson $15.00
16. Evil Side Of Money III, Jeff Robertson $15.00
17. Flippin' The Game, Alethea and M. Ramzee, $15.00 Available
18. Flippin' The Game II, Alethea and M. Ramzee, $15.00 Dec. 2009
19. Cater To Her, W.S Burkett $15.00
20. Blood of My Brother I, Zoe & Yusuf Woods $15.00
21. Blood of my Brother II, Zoe & Ysuf Woods $15.00
22. Hoodfellas, Richard Jeanty $15.00 available
23. Hoodfellas II, Richard Jeanty, $15.00 03/30/2010
24. The Bedroom Bandit, Richard Jeanty $15.00 Available
25. Mr. Erotica, Richard Jeanty, $15.00, Sept 2010
26. Stick N Move II, Shawn Black $15.00 Available
27. Stick N Move III, Shawn Black $15.00 Jan, 2010
28. Miami Noire, W.S. Burkett $15.00 Available
29. Insanely In Love, Cereka Cook $15.00 Available
30. Blood of My Brother III, Zoe & Yusuf Woods September 2009

Name_____

Address_____

City_____State_____Zip Code_____

Please send the novels that I have circled above.
Shipping and Handling: Free
Total Number of Books_____
Total Amount Due_____
        Buy 3 books and get 1 free. This offer is subject to change without notice.
Send institution check or money order (no cash or CODs) to:
RJ Publications
PO Box 300771
Jamaica, NY 11434
For more information please call 718-471-2926, or visit www.rjpublications.com

Please allow 2-3 weeks for delivery.

Use this coupon to order by mail
31. Neglected Souls, Richard Jeanty $14.95
32. Neglected No More, Richard Jeanty $14.95
33. Ignorant Souls, Richard Jeanty $15.00, October 2009
34. Sexual Exploits of Nympho, Richard Jeanty $14.95
35. Meeting Ms. Right's Whip Appeal, Richard Jeanty $14.95
36. Me and Mrs. Jones, K.M Thompson $14.95
37. Chasin' Satisfaction, W.S Burkett $14.95
38. Extreme Circumstances, Cereka Cook $14.95
39. The Most Dangerous Gang In America, R. Jeanty $15.00
40. Sexual Exploits of a Nympho II, Richard Jeanty $15.00
41. Sexual Jeopardy, Richard Jeanty $14.95
42. Too Many Secrets, Too Many Lies, Sonya Sparks $15.00
43. Stick And Move, Shawn Black $15.00 Available
44. Evil Side Of Money, Jeff Robertson $15.00
45. Evil Side Of Money II, Jeff Robertson $15.00
46. Evil Side Of Money III, Jeff Robertson $15.00
47. Flippin' The Game, Alethea and M. Ramzee, $15.00 Available
48. Flippin' The Game II, Alethea and M. Ramzee, $15.00 Dec. 2009
49. Cater To Her, W.S Burkett $15.00
50. Blood of My Brother I, Zoe & Yusuf Woods $15.00
51. Blood of my Brother II, Zoe & Ysuf Woods $15.00
52. Hoodfellas, Richard Jeanty $15.00 available
53. Hoodfellas II, Richard Jeanty, $15.00 03/30/2010
54. The Bedroom Bandit, Richard Jeanty $15.00 Available
55. Mr. Erotica, Richard Jeanty, $15.00, Sept 2010
56. Stick N Move II, Shawn Black $15.00 Available
57. Stick N Move III, Shawn Black $15.00 Jan, 2010
58. Miami Noire, W.S. Burkett $15.00 Available
59. Insanely In Love, Cereka Cook $15.00 Available
60. Blood of My Brother III, Zoe & Yusuf Woods September 2009
Name_____
Address_____
City_____State_____Zip Code_____

Please send the novels that I have circled above.
Shipping and Handling: Free
Total Number of Books_____
Total Amount Due_____
Buy 3 books and get 1 free. This offer is subject to change without notice.
Send institution check or money order (no cash or CODs) to:
RJ Publications
PO Box 300771
Jamaica, NY 11434
For more information please call 718-471-2926, or visit www.rjpublications.com

Please allow 2-3 weeks for delivery.

Use this coupon to order by mail
61. Neglected Souls, Richard Jeanty $14.95
62. Neglected No More, Richard Jeanty $14.95
63. Ignorant Souls, Richard Jeanty $15.00, October 2009
64. Sexual Exploits of Nympho, Richard Jeanty $14.95
65. Meeting Ms. Right's Whip Appeal, Richard Jeanty $14.95
66. Me and Mrs. Jones, K.M Thompson $14.95
67. Chasin' Satisfaction, W.S Burkett $14.95
68. Extreme Circumstances, Cereka Cook $14.95
69. The Most Dangerous Gang In America, R. Jeanty $15.00
70. Sexual Exploits of a Nympho II, Richard Jeanty $15.00
71. Sexual Jeopardy, Richard Jeanty $14.95
72. Too Many Secrets, Too Many Lies, Sonya Sparks $15.00
73. Stick And Move, Shawn Black $15.00 Available
74. Evil Side Of Money, Jeff Robertson $15.00
75. Evil Side Of Money II, Jeff Robertson $15.00
76. Evil Side Of Money III, Jeff Robertson $15.00
77. Flippin' The Game, Alethea and M. Ramzee, $15.00 Available
78. Flippin' The Game II, Alethea and M. Ramzee, $15.00 Dec. 2009
79. Cater To Her, W.S Burkett $15.00
80. Blood of My Brother I, Zoe & Yusuf Woods $15.00
81. Blood of my Brother II, Zoe & Ysuf Woods $15.00
82. Hoodfellas, Richard Jeanty $15.00 available
83. Hoodfellas II, Richard Jeanty, $15.00 03/30/2010
84. The Bedroom Bandit, Richard Jeanty $15.00 Available
85. Mr. Erotica, Richard Jeanty, $15.00, Sept 2010
86. Stick N Move II, Shawn Black $15.00 Available
87. Stick N Move III, Shawn Black $15.00 Jan, 2010
88. Miami Noire, W.S. Burkett $15.00 Available
89. Insanely In Love, Cereka Cook $15.00 Available
90. Blood of My Brother III, Zoe & Yusuf Woods September 2009

Name_____
Address_____
City_____State____ Zip Code_____

Please send the novels that I have circled above.
Shipping and Handling: Free
Total Number of Books_____
Total Amount Due_____
        Buy 3 books and get 1 free. This offer is subject to change without notice.
Send institution check or money order (no cash or CODs) to:
RJ Publications
PO Box 300771
Jamaica, NY 11434
For more information please call 718-471-2926, or visit www.rjpublications.com

Please allow 2-3 weeks for delivery.

Use this coupon to order by mail
91. Neglected Souls, Richard Jeanty $14.95
92. Neglected No More, Richard Jeanty $14.95
93. Ignorant Souls, Richard Jeanty $15.00, October 2009
94. Sexual Exploits of Nympho, Richard Jeanty $14.95
95. Meeting Ms. Right's Whip Appeal, Richard Jeanty $14.95
96. Me and Mrs. Jones, K.M Thompson $14.95
97. Chasin' Satisfaction, W.S Burkett $14.95
98. Extreme Circumstances, Cereka Cook $14.95
99. The Most Dangerous Gang In America, R. Jeanty $15.00
100. Sexual Exploits of a Nympho II, Richard Jeanty $15.00
101. Sexual Jeopardy, Richard Jeanty $14.95
102. Too Many Secrets, Too Many Lies, Sonya Sparks $15.00
103. Stick And Move, Shawn Black $15.00 Available
104. Evil Side Of Money, Jeff Robertson $15.00
105. Evil Side Of Money II, Jeff Robertson $15.00
106. Evil Side Of Money III, Jeff Robertson $15.00
107. Flippin' The Game, Alethea and M. Ramzee, $15.00 Available
108. Flippin' The Game II, Alethea and M. Ramzee, $15.00 Dec. 2009
109. Cater To Her, W.S Burkett $15.00
110. Blood of My Brother I, Zoe & Yusuf Woods $15.00
111. Blood of my Brother II, Zoe & Ysuf Woods $15.00
112. Hoodfellas, Richard Jeanty $15.00 available
113. Hoodfellas II, Richard Jeanty, $15.00 03/30/2010
114. The Bedroom Bandit, Richard Jeanty $15.00 Available
115. Mr. Erotica, Richard Jeanty, $15.00, Sept 2010
116. Stick N Move II, Shawn Black $15.00 Available
117. Stick N Move III, Shawn Black $15.00 Jan, 2010
118. Miami Noire, W.S. Burkett $15.00 Available
119. Insanely In Love, Cereka Cook $15.00 Available
120. Blood of My Brother III, Zoe & Yusuf Woods September 2009
Name_____
Address_____
City_____State_____Zip Code_____

Please send the novels that I have circled above.
Shipping and Handling: Free
Total Number of Books_____
Total Amount Due_____
Buy 3 books and get 1 free. This offer is subject to change without notice.
Send institution check or money order (no cash or CODs) to:
RJ Publications
PO Box 300771
Jamaica, NY 11434
For more information please call 718-471-2926, or visit www.rjpublications.com

Please allow 2-3 weeks for delivery.